The
Game
Can't
Love
You
Back

The Game Can't Love You Back

KAROLE COZZO

Swoon **READS**

NEW YORK

A Swoon Reads Book
An imprint of Feiwel and Friends and Macmillan Publishing Group, LLC
175 Fifth Avenue, New York, NY 10010

Our books may be purchased in bulk for promotional, educational, or business use.
Please contact your local bookseller or the Macmillan Corporate and Premium Sales
Department at (800) 221-7945 ext. 5442 or by e-mail at MacmillanSpecialMarkets@
macmillan.com.

Library of Congress Cataloging-in-Publication Data is available.
ISBN 9781250163899 (hardcover) / ISBN 9781250163882 (ebook)

Book design by Danielle Mazzella di Bosco
First edition, 2018

10 9 8 7 6 5 4 3 2 1

swoonreads.com

For all my fellow feisty girls

ELECTRICAL FIRE DESTROYS GYM, SENIOR WING OF FARMINGTON SOUTH HIGH SCHOOL

Staff Reporter

In a fortunate turn of events, Farmington South High School was closed for winter break when an electrical fire broke out at approximately nine o'clock Tuesday morning, and no staff, students, or family members were present at the time. The fire raged for over an hour before it was contained, ultimately destroying the gym and senior hallway of the building. Investigators report that the fire is being attributed to a wiring system compromised by age and wear.

Farmington South High School, originally the sole high school within the district, was slated for renovations at the close of the school year, which were scheduled to run the entirety of next school year as well. However, in light of the fire, students will be absorbed by Farmington East High School for the remainder of the current school year, effective January 4.

This announcement from the superintendent, Dr. Gerald Coyle, was met with concern and disappointment, especially from members of the Farmington South senior class and members of sports teams that are midseason. While sports that are currently in season will continue to represent Farmington South, spring sports athletes will also be absorbed by Farmington East teams.

"Our hearts go out to the students who will have their lives, academic plans, and extracurricular activities disrupted by this event," Superintendent Coyle said on Wednesday evening. "However, I urge everyone to remember that while Farmington has been operating with two high schools, at heart we are one community, and I know we will all come together to support the students from Farmington South as they cope with the loss of their school earlier than anticipated."

The superintendent announced that Farmington South students will receive their class schedules in the mail prior to school recommencing in January, and that school staff is working overtime to rework the existing Farmington East schedule to accommodate the influx of new students.

Dear Superintendent Coyle:

On behalf of Farmington South varsity athletes, I'm writing to ask for your reconsideration of the decision to integrate the Farmington athletic teams for the upcoming spring season. We understand that this will put somewhat of a strain on resources and practice facilities available at Farmington East, but we are willing to be flexible and understanding if allowed to continue to represent the Farmington South Bulldogs for the remainder of the school year.

For many of us, the bulldog is more than an emblem we wear on our uniforms—it is a source of pride and a tradition of excellence that we are passionate about upholding. We have been asked to adjust to many sudden changes, and being allowed to keep our teams together would go a long way in terms of bolstering our spirits at this time.

To show my level of commitment to this effort, I have spent the last twenty-four hours of my winter break driving around the community, collecting signatures from 152 fellow student athletes in support of this petition, which are included below. We are willing to do whatever it takes to remain Bulldogs, and we sincerely hope you understand our feelings at this time, and will reconsider what seems to be the "easy" decision to collapse the teams for the spring season. Not only are team titles, personal awards, and scholarships for graduating athletes on the line, our very identity as Bulldogs is being stripped away. We beg you to rethink and rework this.

Respectfully,

Eve Marshall

Eve Marshall

Varsity Soccer—Cocaptain

Varsity Basketball—Cocaptain

Varsity Baseball

National Honor Society—Treasurer

Peer Tutor

Spanish Club

Bulldogs Go Green Club

Mock Trial

Future Business Leaders of America

Choral Club

Dear Miss Marshall:

Thank you for your thoughtful, well-written letter on behalf of your fellow student athletes—it is a testament to the intelligence and spirit that students from Farmington South will bring to their new school tomorrow!

However, unfortunately, I am unable to grant your request that Farmington South athletes be able to continue as separate teams for the spring season. In considering facilities, transportation, staffing, and scheduling with the schools coming together, it is simply not possible.

I assure all Farmington South athletes that you will find your rightful place on Farmington East Pirates teams, and that these teams will be even stronger when you come together. I ask you to keep an open mind and consider the benefits of our teams joining.

I wish you all the best in this transition. I'm certain you will rise to the occasion.

Go Pirates!

Kindly,

Dr. Gerald Coyle
Superintendent, Farmington Area School District

 **Eve**
@EveM#13Bulldogs

You've got to be kidding me. #BS

♡   ⇄   ♡   ✉   2 Jan

 Eve
@EveM#13Bulldogs

#NeveraPirate

♡   ⇄   ♡   ✉   2 Jan

Eve
@EveM#13Bulldogs

#Bulldog4Life

♡   ⇄   ♡   ✉   2 Jan

Two months later . . .

Chapter 1

March 1

Eve

I'm seeing stars.

I wake up at six forty-five a.m. and hazy early morning sunbeams illuminate my sheer curtains, but after my eyes adjust to the light, I'm still seeing stars.

Three smaller stars shoot out from the marble base of the trophy, aspiring to reach the bigger, central star they frame, the one that's engraved with a golden basketball. The trophy is draped in the net from the championship game. The W was a team effort, and some might say the net should be displayed with the big team trophy at school. But most people would say the net belongs to me, so here it is.

I smile, the same smile I've woken with for the past week, since the trophy came home with me. My trophy spent the first night on the pillow beside my head, but now it's in its permanent home so I can wake to the sight of it every morning. *State champions*. It has a damn fine ring to it.

My gaze drifts to the left of the trophy, coming to rest on the framed certificate commemorating my selection to the All-County Girls' Soccer First Team in the fall. EVE MARSHALL, FARMINGTON SOUTH, JUNIOR, 5'8", FORWARD. Not as newsworthy as a state championship, but the best I could hope for. Offense wins games; defense wins championships. And on the soccer field, I didn't have the defense to back me up and take us all the way. A familiar sense of satisfaction fills my chest as I look at my name. I don't say it out loud, but maybe I prefer individual accolades anyway. I was pumped I'd been recognized as an individual, at least.

And then my gaze drifts right, past the stars, to the empty spot I'd reserved on my shelf. Before, a Cy Young trophy ending up there was inevitable, but now . . . My smile disappears as I grind my molars together. Stupid fire. Stupid Dr. Coyle and heartless administrative decision-making. They've effed up everything.

I whip my covers back, my feet hit the cold wood floor, and I storm into the bathroom for a quick shower. My thick, long dark hair is so routinely plaited into two French braids to keep it out of my face, it could probably braid itself by now, and it stays in place despite the shower.

Then, feeling subversive—and ready, willing, and able to show it—I tug a Farmington South Bulldogs hoodie over my head and pull on a pair of black sweatpants. My sneakers are the only clothing I put any time into selecting. Studying all eleven pairs of Nikes, I finally select the black-and-fluorescent-green Cross Bionics. They're badass. Superhero colors.

After bounding down the stairs, I'm in and out of the kitchen in a flash, grabbing a Clif Bar from the pantry and a bottle of Minute Maid from the fridge. Marcella's already behind the wheel of the cheery red Jetta parked in the driveway next door. She's bobbing her head, shiny brown hair gyrating right along with her, and her lips are moving. Taylor Swift. I inhale a deep breath. I just *know* it's Taylor Swift.

I sling my backpack onto my shoulders and cross the narrow patch of grass that separates our houses. As I climb into the passenger seat, she quickly swipes her index finger across the face of her iPhone to silence the music, but not before I get a glimpse of the cover art on the screen, a wild mass of blond curls and red lips. Swifty. Knew it.

"Good morning, Eve," she greets me.

I glance at Marcella's colorful outfit. Mustard wool miniskirt, tight red sweater worn over a shirt that she'd referred to as "chambray" when I'd questioned if jean shirts were really in style outside of Nashville. She should look like a walking advertisement for hot dog condiments, but somehow, on Marcella, it works. It always works. "Why are you so fancy today?" I ask.

"It's not fancy, it's classy. There's a difference." She gives me a once-over and scrunches her face up. "Why are you so *un*fancy? You look like you just rolled out of bed."

"Look at my face." I give her my death stare and toss my bag onto the floor with more force than necessary. "Does it look like I'm in the mood?"

Marcella shrugs once and backs out of the driveway. I'm pretty sure she knows better than to take my moods personally.

For the record, probably the only, and I mean *only*, reasons Marcella and I became best friends are (1) we were born exactly one week apart, and (2) we have lived next door to each other our whole lives. There's no undoing a friendship that was an entire childhood in the making, regardless of how totally different we've always been.

So we drive in comfortable silence the two and a half miles to Scott's house, finding him sitting at the curb, eating a sausage-and-egg breakfast sandwich. A second one is wrapped in foil on the sidewalk beside him. His face breaks out in that wide, patented Scott grin the second he sees us, for no damn reason at all. Scott's always smiling for no damn reason at all, and usually the sight of his smile makes me smile, too. Scott MacIntyre's my other best friend, the "mac to my cheese" as he likes to say, but nothing can shake my surly mood today.

Scott is short and squat, as if his body's been compressed from all the time he's spent behind the plate, catching for me, and he lumbers into the backseat. He leans over the headrest and grips my shoulders with both hands. He shakes me a little bit. "Pitchers report today, baby!"

I twist in my seat and give him my best *Really?* face.

He collapses back with a sigh and buckles his seat belt. "The team is going to be stronger than ever," he says. "You just need to get with the program."

"You're delusional if you think it's going to be that simple." I flick my braids over my shoulders and reach down to pull my chem binder from my bag, promptly ending the conversation. I have an exam today, and it won't hurt to work out a few more practice equations now, especially since I'm supposed to be picking trash up with the Go Green Club during my study hall. And it's a waste of his breath to try to convince me that what's happening today is a good thing.

I inhale sharply as I remember last season's first practice. I jumped out of bed that day, counted down the minutes of every single class. The memory brings a stabbing pain of loss to my gut. I used to relish the first day of practice. Today I'm dreading it like nothing else. I clench my fists around the binder edges, my mixed-up emotions simmering down to a bitter anger as I consider—for about the hundredth time—the injustice of it all.

....

When we enter the lobby, which still smells and feels unfamiliar—even two months in—an invisible magnet draws Brian to Marcella. Literally. Their bodies make contact at several points, simultaneously. Fingertips. Hips. Lips. It's all a little bit too much for 7:40 in the morning. Okay, a lot bit too much. I should be used to it by now, since Brian and Marcella are pretty much an institution. Brian and Marcella. Marcella and Brian. They've been together for so long now, sometimes it's hard to tell where Marcella ends and Brian starts.

They turn back toward me and Scott. We huddle close together in the crowded space, still working at recognizing faces, trying to find friends among strangers. The lines are starting to blur some, which aggravates me. Hands in fists, I fold my arms across the bulldog on my chest, just as a rowdy group behind me shoves its smallest member, a short girl with pink hair the color of Bazooka gum, right into my back, pushing me into Scott.

"Whoa, sorry." She giggles as she attempts to right herself, pulling her oversize black hoodie back up on her shoulder.

I get a better look at her. In addition to the cotton-candy-colored hair, she has pink-and-blue gauges in both earlobes.

Two round studs pierce the skin above her lips. Underneath the heavy eye makeup, she looks like she's about twelve.

Then she scampers off, losing herself among the group of ripped-black-shirt-wearing guys who were jostling her about.

I quirk an eyebrow and shake my head.

"Your judgment is showing." Scott grins, nudging me in the ribs. "You might want to tuck that back in."

"No judgment," I lie. "I just don't get people like that. Who works so hard at not fitting in?"

Marcella snickers.

"What?"

I swear her gaze flicks to my Bulldogs sweatshirt, but she just smiles at Brian and shakes her head. "Nothing." She tugs on his hand. "We should go. The student council meeting's all the way down in Mrs. Trimble's room. And today we're taking the final vote on the prom theme!"

"Okay, babe."

Marcella, the eternal good sport, is handling the loss of her presidency over the junior class of Farmington South with grace and dignity, jumping right back into school politics at Farmington East without missing a beat. She separates herself from Brian for a quick second to give me a hug, the scent of her trademark Burberry perfume washing over me. "See you at lunch." She tugs on a braid before reaching for Brian's hand again.

"See you."

My gaze follows them as they're swallowed up by the sea of bodies, and I catch a glimpse of some of my friends from the South girls' basketball team in the alcove near the ramp. I gesture toward them and Scott nods, down for whatever. I take three steps in their direction . . . and then stop in my tracks, fingers tightening into an angry claw around my black backpack strap.

Blocking my path is the Farmington East baseball team. Its members are loud and amped, several of them dressed in last year's T-shirts, bearing the words THERE'S NO "I" IN TEAM. And as I watch them, they get even louder and more amped, calling out and slapping fives. Because their captain has just arrived, whipping them into a frenzy.

And God grant me patience. Because if his entrance wasn't so damn *irritating*, I would walk over and *laugh* in his pretty face.

Jamie Abrams.

He swaggers across the lobby with the air of a rapper who's sustained a gunshot wound or something. I mean, I swear, he might actually be faking a limp. It's early March and partly cloudy, yet he has sunglasses on. Inside. Jamie's got his East baseball cap on backward, and he's wearing his Windbreaker, embroidered with his cocky nickname—ACE—in gold over his chest.

Jamie Abrams, God's gift to Farmington baseball. God's gift to Farmington girls.

I can't stand him.

Not that I've ever spoken to him. I've been avoiding him like the plague the past couple of months.

But that doesn't stop me from hating him, or more specifically, hating the idea of him. From what I've observed—discreetly, of course—his prime objectives for coming to school include flaunting his overhyped image and finding his next hookup. He's always talking, always laughing, always whispering in one girl or another's ear. I can't really believe he takes anything that seriously, so I highly doubt that baseball is an exception.

Even if he has been the star pitcher for two years and

counting, securing the position his freshman year, which is pretty much unheard-of. He's good, sure, but there's no way in hell he's as dedicated as I am.

Yet I'm willing to *bet* he feels entitled to that Cy Young trophy. Because everyone makes him out to be such a rock star. Because this team is more his than mine.

That trophy belongs on my shelf.

And there's only one for the taking now.

My natural competitive impulses flare, and I realize I'm glaring at him. I shake my head in frustration. I'm used to glaring at the person in the batter's box, not the one wearing the same uniform.

As I stand there, shooting daggers, something weird happens. I see the muscles in his back tense beneath his Windbreaker and he stops running his mouth, midsentence. He turns and looks right in my direction, as though he can feel my fiery gaze upon his back.

Slowly, he removes his hat, running one hand over the top of his close-cropped light brown hair. The glasses come off next, and before I'm ready for it, his cool, steady, slate-blue eyes are piercing mine. The look on his face bears no trace of the sleepy-eyed, cocky smirk combo I usually see him using when he focuses on other girls.

All laughter has drained from his face, and his glare is as ice-cold as the one I've got trained on him is hot.

I think it's the first time he's ever really looked at me. And in that instant, it's crystal clear—as crystal clear as those blue eyes of his—that he feels the same way about me as I feel about him.

This is why it doesn't matter that I'm wearing a Bulldogs

hoodie. Why I couldn't embrace Marcella's cheerful mood this morning and why I dismissed Scott's contention that our teams coming together will make Farmington baseball even stronger.

At the end of the day, it doesn't matter where we go to school or what mascot I wear on my shirt now. Locked in a staring contest with Jamie, I know I'm right. We're not on the same team. Not at all.

Chapter 2

March 1

Jamie

"**M**orning, handsome."

My mom's in the kitchen when I come downstairs, standing at the counter, stirring artificial creamer into this huge travel coffee mug. She tries to assault me with a hug as I pass her, but I shrug her off. She knows I'm not a morning person.

"Morning, Ma," I mutter, opening the pantry, considering my options. Half-empty box of Target-brand reduced-fat granola. Probably half-stale, too. Unopened box of Froot Loops. No-brainer. I grab Toucan Sam and rip open the cardboard.

When I turn back around to get a bowl, I see the tension in her shoulders. "What?"

Her lips twitch nervously. "What's wrong with granola? It's healthier."

"I like Froot Loops."

She doesn't say anything right away, but eventually she gives me the usual reminder. "You two can't keep letting open boxes of cereal go to waste."

I stare down at my full bowl of cereal, wishing she wasn't standing there making me feel guilty about my breakfast. "It's just cereal."

"Everything can't be 'it's just.'"

I pick up the box and set it back down on the table for emphasis. "It's just cereal," I repeat.

She takes a big swig of coffee and resets her smile, backing off. "So practice starts today, huh?"

I shovel cereal into my mouth, nodding while I chew and swallow. "Yep."

My mom approaches me again, smiling warmly, and rubs at one shoulder. "You feeling good?"

"Always."

Then she leaves her hand there. Lately, it's like she's always trying to make contact, like she needs someone to hold on to. I don't really like the way it feels, being that someone, but she's trying to do things differently these days, so I let her lean on me sometimes. "Text me and let me know how it goes, okay? I have to work a double today."

"Okay."

"Have you gotten to know some of the guys from South?"

"Yeah, I knew a bunch of them already from summer ball. You know Brayden and Noah Turner, right? And Jake Pawlings, who was on the Padres with me back in the day?"

"I recognize those names."

I shrug, pouring some more cereal into my bowl. "The other guys, I met them at tryouts this past week. They're all right."

A half smile lifts her left cheek, and her eyebrow goes up at the same time. "Any threats?"

A *psssh* sound escapes my lips. "Not even close."

Although . . .

I narrow my eyes at the milk, thinking of the one person I *didn't* meet at tryouts last week.

Not even close, I think again.

There's an obnoxious clatter on the stairs, and a second later, O appears. My hand freezes, spoon halfway to my mouth. My half sister has done lots of things to make herself look silly, but this takes the game to a whole new level. I stare at her as I chew my last spoonful of cereal. Shaking my head as I take the empty bowl to the sink, I murmur my opinion to no one in particular. "You look completely ridiculous."

She rolls her eyes comically. "Annnd, good morning to you, too, Sunshine." Olivia glances at the table and claps her hands. "Yay, Froot Loops!"

Mom's pursing her lips again, over the cereal or O's latest makeover, I don't know. But she chooses not to comment on either and digs around in her purse for her keys. "All right, kiddos, I'm off." She squares her shoulders and lifts her mug, ready to take on the working world.

In actuality, I've been a part of the working world longer than she has. George is a good guy, and he let me start taking shifts at Best's Burger Barn and Shake Shack, paying me under the table before I could legally work.

Mom plants a kiss on the top of my head, and then more hesitantly on the top of my sister's—God only knows what chemicals were responsible for that train wreck—before opening the back door. "Hit the road. Don't be late."

I pull my Windbreaker on and look down at my half sister. She looks more like a caricature of Olivia than her actual self.

I inhale through my nose, trying to see past the pink and the piercings. "You need a ride?"

Olivia shakes her head absently, concentration focused on arranging her Froot Loops into a rainbow pattern inside her bowl. "Justin's getting me."

I bite my tongue rather than voicing my opinion on her latest guy, who's a senior, and really has no business "getting" her. "All right. See ya later, O."

It's not till I'm out the door that I feel like I can breathe again. I'd always thought our home would feel better if my mom got herself a backbone, but now that she has one, there's a whole bunch of new issues. Single parent means single income, and hers isn't very substantial regardless of how many hours she works the checkout at Target.

My Jeep Cherokee's parked on the street, all prettied up, rims shining. It's a bitch to keep the tank filled anymore, but at least I still have my car. Just about the only good thing Doug contributed around here.

Used car salesman. Such a perfectly fitting job for that jerk-off.

I climb behind the wheel, checking my reflection in the mirror as I adjust my hat, grab my Ray-Bans out of the glove compartment. They're sitting on top of a purple hair tie someone left behind. Probably Naomi.

That's when I remember she texted me late last night, to see about me picking her up on the way to school. But I know it's not transportation that she's really interested in on the way to school, and I have to focus today. The season is officially under way, and baseball means more to me than any girl could, that's for sure.

I take the long way to school, stopping at Wawa for some gum. The school lobby's overcrowded when I get there, with all the kids from South here, but still I'm spotted the minute I walk through the door.

Lise scampers over to me, wrapping herself around my biceps like an eel. "I'm pulling some major strings to make sure I get picked as your spirit girl," she hisses in my ear.

"That'll be sweet." I give her an easy smile, cracking my gum.

One time Naomi told me that maneuver makes my jaw look sexy. I didn't know that was a thing, but hey, whatever works.

Out of nowhere, I feel someone damn near grab my ass. It's one of the new girls, and I can't remember her name. I do, however, remember *her* ass, which is encased in a pair of supertight cream-colored cords. "Thanks for saying hi to me," she says with a pout.

I put my hand over my heart in apology. "I'm sorry, sweetheart," I say. "Won't happen again."

Finally I make it through the gauntlet and see my boys in the center of the lobby. I nod confidently and saunter toward them. I insert myself into their circle, jostling a couple of sophomores, giving fist bumps to my fellow upperclassmen. Everyone turns to greet me, a few with enthusiastic slaps to the back, ready for today to get under way. Ready for this season to get under way. It's about damn time.

Throughout the rest of the lobby, people are packed like sardines, but they give my team—most members dressed in gold and black, too—plenty of room. They get it.

This is our turf. My turf.

Then I feel the hairs on the back of my neck stand up.

It's a weird, disturbing sensation, like a sudden drop in atmospheric pressure or something. I actually feel someone's eyes on my back.

I turn in the direction of the feeling, toward the owner of the eyes. *Of course.* I'm tempted to laugh, except she's so ridiculous, I can't. She's the worst joke I've heard all year.

Eve Marshall. Female baseball player.

The Phenom.

They actually called her that, the city paper that featured a front-page story on her athletic prowess. And not just our local bullshit paper, but *Sports Illustrated*, when they featured her in their recent monthly segment on standout high school athletes across the country. When I saw her face on the cover of my favorite magazine as I pulled it from our mailbox, I launched it into the recycle bin without a second glance.

She's difficult, you can tell just by looking at her. She's staring me down right now, those huge amber wolf eyes taking me on *as if she can*. Bucking tradition, just for the sake of being difficult. I mean, both schools had perfectly respectable softball teams.

Exceptions are already being made for her. State championships for girls' basketball overlapped with pitcher tryouts, and she got an automatic spot. You wanna tell me there wasn't some kind of favoritism at play there? No new *guy* would have had it so easy.

And already . . . everyone's talking about her.

She's not backing down, and it's pissing me off. So I let her know, with my eyes. *I'm not gonna make this easy for you.* I fold my arms across my chest and glare at her, hopefully driving the point home.

My school, my turf, my mound. My time in the spotlight. My second Cy Young trophy.

Bring it on, sweetheart.

Chapter 3

March 1

Eve

I change for practice in the girls' locker room. I've never really minded being separated from my team in this sense. The girls' locker room smells like powdery deodorant and floral body sprays with only subtle undertones of sweat. The boys' locker room must smell like . . . I don't even want to know. Various funk mixed with other funk.

Usually, the only times I mind my separate-but-equal status are game days. Back at South, I could actually hear my team on the other side of the cinder-block walls. Getting pumped. Making memories. Telling jokes. By the time I joined them, I'd usually missed the punch lines.

I set my bag on a bench in front of an empty row of lockers and start changing. The softball team is on its way down to the field. Some of the members of the team from South call hi to me. I've never gotten the sense that they resent me or anything—my choice to play with the boys—but they're a tight unit, and I'm just not part of their group.

Members of the team from East . . . they stare at me like an alien as they pass. The girl wearing catcher's pads mutters something under her breath, and her teammate snickers in response. Shaking my head, I tie on my cleats. I just wish they got it, that it was never a choice. It just was what it was. Having three athletic older brothers, I spent my weekend afternoons during the spring at Little League games. My mom, already frazzled with the family's hectic schedule and my dad working a lot of weekends, had just shrugged when I reached an age when I, too, could play. "You want to play ball, you play baseball," she'd said. "We can't be four places at once."

My mom had been a star forward at UConn and even played basketball internationally until she met and married my dad. She wasn't exactly dying to schlep me to ballet or cheerleading.

So I learned to play a game that had nine innings instead of seven, learned how to catch a ball that was nine inches around instead of eleven. I learned to pitch it overhand instead of under.

And I learned I was good at it, really good. Better than most of the boys.

I found out I could stare down those boys who had three inches of height and twenty pounds of muscle on me. From the mound, I could take them down, take them out. I still can. It's an awesome feeling, exhilarating and powerful and fun as hell.

So why would I ever even think about going out and learning how to "throw like a girl"?

Phenom.

Exception to the rule.

Freak of nature.

As long as I'm winning, I don't really give a hoot what they call me. I love this game.

And suddenly, in the locker room, the mound only moments away, reflecting on all this, my sour mood dissipates. Feeling invigorated, I jump to my feet and tie my lucky bandanna around my head.

I'm ready.

Catching a glimpse of myself in the mirror, I inhale a quick breath. Except for one thing.

I walk to the end of the aisle, craning my neck back and forth, making sure I'm truly alone. When I'm certain I am, I retrieve the thick Ace bandage from my bag, push up the elastic bottom of my sports bra, and wrap the bandage around my chest.

The Ace bandage is a recent addition to my uniform. It wasn't necessary before. My mom's been warning me for years about how she was a "late bloomer," but I'd looked down at my flat chest and scoffed. This past summer, I stopped really being able to scoff anymore. I have boobs, and as far as my form goes, they suck. I've learned to work around them, but there's a part of me that really wishes I didn't have to.

Plus.

The idea that any of my teammates would be *looking at my boobs* when I'm trying to concentrate . . . oh hell no.

After turning sideways and studying my silhouette in the mirror, convinced I've minimized the problem, I grab my dusty glove and head down to the field. It still feels more like winter than spring, and goose bumps instantly break out on my thighs as I jog down the hill to the diamond. Wind whips the hood of my Windbreaker against my braids and flips my bandanna, and I pick up the pace, hoping to warm up. I'm relieved to see members of the team gathering inside the dugout, which blocks the chill.

I'm not the first to arrive and I'm not the last. Scott scoots over on the bench to make room for me, and I smile gratefully at him. He stays close enough that I can feel the warmth of his body and wraps a thick arm around my shoulders for good measure. It doesn't escape my notice that you could easily divide the dugout in half: players from East on the left, players from South on the right.

Our three coaches appear over the crest of the hill, and my heart starts pounding against my chest, even though my old coach from South is part of the group. The pounding makes my entire rib cage vibrate, constricted by the tight elastic of the Ace bandage and sturdy Under Armour sports bra.

I feel a lingering sense of gratitude as I study Coach Karlson, my new head coach. He did me a solid by letting me try out in private because of the overlap with states, which gave me hope that those of us from South would get a fair shot as Pirates. But now it's time to prove myself for real. Prove that I can hang, that I actually belong here. Not in the quiet gym, but out here on the field. Where the pressure's real.

As the group comes into view, I recognize a fourth figure walking with the coaches.

Jamie.

They come closer still, and his face is more serious than I've ever seen it. It transforms him, and I can't help but stare, heart hammering anew in a way I can't make sense of.

Until he catches me staring, and he lifts his chin and narrows his eyes at me at the same time. *What the hell are you looking at?*

I drop my head and concentrate on the dusty cleat prints on the ground. I don't even know what I'm looking at. Or why I bowed out of our staring contest.

I can't let this boy intimidate me. I pick my chin back up, staring grimly out at the mound instead. It's time to focus.

Coach Karlson comes to stand in front of us, clipboard against his chest, legs spread hip-width apart. He looks left. He looks right. He looks left and right again. He chuckles once and shakes his head. "Here's the deal, guys," he tells us. "I'm not gonna force you to sit next to someone new on the bench. I'm not gonna recite some *Remember the Titans* team-building bullshit." He raises one shoulder. "Frankly, we don't have time for that, not if we want to win ball games. We have real work to do."

From the corner of my eye, I glimpse Jamie. He hasn't joined the team on the bench; he's leaning against a side wall instead, like he's above the rest of us somehow. We're not going to be forced to get along.

Good.

"So if there's any drama going on about two teams becoming one, I don't want to hear about it," Coach continues. "And I damn sure don't want to see it, not on my field. You got personal problems, you work them out. Off the field. This is the situation that's been handed to us, and I expect every one of you to be mature enough to rise to the occasion."

I feel a mild warmth in my cheeks, thinking that if Coach had been inside the car this morning, I wouldn't have made the best impression.

"One thing those of you who don't know me very well will quickly realize is this: I'm fair. And I don't play favorites. Obviously, with the recent changes, some people aren't going to be able to lay claim to positions as easily as they may have before. That's life, my friends, and my personal belief is that this can boost everyone to their best performance. There's no room for laziness anymore. You get lazy, there's going to be another talented player breathing down your neck, ready to take your spot in the starting lineup."

Ready to steal your accolades, I think.

"Our first game is less than two weeks away. The lineup won't be set until the night before. So I expect to see everyone busting their asses for the next two weeks if you feel that lineup should have your name on it. I don't play favorites," he repeats. "This will be a new lineup." He gestures over his shoulder, in the direction of the diamond. "Now hustle out there and earn it."

But as the rest of us stand and scoop up our gloves as quickly as possible, I notice that Coach wraps his arm around Jamie's shoulders, giving him a squeeze. So much for not playing favorites. As if I don't already have enough hurdles to overcome to secure time on the mound, I have to deal with the fact that Coach and Jamie appear to be pretty buddy-buddy.

The structure of practice is pretty similar to what I'm used to, especially with Coach Parsons from South still on the field. Jamie and the senior cocaptains lead us through stretches and warm-ups in the outfield. Then we break into groups and rotate through fielding drills, hitting practice, and base running. Scott and I are in different groups, and I don't say a word to any of my teammates during the drills, not even my teammates from South, even though others are chatting during rotations. I stay laser focused, hang on every word from our coaches, and bust my ass every time my name is called to step forward. Despite the slight tremble in my hands, I do okay. I hold my own.

Then, in the final half hour before wind sprints, Coach Jackson calls the pitchers and catchers together. "Let's run through this rotation twice. We'll start off slowly. Fifteen fastballs from windup, rotating to the inside and outside each pitch," he says. He twists toward the outfield, pointing to my old shortstop from South. "Jamison, right?" Chris Jamison nods. "Grab a helmet and come stand in at the plate."

As he takes position, grabbing a bat and adjusting his helmet, my heart starts pounding. This is getting real. Then I notice the other assistant coach setting up the video camera on the tripod, ready to record our throws so we can review and discuss mechanics later. My heart threatens to escape my chest altogether, and it's downright painful, thanks to the damn Ace bandage.

Coach Jackson looks back at us. "Line up, gang."

I end up third in line of the four pitchers who made the team—two of us from South, two from East. Jamie ends up behind me, and even though he definitely keeps his distance, I swear I can feel the tension and anger radiating off his body.

I'm surprised at his positioning. From the way he seems to like to steal the show, I would have assumed he'd be first in line.

To the left of the plate, I see Scott move so that he's third in line of the catchers. I catch his eye and smile, and he gives me a thumbs-up in return.

The rest of our teammates keep busy in the outfield as the first two pitchers take their turns on the mound. I can't help but be impressed by Matt Sanders's speed, but he definitely pays the price in accuracy. Pat Bechtel, my former reliever from South, goes next. He's solid, but his range is somewhat limited.

Thirty pitches from the two of them, and I'm up. Scott must

notice the way I close my eyes for a minute, blowing deep breaths through my pursed lips, because he takes a moment to lift his mask. He doesn't say anything out loud, but I'm practiced at reading his lips. I've been seeing Scott behind the plate for almost a decade. *You got this.* He raises his index and middle finger, pointing at my eyes, then turns his fingers around, pointing into his own eyes. *Eyes on me. Right here only. You got this.*

But despite his command to focus, I glance behind me in the final moment. I realize there are about twenty pairs of eyes on me. My teammates have abandoned their drills, and no one is redirecting them. Coach Karlson is standing in the outfield, bat across his shoulders, watching me, too. The occasional breeze across the infield is the only sound for miles. I look down and realize the ball is quaking in my trembling hand.

Pissed and frustrated, I force my fingers into a vise around the ball. I mean, how the hell am I going to face our opponents if I can't even face my own team?

I stare into Scott's steady green eyes and repeat his words to myself. *You got this. Eyes on me. You got this.*

I take a final deep breath and let the rest of it go blurry. Chris at the plate, holding his bat in position. The coach with the video camera in my peripheral vision. Jamie, glowering from the third baseline.

I close my eyes so I can't see any of them, and then right before I wind up, I open them. I refuse to let my focus shift even minutely from Scott's glove, at the ready. Muscle memory kicks in before my mind even tells my body what to do, and I fire. Mere seconds later, I hear the familiar, satisfying *thwack* of leather pummeling leather. Scott's glove hasn't moved at all.

He nods once, all business, and rises slightly to return the ball to me. Fourteen more times I fire, fourteen more times I nail it.

Only then do I breathe, shoulders going lax, a wide, gleeful smile lifting my cheeks. I point at Scott and raise my arms in triumph. He pumps his fist in the air three times.

That's when I hear it, behind me, surprising the hell out of me. Applause. I whirl around, finding that most of my teammates— my teammates from both South and East—are clapping. Even Coach is clapping.

Any trace of this morning's gloom is obliterated. The mound still feels like home, and my team is making me feel welcome there.

Before they can see my smile, I wipe it off my face and adjust my bandanna as I trot off the infield and get back in line. The look on Jamie's face as I approach him tells me, in no uncertain terms, that he has not been clapping along with the rest of them. He storms past me, eyes narrow slits, our shoulders bumping as I leave the mound and he claims it for himself.

Chapter 4

March 3

Jamie

Cutting my headlights, I turn into the school's back parking lot. I don't think there's any monitoring or recording going on, but the stealth aspect's cool.

I'm the first to arrive. So maybe I'm overeager—I dragged myself off Kaitlyn's couch, out from under Kaitlyn, about twenty minutes sooner than I probably needed to. Kaitlyn, owner of the tight cream cords. My hand grazes my neck; I can still feel her teeth. Yeah, I don't think I'll forget her name again.

I head down to the track, glancing over my shoulder after every few steps to make sure no one's trailing me. They're not, so I hop over the chain-link fence, unlocking it from the inside so my teammates have no trouble getting in. We made sure they all got the text. *Pirate newbies. Practice track. Ten o'clock. Be there, or don't bother showing up for practice on Monday.*

The night is completely still as I make my way to the middle of the track, right around the fifty yard line, and wait. Nathan and Brendan, my cocaptains, show up next, arriving together. They're both dressed in black, and Brendan has a knit beanie pulled low on his forehead.

"What are you fuckers doing? This isn't *Mission: Impossible*."

Nathan grins as we slap hands. "You're right. It's better."

"You ready for this?" Brendan asks.

I grind my heel into the gravel of the track. "Absolutely."

"It's a lot more fun as an upperclassman, right?"

Laughing, I nod. I've paid my dues already. And now, even as a junior, I've been elected as captain. I'd be lying if I said I didn't like the authority.

As the others arrive, I stand with my arms crossed, following their path to the bleachers with stern eyes. We don't greet them, and they don't talk to each other. Without being told what to do, they figure it out. The other juniors and seniors from East, who are exempt, join us on the track. The sophomores and the kids who transferred from South take to the first row of the bleachers, arranging themselves in a solemn line.

She arrives with her buddy, the catcher, at the last minute. I guess they thought there was strength in numbers. I'm almost gleeful, thinking about how wrong they are. There's no way to take cover tonight. My eyes stay on her as I envision her discomfort. Serves her right. She asked for this.

The resentment flares like a lit match, leaving me scowling down at my feet.

I think about the way everyone went back to the outfield when she had done her rotation on the mound. I'd gone last, expecting to steal the show, redirect their attention back where it belonged. When her turn was over, no one even looked up.

I swallow hard, thinking of how Coach had hugged her, frea-kin' *hugged* her, at the end of our first practice. The memory feels like a steel boot to my lungs, kicking the air out of them, and I refocus my attention on the bleachers, gritting my teeth, glaring at her.

Let's do this.

Nathan spits into the gravel beside me, cups his hands in front of his mouth, and calls up into the bleachers. "Good evening, gentlemen." He doesn't adjust his language for her, and I notice her rolling her eyes.

It's a subtle response, but for whatever reason, it increases the pressure inside my chest. It's a baseball team. *Get over yourself.*

"Let me explain why we're here tonight, for you sophomores or transfers who might not know." He pauses for effect. "Tonight is about the spirit of tradition alive and well within the Farmington East baseball team." He nods at Brendan, who pulls a folded piece of paper from his pocket.

Brendan raises his hand. "But before we go any further," he tells the group, "I need to read something to you guys." He squints at the paper in the darkness. " 'Farmington School District Administrative Guideline 5213, Student Anti-Hazing.' "

Eve swallows hard and a second later, her hand goes to her throat, trying to hide her reaction a beat too late. There's a sudden trace of fear in her eyes. As I survey the guys beside her, it's evident she's not the only one starting to worry.

" 'The purpose of this guideline is to maintain a safe learning environment for all students and staff members at Farmington schools. Hazing in any form is neither tolerated nor consistent with any educational goals of Farmington schools.' "

Brendan goes on to read from a list of examples of activities referred to in the policy. I catch phrases like "degrades or risks emotional and/or physical harm," "physically abusive, hazardous, or sexually violating." Eve's shoulders jump, and I wonder what she's imagining. We're not *that* depraved, for Christ's sake.

"'. . . any activity that subjects a student to extreme mental stress, embarrassment, shame, or humiliation that adversely affects the mental health or dignity of the student or discourages the student from remaining in school.'"

He looks back up into the bleachers. "Y'all got that?" he asks.

The newbies nod.

Then Brendan nods, too. "Good." He turns in my direction, hands the policy to me.

I keep my eyes on the bleachers as I rip it into tiny pieces that fall and litter the ground.

"Get down here," Nathan orders them.

Heads down, the group drags their feet as they make their way to the track and huddle together before us. Even though they're only a year younger than me, the sophomores look like kids, nervous and small. The juniors and seniors from South still look more annoyed than anything else.

"This long-standing tradition," Nathan explains, "is known as the half-naked mile." He smirks. "Or to some—the brave, those confident in their manhood—it's known as the naked half mile."

"You have seven minutes to finish the run," Brendan chimes in. "If you don't finish the run in seven minutes, you're on equipment duty the whole season. There's no rotation, no trading off.

If your ass isn't across the line in seven minutes, it's you and anyone else who's dragging."

"A seven-minute mile?" one brave, stupid sophomore asks. "Come on, man, that's nuts."

"You have a choice." Nathan shrugs. "I said half-naked mile . . . or naked half mile."

We wait for their understanding to set in, but none of them really seem too swift.

Impatient, I step forward to explain. "You do the run in your boxers, you have to run a mile in seven. You go commando, you only owe us two laps around the track. Half mile. Which is plenty easy in seven minutes."

A senior from South crosses his arms and cocks his head at me. "You're serious? I'm a senior. I outrank you. This is a joke."

I flash him a tight-lipped smile. "No, it's not a joke. It's an East tradition. You want to play ball at East, you're a part of the tradition."

"Whatever. Let's just get this done so we can go home. I have better shit to do." Chris Jamison pulls his shirt overhead and tugs off his sweats. He's undecided about his boxers, I guess waiting to see what everyone else will do, and stops there.

Slowly, following his lead, the rest of the guys do the same. Moving unnaturally slowly, they pull shirts overhead, hop on one foot as they remove pants. Then stand self-consciously before us in their underwear.

They're in a circle and end up taking a few steps back, turning inward and staring at the last two people in the group, who are still fully clothed.

This is the moment I've been waiting for. I wonder if she's

going to cry. Most girls cry so easily. "I'm sorry—is there a problem?"

My words don't register on her face, which is carved from stone. All but her eyes, which blaze with disdain.

"Come on, Jamie," Scott says, his voice small. "You can't possibly ask her to do this, too."

Scott seems like he'd be an okay guy—friendly and easygoing and shit—if he didn't live so far up her ass. But he's making a mistake right now.

"Why can't I? She wants to play with the boys"—I turn and meet her gaze—"then she needs to be willing to play with the boys." I shrug. "It's not like we made this up on her behalf. The naked half mile's been around a lot longer than she has."

"This is different," he protests. He extends his neck, but it does nothing to intimidate me. "It's not cool and you know it."

Those eyes of hers are still on fire, but you'd never know it from the chill of her voice when she finally speaks up. "It's cool, Scott."

"No, it's n—"

"Scott, I said it's cool," she repeats, cutting him off. And before I know what's happening, her shirt is off. My eyes widen in shock, but before they even process what they're seeing, her pants are off, too.

And there stands Eve, in the middle of a group of twenty or so guys, in her underwear. Not surprisingly, it's not any kind of pink lacy shit. She's just wearing a black sports bra and red boy shorts. But holy shit. The length of her legs and the muscular curve of her ass and her . . . Where the hell did *those* come from? They definitely had not been there during practice.

She looks at me, seething with anger. "What? Haven't you

ever seen a girl in her underwear before?" Her hands go to her hips. "Who knew? Maybe your reputation is as overinflated as your ego."

A few of the guys behind her start laughing.

My temper flares to life, jaw twitching as I try to keep my rage from showing itself on my face. This is not how this was supposed to go! This was supposed to *break* her. This was supposed to put her in her place. But she's standing there, all haughty and shit, even in her underwear, like she's trying to put me in mine.

She is, far and away, the most aggravating, loathsome female I've ever encountered.

"Line up," I growl. "Scott, get your clothes off."

He seems just as stunned by Eve's little striptease as I am and nods robotically as he loses his clothes. He lines up beside her, in shamrock boxers. I shake my head at what a mismatched pair they are. I steal another quick glance at Eve, eyes roaming her body. I bet he'd give anything . . .

I whirl away from them, agitated. Why the hell am I thinking about this?

Brendan is setting the stopwatch on his phone, so I step back and out of the way. Some of the guys—mostly seniors from South and sophomores from East—have the nerve to lose their boxers at the last second. I don't really want to see that shit, and my eyes are drawn to the red of Eve's underwear. I try to tell myself I really don't want to see that, either. It's not so easy.

She and Scott jostle for position near the front of the pack. A new look of concentration and concern takes over her features. Unless in addition to being a baseball wunderkind she's also the next Lolo Jones, she's going to be hard-pressed to run the full mile in under seven.

"Go!" Brendan bellows, and the pack takes off.

As they run their first lap of the quarter-mile track, all I see is flashes of flesh against white socks, flying appendages—I tell myself I'm only seeing arms and legs—and a spot of angry red in the middle of the pack. They make the turn and sweep by us, creating a cold breeze in the dark night.

The sprinters lose some momentum on the second lap, especially those who are naked and know they're almost done, easing across the finish line and making beelines for their pile of clothes before collapsing and panting against the fence. I glance over Brendan's shoulder at his phone. Three-eighteen down when the first naked runner crosses the line.

A pack of eight remains on the track for the final two laps. Each of them seems to be doing everything in their power to stay near the front, lest they fall behind and out of luck. Eve's holding her own—she's not out front, but she's not bringing up the rear, either. Her buddy Scott is.

Taking another look at Brendan's watch as they finish their third lap, I decide they're in decent position to finish under seven, all of them, which is fairly impressive. Eve's gait doesn't seem strained; she sort of runs like a deer. She's just behind the leader going into the fourth lap.

But she breaks her own stride as she passes us, glancing back over her shoulder, looking for Scott. It's obvious he's struggling, that he went out too fast, and that his stubby legs are churning and churning but not getting him very far. I look down at the phone again. He's not gonna finish in time.

One teammate passes Eve. Then another. Then a third. She is not breathing heavily and her face isn't red—she hasn't even broken a sweat. Falling back is by choice, purposeful, for Scott's sake.

I can hear her clear across the track, encouraging him. "Homestretch, MacIntyre. Homestretch now."

He tries to respond to the motivation, but he's got nothing left. The timer starts beeping on Brendan's phone just seconds before they cross the finish line, together. Scott instantly bends forward, mouth open like a fish, gasping for air, while Eve is unaffected. Her hands are back on her hips and she stares into the distance.

Nathan approaches them and claps them on their backs. "Valiant effort. Congrats on equipment duty."

Brendan flips open the top on the cooler he dragged down to the field with him, which is filled with cold bottles of water and cans of Natty Ice. "Welcome to the team, gentlemen. You're officially Pirates now."

Eve doesn't roll her eyes this time. Her brows come together in the middle, and there's something I can't read in her expression. Her gaze falls to the ground.

When Scott's regained his breath, he seems to get his spirit back at the same time, and good-naturedly endures some ribbing and accepts pats on the back from the guys. He doesn't bother putting his clothes back on, but ambles over to the cooler to pop open a beer in his bright green boxers and running shoes. Then he fishes out a water bottle and holds it up in the air. "Eve. You want?"

She's already put her T-shirt back on and is fiddling with the tie on her sweats. "Nope," she says succinctly, pulling on the drawstring with unnecessary force. "I'm good."

She looks over at Nathan, Brendan, and me. "Are we excused now? Or is the party mandatory, too?"

"Uhh, parties are supposed to be fun?" Brendan says.

"Yeah, come on, Eve, stay and hang out," Scott coaxes her. He sits down on the cooler. "We all survived, right? Come have a drink."

She just presses her lips together and shakes her head sternly. "Thanks, but I'm good."

Scott stands and walks over to double-check with her. "You want me to come with?"

She shakes off the offer, and he takes her arm and pulls her aside. It looks like there's some back-and-forth, but Eve must win out, because Scott eventually returns to his buddies on the team while she fishes for her keys. She offers a vague wave to the group, and several people take a break from their beers and conversations to say good-bye. I'm not one of them.

Then Eve turns on her heel and marches off toward the gate. She doesn't look back.

Good. She's gone. Things can be normal now, for a few minutes at least.

But even fifteen minutes later, I can't get into the party. Frustrated as hell, I down a second beer in thirty seconds, crushing the empty can in my fist. This was supposed to be the thing that would break her spirit. And if this didn't do it . . . then what the hell will?

Chapter 5

March 3

Eve

Parked in my driveway, I look at the front door of my house. Then I glance over at Marcella's. There's only one car in the driveway—her parents aren't home from date night yet, and Brian's surprisingly not taking advantage of the empty house. I look at my front door again. Evan and Eric, my two oldest brothers, have been out of the house for a few years, and Ethan left for NYU in August. Which means I have the *full* attention of our parents now, and they'll probably ask questions about where I've been.

It's a no-brainer. I climb out of my car and head toward Marcella's, opening the door without knocking. Even though I clomp up the stairs, she doesn't hear me coming over the noise from the television in her room, and she practically jumps off her bed when I open the door, whatever she's holding in her hands flying into the air before her.

"Good Lord, Eve! You almost gave me a heart attack!"

"Sorry." I flop down onto the other side of her queen-size bed, which allows me to identify the chicken-cutlet-looking things that went flying into the air a moment ago. Marcella's squishy, plasticky falsies. The ones she shoves inside her bra for pageants. And, I suspect, most normal school days. She's hand washed them and was apparently drying them with a towel.

"I didn't expect you back so soon."

We'd been having a perfectly nice Friday night, fighting over the remote to tune her TV to Bravo (her choice), or TBS, which was showing *A League of Their Own*, when the text came in.

My lips form a hard line, and I stare down at the familiar floral pattern of her quilt, tracing the stitch work with my finger. "Didn't take long."

"What happened?"

I tell the story, Marcella's eyes growing wide when I get to the part about the captains ordering us to lose our clothes.

"Oh my God, what did you do?"

I shrug. "I went ahead and took my clothes off."

Marcella's hand flies to her mouth. "Are you freakin' kidding me? They probably could've gotten suspended or even kicked off the team for something like that! Why didn't you say *no*?"

My chest tightens. "Because screw them."

Screw them. Maybe they've done it for years, to humiliate everyone. But no way in hell I was going to let them find a way to humiliate me *more*. My underwear covered up just like—better than—a bathing suit. I refused to let them, *him*, see me hesitate for more than a second before following their stupid instructions.

Marcella shakes her head, looking frustrated. "Sometimes I really don't understand how your mind works, Eve Marshall."

Screwing my face up, I point to the falsies, which she's patting dry with inordinate care. "Same."

This makes her crack a half smile, and she prompts me with her hand. "So? What happened? Did you smoke 'em?"

"I would've, but . . . Scott was struggling. I couldn't let him go down like that. I dropped back to finish up with him."

"You went through all that and still ended up losing out?"

"I couldn't do that to Scott. He's always stuck up for me. I owe him."

Then I'm quiet for a minute, outlining a peony on her quilt with my finger. "And . . . I guess some dumb part of me was trying to prove something." Looking up, I stare out Marcella's window. "Hanging back with Scott, I guess I thought maybe it would . . . show them something. Someone they want to have around. A team player, if they'd just give me the chance to be. But then when the stupid run was over"—I shake my head—"it just became obvious again that I'm odd girl out, no matter what I do. Maybe I was never 'one of the boys' back at South, either, but it's like starting back at square one now with all this East bullshit." My shoulders slump. "It's a crappy feeling. And it's an even crappier feeling that I fooled myself, for five minutes, into thinking it was worth it to try to prove myself to them," I finish.

She stares back at me helplessly, big brown eyes sympathetic, finally putting the chicken cutlets down. Marcella has no idea what to say to me. She's always played with the girls; she has no idea what it's like playing with the boys. "I have Phish Food downstairs?" she says.

"Sure," I tell her, smiling wanly. "Why the hell not."

Marcella hops off the bed and returns five minutes later, carrying a tray holding two ceramic cups shaped and painted to resemble ice-cream cones. The ice cream is scooped artfully and topped with swirls of whipped cream.

"Your presentation never fails," I tell her, taking my cup off the tray.

She smiles broadly.

"What time are you going with my mom tomorrow?"

My mom has arranged a meeting for Marcella with the owner of the fitness and nutrition center that she manages. Marcella's deep into fund-raising mode at this point. The Girls Across America Miss Pennsylvania Teen Pageant has been Marcella's dream since she started competing. At the end of the year, she'd gotten "the call" that she'd been selected as a contestant. Sponsors help cover entry costs and related pageant costs, and Marcella needs to come up with nearly three thousand dollars.

She nods. "Ten o'clock. I'm all set." A fierce look of determination takes over her face. "I just want to reach my goal. Until then, the waiting is driving me mad."

I refrain from sharing my belief that she's already mad, actually *fund-raising* to participate in something as antiquated as a beauty pageant.

I arrange myself against her pillows, digging into my ice cream. "So where's Brian tonight?" I ask around a full mouth. "I thought he'd be here."

Her smile falters minutely, but it doesn't escape my notice before she plasters it back into place.

"He must've gotten hung up. He was supposed to be here at nine thirty, but"—she picks up her phone, which is sitting beside her on the bed—"he hasn't texted me to say he's on his way yet."

"That's weird." The words are out of my mouth before I consider their potential impact. But it *is* weird. Brian's usually stuck on Marcella like white on rice.

Her smile falls away altogether. "Is it?"

"Or not," I say quickly. "It's just one night. People do get sidetracked. It's only because Brian's such an attentive little puppy dog that it seems odd."

She hits me with a stuffed pink poodle wearing a beret. "He's not a puppy dog."

"He sort of is. And I mean"—I shrug—"you kind of keep him on a tight leash."

Irritation—or worry, I'm not sure which—glints in her eye. "What do you mean?"

"Come on, Marcella," I start, trying to keep my voice light. "You run his shit, and you can't deny that. There's this look you give him, when he says or does something you don't entirely approve of, that instantly puts him back in his place. It's funny."

She doesn't seem to see the humor. "Brian's never once complained about how things are between us."

I notice the way her arms are suddenly tensed at her side, how I can see the tendons in her neck.

"Marcella, I'm just joking. You guys are going to be Class Couple, Most Likely to Get Married and Have a Million Babies, and all that jazz," I assure her, dragging my spoon along the bottom of my cup. "It's a given."

Then I set the cup on her nightstand and start undoing my braids. I ended up letting my mom schedule a haircut for tomorrow, after she actually looked at the calendar and pointed out I haven't had even a trim in nine months. I'm not sure the last time

I actually combed my hair before putting the braids back in, and if I don't at least try to detangle it tonight, I won't be able to sleep in like I want to.

I stare at Marcella's face as my fingers busy themselves on my braids. She's still not laughing and has set her ice cream aside.

"I'm just teasing," I say. Then I pause. "You're not honestly concerned, are you?"

She considers for a minute. Then she waves her hand. "No. You're right. It's fine. I'm sure it's fine."

She's lying. But if she doesn't want to say whatever's bothering her, I'm not gonna press.

"Want me to help?" she suddenly asks brightly.

I nod and she crawls behind me, some oddly shaped purple plastic rock in her hand. She tries to bring it near my head, and I recoil. "What the hell is that?"

She rolls her eyes. "It's a Tangle Teezer. I can't believe you don't have one of these. All that hair."

"Somehow I've survived," I answer dryly.

I let my best friend brush my hair. It feels good, actually. We sit there in silence as Marcella works; she has a nice rhythm going, except for when she stops, every two minutes or so, to check her phone.

When she's done, I shake out the wild, crimped mass that is my hair. It's longer than I remember, ghosting over my shoulder blades.

Marcella slides back over to the side of her bed, lying down and propping herself up on one elbow. She stares at me and smiles. "So did your new teammates totally lose their minds when you got all nekkid? I bet their eyeballs popped right out of their heads."

Funny thing is, the only person's reaction I can remember is Jamie's. I don't know what anyone else did. And yeah, there'd been some eyeball popping going on, but that was only because I'd obviously surprised the crap out of him. He'd underestimated me, again.

"Hardly. It was a test. It wasn't, like, a sexual thing."

"Oh my God, Eve." Marcella huffs in exasperation and yanks on my elbow, pulling me off the bed. She directs me in front of the full-length mirror attached to the back of her door. "Look at you. With your hair all down and wild? And your *body*? You look like a before picture from the makeover show on *America's Next Top Model*. All fresh-faced and naturally gorgeous. You're like a young Adriana Lima or something."

This actually makes me chortle, even though I don't know who Adriana Lima is. This look is not gorgeous—my hair is its own entity right now. "More like someone who just stuck her finger in an outlet."

"You don't always have to make a joke out of it, you know," she informs me. "When you get a compliment. You're such a confident person. Why's it so hard to acknowledge that part of you that's beautiful?"

I roll my eyes. Marcella's practically made a *career* out of acknowledging the part of her that's beautiful. She doesn't get it.

"That's just not the way I see myself. When I look in the mirror, I just really don't see . . . that."

The packaging. The body. Rather, I've always looked in the mirror and seen what my body can *do*. Its strength. Not its . . . beauty.

"Yeah, well, Eve, my friend? Those teenage boys with the raging hormones you just got half-naked in front of?" She regards me, eyes serious. "I can assure you . . . they do. And I know you probably hate it, but it's only going to get harder and harder for them to accept you as one of the guys."

Looking at myself in the mirror, seeing the way my tight T-shirt hugs my new curves, noticing the way my sweats cling to my butt, suddenly I can actually feel Jamie's gaze on me in that second I shucked my clothes. It's an uncomfortable feeling, the remembering, and I turn from the mirror to get away from it.

I can't control the way my shape is changing and how it impacts my game; I can't control how my teammates respond to it. And after being forced to change schools and become a Pirate, I'm just about sick to death of things beyond my control.

Chapter 6

March 7

Jamie

"Ugh, I'd do anything to have gym every day and skip the health class rotation," Naomi complains as we head toward the gym after lunch. "Mrs. Syler is such a troll. She pulled me aside the first day we were back from break, all dramatic about my attendance. She seriously acts like I get off on skipping her class."

"Well, you did miss more than once." I glance down at her and smirk. "If I'm remembering."

"Whatever. Her class is boring as hell."

I grab for her hand and draw her closer. "Feel like skipping today? If she's harassing you anyway . . ."

From the corner of my eye, I see Coach Karlson pop his head out of his office. He does a double take and focuses on me.

"Abrams, get your hands off the lady and your butt in my office," he orders.

Naomi takes advantage of the situation and frees herself from my grasp, purposely rubbing up against me as she heads toward the health classroom. "We can revisit the topic later," she promises, tongue poking out the side of her mouth as she saunters away from me.

I watch her for a long minute before sighing and doubling back toward Coach's office. "What's going on, Coach?" I lean against the wall, looking down at him. He's sitting at his desk, riffling through a stack of mustard-colored papers.

Report cards.

Shit.

He points to the chair across from him.

"I'm cool." I'd rather keep my distance.

Coach finally looks up, and he's not happy. "Sit."

Slowly, I pull out the chair and sit. He gets up to close the door, and then sits back down, directly across from me. I don't meet his eye.

"Your GPA last quarter? Garbage."

"Jeez, be blunt already," I mutter out the side of my mouth, looking toward the window, wishing I could teleport myself through it.

"Jamie."

I don't want to, but him saying my first name, it makes me look at his face. When Coach says my first name, he's going above and beyond being my coach. The softening of his voice reminds me how much I respect him. How much I respect the idea of a man who knows how to soften his voice.

My sneakers tap against his floor while I try to squelch his worries. "Come on, Coach. I know the eligibility requirements. It won't drop too low. Spring semester, I always buckle down so it doesn't."

"I'm not just talking about the eligibility requirements," he says. "You have college applications to think about in the fall."

This makes me laugh out loud. "Yeah, right. Because my grades are going to have anything to do with that." I square my shoulders and stick my chin out. "I'm going to college to play ball."

"Mm-hmm." Coach chews thoughtfully on the corner of his lip for a minute. "You have any idea how few full D1 scholarships are out there? They don't go to the kids who care only about playing ball anymore, not when there are kids who can play *and* keep their grades up."

I keep my chin high.

"Well, then maybe I'll just get drafted next spring. Skip college altogether." I grin, but Coach isn't in a joking mood.

"Be serious," he chastises me. "Just for a minute." He stares at me hard, wanting me to get this. "Most athletic scholarships are only partial. And more and more, schools don't want to invest in kids who aren't there for an education, too. Sure, you can take out a shitload of loans, but I don't think you want to do that. And loans might not be enough if a scholarship doesn't come through at all."

A sense of powerlessness, a feeling I fucking hate, presses against my chest. "You've always said I was good enough."

"You are good enough. You're so good I have no doubt that plenty of schools will want to offer you a full ride." He shakes his head. "But no college coach is going to want to take the risk on a starting pitcher if he's concerned he's going to drop out or fail out after one semester." He gestures toward the hall. "Lord knows you like your 'distractions.' Class isn't really your thing, either. But from now until next year? You've got to be a little smarter."

I have nothing to say to him. So I keep staring at my toes, which are still tapping, now with frustration and irritation, too.

His eyes are still on me. It feels like hours that he sits there staring me down. But his voice is kinder when he starts talking again.

"Doug staying away?" he asks.

I inhale sharply, rub at the back of my neck. Stare at the ground some more. "Yeah," I murmur.

"Your mom give any more thought to pressing charges?"

"Nah." I glance up, just for a second, then look down again. "She doesn't want to get involved in all that. Lawyers are expensive."

Coach looks at me some more. "You and Olivia doing okay? You need anything?"

"You did enough." I'm quiet for a minute. "We, uh, saw your car out front those first few nights." I chuckle, but it sounds as forced as it feels. "More dependable than the cops. So thank you, but . . ." I stand up and push the chair in. "We're good."

He gets the hint and drops the subject. He stabs one finger at the mustard-colored paper on top of the pile. "You gotta do something about your English grade. You're walking a real fine line between a D and an F. You start failing, I'll have to bench you until you bring it back up."

I exhale loudly and shift my backpack between my shoulders. "Come on, Coach . . ."

He raises both hands. "Not up to me, Abrams. It's school policy. And like I said, you're walking a fine line here. When's your next test?"

I don't answer him for a while. I don't really know. "Thursday?" I guess.

He hands me a paper. "Go to tutoring today. There's a session during your seventh-period study hall."

I shake my head and smile. "Man, you have my schedule memorized?"

Coach cocks an eyebrow and smiles back at me. "Yes, I do." He flips through some more papers. "Eve Marshall's a peer tutor, you know. And I understand she's a really bright girl."

I laugh, exactly three times, even though I'm far from amused. It feels like my head could explode. I stare at him, my *you must be shitting me* expression written all over my face. "No thanks. I'll find someone else. Anyone else."

"She's a teammate."

"She's a bad joke."

The humor drains from Coach's eyes. "She's a teammate," he repeats. "And it's pretty damn obvious that you're having more difficulty with that concept than most."

I stare out the window. Okay. So it's obvious.

Coach sits back in his chair and crosses his arms. "All right, it's no longer a request, it's an order," he says firmly. "You *will* schedule a tutoring session with Eve. She has a ninety-eight percent average in English, and she has Mrs. Jabrowski, too. I'll even set it up for you." He picks up his phone.

"Why are you doing this to me?" I mutter under my breath, kicking at his desk leg as he makes the call.

Pushing the receiver away from his mouth, he tells me, "Because sometimes you have one hell of a time getting out of your own way."

My forehead falls into my hands and I groan aloud, even though no one's listening and no one cares.

This has to be some kind of really messed-up reverse psychology, I decide. I wasn't scared by his reality check about missing out on a scholarship. But threaten me with the prospect of ongoing "tutoring sessions" with Eve Marshall?

You can bet your sweet ass I'll never fail an English test again.

Chapter 7

March 7

Eve

Making my way down the 200s hallway, I glower at everyone I pass without really meaning to. Seventh period is only minutes away, and I can't avoid it any longer.

I hate peer tutoring.

There are those extracurriculars I truly enjoy, the ones I live for: soccer, basketball, baseball. There are those extracurriculars I endure for the sake of rounding out my "college résumé": chorus and Spanish Club and mock trial. And then there is the one extracurricular, year after year, my guidance counselor has guilted me into doing.

Peer tutoring.

"Please, Eve, we can never round up enough student athletes," she begged me. "You're such a good example. So wonderful with time management, with all the things you juggle. You're a *natural*."

I'm not. Not really. I work my butt off for my grades; there's nothing natural about it. In my family, straight As is the expectation, and I do what it takes to bring them home. But God only gifted me with one thing, and it has to do with how my body works, not how my brain works. My teachers don't really see it that way, because I've mastered my game face and just keep grinding. Secretly, I stockpile extra-credit points, just in case. I actually use study halls to *study*, even when I've got the material down pat.

It's tiring, for sure. Far from natural.

I pass Jamie Abrams, camped out in the alcove by the water fountain, in some half-teasing, half-inappropriate embrace with his go-to girl, Naomi, I think. I don't look at him, holding on to a few final seconds of denial, pretending we're not approaching room 207 for any type of shared purpose.

This is not happening, I tell myself as I walk through the door.

But really, why is fate so cruel? It's not my damn fault that he doesn't have two brain cells to rub together—why is it my job to help him get by?

Oh riiiiight, the whole "teammate" argument again. Because he's really treated me like one.

The only reason I stopped protesting this super-stellar little arrangement is because it dawned on me that in the peer tutoring room he would have to look at me. He would have to talk to me. He would not be able to dismiss me. And I could guess how much he wouldn't want to be there. It seemed like a way to exact some revenge for what he did to me on Friday night. This time, he would have to listen to *me*.

It would be more torturous for him than me. So after ten minutes with Mrs. Parente in the guidance office, I gave up the fight. But right now . . . I wish I hadn't.

I want him to acknowledge me. I want something to be on my terms. But I don't really want to look at him. And I don't want to talk to him.

There are already several groups of students paired off inside the classroom, but when the bell rings, Jamie still hasn't walked through the door. I busy myself pulling two desks together, leafing through my English binder, like I'll find *any* tool in there that will help me get through this.

Finally, six minutes later, Jamie comes strolling through the door. He takes his time crossing the room and drops unceremoniously into the chair across from me. "English. Good times. Let's get this party started," he announces breezily.

Without looking at him head-on, I try to read his expression. He doesn't seem overtly hostile or aggravated. What the hell was Naomi able to accomplish in the ten minutes between classes to wipe that usual smug, combative expression off his face?

He's sitting too close for comfort—his cologne overwhelms me; I smell his fresh minty gum every time he snaps his jaw. The realization of this proximity makes me angry, as always, at how he seems to viscerally ruffle me. I shake my head and flip through my binder again, all business.

"Can you at least bother to say hello first?" I blurt out. "Look me in the eye?"

"Can you?" he snaps back immediately, sitting back against his chair and crossing his arms. "Without . . . snarling?"

"I asked you first."

He chuckles, snaps his gum some more. "Man, you are . . ." Jamie looks almost amused. "Never mind." *Snap, snap.* "It's not worth it." He smiles, but his expression doesn't warm. "Hello, Eve."

"Hello," I respond. Begrudgingly. I hadn't really been expecting him to comply with the request. "We only have forty-two minutes left," I say, looking up at the clock. "What do you need help with?"

Jamie chuckles. "Look, I don't need help. You don't get it." He quirks an eyebrow at me. "This your first quarter with Jabrowski?"

I nod.

"She hates athletes. You'll see. If you haven't figured it out already, you will."

It occurs to me he's probably just spoken more to me in the last three minutes than he has in a week on the diamond. It also occurs to me that he's just acknowledged me as an "athlete." Which I guess is something.

"She's just a miserable person, and she seems to enjoy making other people miserable," he continues, leaning back in his chair. "She totally plays favorites with the kids who aren't involved in anything. Gives them special treatment. And is extra hard on athletes. Acts personally offended when we have to leave early for games, talks to us differently and stuff."

I shake my head. "That's ridiculous."

"Trust me. You'll see."

Then he comes toward me again, suddenly, leaning on the desk with his arms crossed, his face only inches from mine. His eyes make me think of the sea—not warm, tropical waters, but the gray-blue of the Atlantic during a storm.

I grip my pencil tightly. "You've just wasted another minute with that bullshit theory."

He offers up a small, prim, sarcastic smile. "Sorry, Miss Marshall. I'll try to focus."

"What do you have coming up this week?" He's not in my class, and I can't remember if all the eleventh-grade sections are on the same unit.

"The final *To Kill a Mockingbird* essay test. The only good thing about it is that we'll finally be done with the damn book."

"*To Kill a Mockingbird*'s not so bad." I shrug. "Better than Shakespeare."

Jamie shakes his head. "I can't get into it. I'd rather read it myself than be tortured by Jabrowski reading it aloud. That stupid, fake Southern accent she puts on makes me really angry."

I have to look away, because out of nowhere, surprisingly, I'm biting back a smile. Jabrowski's terrible accent makes my blood boil, too. Sometimes I've had to actually clamp my lips together to keep from begging her, out loud, to *stop it already!* But no one else in my class seems the least bit perturbed.

"Plus, it's totally a book for girls. I don't get how it's sup-posed to appeal to guys. It's a book about this little . . . brat."

"You can't call Scout a brat," I protest.

Jamie cocks his head and smirks at me, long lashes flutter-ing at the edges. "You like her. Go fucking figure."

I literally *feel* my hackles go up. "What's that mean?"

Jamie takes it upon himself to flip through my English notes until he finds the character list, which includes a few descriptive phrases for each of the key players in the story. " 'Scout,' " he reads aloud, " 'a tomboy with a combative streak.' "

He looks so damn haughty and self-satisfied, I start worry-ing that *my* combative streak might propel me to push his chair over. Assault on school grounds would not be good to add to my student résumé. I try to refocus. "Yeah, well, you can't not like

Atticus Finch. Even if you hate Scout's character, guys always like Atticus. He's, like, the quintessential father figure."

A dark look that I can't read displaces the arrogance in Jamie's expression. "Think we've just wasted another four minutes," he says. "Can we just focus, get this done? I want to pass this test."

"Sorry, didn't realize you were so motivated."

He looks at me again. "Trust me, I have my reasons."

I shrug off his cryptic comment and pull out the results from the Google search I ran earlier. "I have a list of common essay questions about the book we can go over. There's a ton of themes and symbolism in *To Kill a Mockingbird*, but there's definitely some popular ones that teachers always hit on, it seems like. That's a good place to start."

Jamie nods blankly. I can't tell if he's really listening or not.

"And from what I've heard, the hard part of Jabrowski's essay tests is that she tries to fit so many damn questions onto the test. It's easy to run out of time. So . . . organizing your answers first is really important. It keeps you on track. Before you start writing, take a minute to make sure you have your ideas for your introduction, supporting details, and conclusion in mind."

I look up again, to gauge his understanding, and find those restless eyes trained on mine. I swallow hard and look back at my page. "So . . . the mockingbird itself is always included in any question about symbolism. . . ."

For the next half hour, we talk—well, I talk—about symbolism and themes. Jamie listens, and every few minutes, begrudgingly, jots down something that I say.

Then the bell rings, and with a tersely muttered "Thank you,"

Jamie shoves his notebook into his backpack and makes a bee-line for the door. Despite managing to keep the peace for one study hall, there's certainly no pretense that we would head toward the locker rooms for practice *together*.

Still, I'm only steps behind him as we approach the corner heading back toward the main lobby. The two of us see the scene unfold at the same time.

"What's up, freak show?"

I recognize the guy doing the taunting—Jeremy Kirkpatrick, senior lacrosse player from South. The lacrosse team is a gigantic, collective douchebag.

And I recognize the target of the taunting as well, the girl who bumped into me last week, the girl with the bright pink hair, piercings, and ear gauges.

She's ignoring him, taking a long drink from the fountain.

"Freak show, I said what's up," Jeremy continues as his douchey buddies watch and laugh. "How can you not hear me with those big holes in your ears?"

Bent over the fountain, she closes her eyes and swallows hard. She doesn't open them, her body freezing, like she's trying to play possum.

But Jeremy's bent on a reaction. "Freeeak show . . . oh freak show . . . ," he keeps calling.

I can't take my eyes off the girl. *Stand up*, I'm mentally willing her. *Stand up and walk away.*

But every muscle in her body is rigid and her eyes are still shut and she's no longer drinking the water. It's running in rivulets down her chin, soaking her black T-shirt.

Then, in an instant, in my peripheral vision I see Jeremy's body slammed into the wall behind him. I turn my body and see that his T-shirt is bunched up in Jamie's fist, and Jamie's about to slam him into the wall for a second time.

"Leave her alone," he growls at Jeremy. He drives his spine into the wall a third time for good measure. "Leave her the fuck alone."

Jeremy is clearly spooked, but he shakes Jamie off and tries to laugh. "Dude. Chill." He pushes Jamie away, straightening his polo shirt, and moseys off with his friends in tow. "Crazy-ass East kids."

Jamie keeps his furious eyes trained on Jeremy's back. "Pussy." He spits on the ground before turning back to the girl, who is propped up on the water fountain with one thin, shaky arm.

Even though a small crowd has gathered, Jamie collects the girl in his arms and pulls her close. I catch him checking in on her. "You okay?"

She nods minutely, trying to escape his hug like a child unwilling to be comforted.

I watch, confused about a couple of things. First off, she doesn't look like his type. And second . . . he's being so nice.

But he's not nice for long. He's glaring again, at the tall, lanky guy who comes running up, holding the waist of his loose black jeans, tugging the girl out of Jamie's arms. "Where were you at during all this, *Justin*?"

He doesn't wait for a response before turning back to the girl. "Just keep away from those assholes, huh?" She nods, and he picks up his backpack from where he dropped it before assaulting Jeremy. Then he heads off toward the gym, not bothering to look back, like nothing ever happened.

Chapter 8

March 14

Jamie

It's our first home game today. Well, it's only a scrimmage, but everyone's acting like it's the real deal. Late last night or early this morning, spirit girls stealthily decorated our lockers with gold and black balloons and crepe paper. Lise came running up to me this morning, like she could barely wait to present me with a paper bag full of sugar cookies decorated to look like baseballs. JV and varsity are both wearing team T-shirts for the school day.

It's the first time our newly combined team is dressed like a team. I see Eve and Scott walk into the lobby together in their shirts. It's like she's finally made the ultimate concession, identifying as a Pirate. But when they walk past, I catch that she's tied those ever-present braids with gold-and-black hair ties. Gold-and-black hair ties are hardly part of the team uniform. Huh. Maybe she *actually* enjoys baseball more than she enjoys protesting something.

I don't say hi to them, though, turning my back before I'm put in a position where I have to. One of our coaches must've just discovered the *Sports Illustrated* feature, because it's hanging on our team bulletin board inside the locker room now. I don't think I can get away with tearing it down. At the same time I turn my back, I close my eyes. I can't let that girl get inside my head today. I need to focus.

I sit in the back of my classes, keep my head down during the day, and avoid Naomi at lunchtime. Avoid Kaitlyn during study hall. By 2:40 when the bell rings, I'm totally in the zone. Inside the locker room, everyone's pumped—there's a natural unifying effect in forcing us to compete against someone besides ourselves, and Overbrook is always one of our biggest rivals. The starting lineup is a mash-up of South and East players, and some of the guys from East are obviously pissed, but it's hard to deny that Coach was fair about it.

Plus, I'm starting. And the road to the trophy begins today, officially or not.

After changing into my uniform pants, I head over to the trainer's office for some pregame stretches. A few of us are in there, shirtless, when Eve marches in with the thermos to fill with ice as part of her equipment duty. She's not going to be able to lift it when it's full, no way.

I swear her cheeks redden when she takes in the scene in the room, a bunch of us half-naked, but she says nothing as she carries the huge orange thermos over to the ice chest.

But Brendan decides not to let her off the hook.

He's stuffing his cup inside his pants but pulls it out to hold it up as he calls to her. "You remembered yours, right, Marshall?"

A few of the guys guffaw, but I just shake my head. There's no time for this shit today.

Our assistant coach lays into him at once. "Watch it, Brendan. Have a little respect."

Eve acknowledges none of it, just coolly goes about her business and then looks around, eyes coming to rest on a metal cart. She wheels it over, then struggles mightily in her attempts to lift the full thermos onto it. I watch her as I swing my right arm around in circles, loosening it up. It's almost painful to watch. *Just admit you need help.*

But she won't. Eve keeps her back to us, I guess thinking we won't see her struggling, but for anyone who's paying attention, it's obvious. She lucks out when Scott appears, grabs the other side, and they heft it onto the cart together.

I shake my head again and shrug into my jersey.

When I get down to the field, I'm sort of stunned by the size of the crowd. The combining of the two teams inevitably means more spectators, but beyond that, it's impossible to miss the extra reporters, some with badges from city papers, and several groups of middle school girls, who can't seem to take their eyes off Eve.

Naomi's there, and she waves to me. Behind her sits that Marcella chick, who comes in with Eve every day. I see my mom, still in her Target uniform. I hope she didn't give up hours to be here. I notice a set of parents and a dude who looks a couple of years older than us wearing buttons with Eve's picture on them, her still in her Bulldogs uniform in the pictures.

I stare at them for a minute. Then, *Focus*, I remind myself.

Doesn't matter how many people are here to see her. *I'm* the Pirates' starting pitcher.

I repeat the mantra to myself in those last few minutes leading up to the game, and then the home plate umpire pulls his mask down and gives Coach a signal, and I jog out to the mound. As the first hitter from Overbrook approaches the plate, I hear the claps and whistles, and I let them energize me.

Then I stop thinking. I switch over to auto mode and do my thing.

First batter up . . . I strike him out looking.

The second batter's a lefty, and he sends a pop-up into right field. Nathan catches it without any effort, and there's two down.

Third batter hits a fast grounder toward second and makes it to first before Chris can throw him out.

Which brings Trevor McFadden to the plate in the cleanup position, arrogant smile clearly visible behind the face guard.

Fucking Trevor McFadden. We all hate that cocky prick.

Unfortunately for me, he also has the bat power to back it up. His presence gets inside my head, because I want to get out of this inning, and I want it badly. I want to get out of this inning with Trevor at the plate. He swings and misses on a fastball, then gets a piece of it for a foul tip on the second pitch. I'm so close, and the realization distracts me. I throw three balls in a row.

I spit into the dirt and pause, and the crowd comes to life to lift me up.

"You got this, Ace!"

"Strike three, baby!"

"All you, man, all you!"

I soak it in, then tune it out, focusing on the catcher's mitt like a laser. I wind up and send a curveball into Timmy's glove. I strike him out looking.

I pump my fist and dash toward the dugout, the crowd

jumping to its feet as we put them away. I enter the dugout whooping and smack my glove onto the bench. "And that's how you start a season, gentlemen!"

....

The innings go by smoothly. During an at bat in the third, I send Phil home and we secure the lead. At the other end, I'm keeping runs from scoring and feeling strong. Things take a turn during the fourth, when on my way to the mound, I notice that Olivia's shown up at the game. She's with two other girls, and they all look like they're struggling to keep their eyes all the way open. She's giggling her head off and keeping her distance from our mother.

Suddenly I'm tense. But I know how to keep home shit off the playing field—I've been doing it for years. I visualize steel bars coming down on the other side of me, blocking it out, providing blinders that let me focus on the plate. Getting the ball to it as quickly and accurately as possible. Right now, nothing else can affect me.

It's a solid opener for me, and I'm surprised when Coach calls a time-out and jogs out to the mound during the sixth inning. Sure, there are two men on base, but I just struck out two batters in a row and I'm feeling confident I can get the third.

Coach kicks the dirt, clears his throat, and looks me in the eye. "How you feeling, Abrams?"

"Good. Strong. Planning to shut this thing down right now."

He flashes a quick smile. "You've had a tremendous start." He clears his throat again. "Let's go out on a high note, all right?"

I shake my head. "I'm good, Coach," I say. "And I thought pitch count didn't really matter till the season officially started."

He shrugs. "The league goes back and forth on that. You should save some regardless."

"Come on, Coach . . ."

"Abrams. Save some." His voice lets me know this issue is not up for debate.

He gives me a quick slap to the rear. "Take a rest."

Before I follow his orders, I stare to the right of the dugout. I should've known who's warming up. I should've known what this was about.

I glare at Coach for a solid twenty seconds before walking off the mound. It doesn't matter that the crowd is loud with appreciation, that they see nothing wrong with what's happening. Sure, it's a rare thing for me to pitch an entire game. But they don't get the picture at all.

And immediately, their attention is diverted when Coach calls Eve into the game. Girls and women are jumping to their feet, letting her know how *supported* she is, how eager they are to stand behind her. Right away, it's evident she's not going to be held to the same standard. If this game gets away from us, which it probably will, they'll still be proud of her. Just for getting out there.

Give me a break.

I slide into the corner of the dugout, ignoring my teammates, who slap my back and extend their hands for high fives, leaving distance between myself and the rest of the team. I glower at her, eyes immediately pulled to her right hand. Even from this distance, I can tell it's shaking. There's no way she's going to be able to deliver.

Eve stands there a long minute, like a statue, attempting to collect herself, and Scott takes off his mask and runs out to the mound to talk to her. He whispers in her ear; he says something that makes her laugh. Then she nods decisively, and with a final thumbs-up in her direction, he returns to his place behind the plate.

Then she does it. She delivers.

She delivers strike after strike. She keeps her cool when the count is full. She keeps her cool when grounders come in her direction.

She's good, damn it, faster than Pat, more consistent than Matty, and we're adding runs to our count while she's keeping them from adding runs to theirs. And regardless of how I hate her up there, I don't have it in me to wish for a loss for the sake of spiting her. I can't begrudge her for getting the job done.

But my newfound respect for her game, along with Coach's decision making, starts to fade during the ninth inning.

That's when it starts slipping away from her, when Overbrook scores two runs and gets a runner to second off a double. And Trevor's up to bat. At the rate she's going, she's on her way to getting lit up.

The pitching coach has Matty warming up. But Coach isn't even glancing in his direction. He's not walking out to the mound. And I feel myself start sweating as I stare at him.

What the hell are you doing?

I look back out at Eve. It's a sink-or-swim moment, and she knows it. It's written all over her face. She's doubtful.

Normally, Coach would pull a pitcher in this scenario, let someone with a fresh arm get us out of the jam. But he wants her to bounce back, regain control. He wants her to prove to herself that out here, with a new team that doesn't fully have her back, she can.

I know what Coach is doing—he's helping her. It's what he does, it's what he's always done for me: helped me. But not like this. Not by giving me a chance when I really didn't deserve one.

I tell myself that if the actual season were under way, he wouldn't be so cavalier with the team's well-being. But I don't even know anymore.

I see Eve's lips moving. She's coaching herself, without even relying on Scott or Coach to boost her. She faces Trevor, who's making some lewd gestures to try to throw her, and glares right at him. She shuts him down. Then their final batter sends a line drive toward third, which is caught by Brayden, who promptly turns and tags the runner who was caught between the bases.

My teammates jump to their feet, fists in the air. I can hear the roar of the crowd outside. And I see Scott throw off his equipment and run toward the mound, swallowing her up in his arms like it's game seven of the fucking World Series.

Coach is beaming, looking toward the mound and clapping.

Because he made the right call, and Eve got the job done.

My anger and disbelief turn to panic, and I'm on my feet at once. *She got the job done.*

Suddenly, I'm gathering my stuff in a flash. I smash my Windbreaker into a ball and jam it into my bat bag, and I crush the paper bag of cookies in my fist, probably destroying them. As I leave the dugout without a word to any of my teammates, I make my way around the back, past the spectators in the bleachers. From the corner of my eye, I catch a glimpse of my mom with her hands cupped in front of her mouth, calling my name over the cheers of the crowd. I rush on up the hill like I don't hear her.

And I don't think anyone else notices me leaving.

I march up the hill, not sure if I feel like trying to get my emotions under some kind of control or just letting them expand and explode. The rational side of my brain reminds me that I was usually relieved midway through a game, midway through even my best games. The W will still be mine, regardless. Resentment swirls inside me. It doesn't feel like that anymore. It doesn't feel like I was the star of the show.

There's a feeling like something is being crushed inside me, and I picture an old car at a junk lot being mashed between the jaws of a huge, remorseless machine. Fuck, it *hurts*, the sensation, and I don't stop it as it transforms itself into bitter, blinding anger instead.

I reach the parking lot, cleats clattering against the pavement as I cross over from the grass. My hands are curling themselves into fists, creating tension in my forearms in keeping with the pressure building up inside me. I wonder exactly how thick the locker room cinder-block walls are, because I have a sudden need to slam my bat against them a few times when I get inside the door. I'm almost there.

"Jamie!"

A voice reaches me from the distance as I stand there, hand on the outside doorknob. It sounds excited and elated. *She* sounds excited and elated.

Eve.

She jogs across the parking lot in my direction. She's lost her ball cap and her face is wide open—she's practically glowing. Downright euphoric.

"We pulled it off," she says with a smile. "That was an awesome start to the season."

Eve steps forward, her right arm outstretched, like she's looking to shake my hand.

I immediately shift my bat bag farther back on my shoulder and jam both hands into my pockets.

Now she looks surprised, chastened, hand hanging foolishly in the air like she made a mistake.

I feel a vein in my neck pulsing, but I work to control it, to keep my voice even. "So you have to feel pretty satisfied about today." I offer up a big, fake smile.

She doesn't respond for a minute, looking unsure. But I keep the smile in place, and eventually she speaks. "Yeah . . . I am. It felt like a team effort and . . ." Eve gazes into the distance, then ducks her head. "That felt good."

I wait until she looks at me again. "No, *you* must feel satisfied," I repeat, letting the smile slide right off my face. "Ultimately, it's all about you, right?" I gesture with my thumb toward the field. "All those people down there, shit, record numbers for a scrimmage, that little 'girl power' crew from the middle school, the goddamn reporters. They were all there to see you." Expression completely flat, I clap three times. "Congratulations. Good for you."

I turn on my heel and open the door.

But she grabs it before I can disappear inside and let it slam behind me, in her face. I spin around in surprise, nearly clocking her with the bat bag.

Her face is right in mine, and she's seething. "What the hell is your problem, dude? I came up here because you pitched an awesome game and I have absolutely no problem saying so. *You* were the starting pitcher, Coach chose *you*, and *you* set up the win." She shakes her head, braids flying. "What the hell reason do you have for being so nasty?"

"You don't get it, all right?" I snap. "Nothing's enough for you, is it?"

She looks frozen and doesn't respond, so I press on, ticking my points off on my fingers. "You have your grades and all the teachers love you. You'd get into any college without being some sort of 'phenom.' You have soccer. You have basketball. And you know that that's your future, that in reality, this is not." My voice becomes sort of high-pitched and screechy. "You don't *need* this!"

I swallow hard. "You don't need a scholarship. Your future's not going to depend on one."

You're not like me. This is all I have. This is everything and this is it.

I take a deep breath, because I can feel my emotions shifting again, and I can't let them slip away from me. Not now.

"I need this, okay? I *need* this. It's not just a game to me; it's the only thing I can even begin to count on. And for that reason, you're always going to be in my way." I look down at the pavement and kick at a rock. "So go ahead and feel satisfied with yourself, tell yourself that it's a team effort. But the truth is, you stole the show just because you could."

I stare into her eyes. I can't read them; I can't tell if she's furious or wounded or confused. But she is quiet for once.

"Without even thinking about what you were stealing. So, congratulations," I whisper.

I turn my back on her and open the door. And this time she has enough sense to stay out of its way. It slams behind me with a satisfying smack, shutting her off and shutting her out.

Chapter 9

March 15

Eve

I should be in a pretty stellar mood.

I closed out the game on a high note, and that's usually a high that lasts at least twenty-four hours. I heard my name mentioned during the sports announcements in homeroom, a first since I'd started at East. My teammates, including some seniors from East who'd continued to keep their distance since practices had started, were quick to come up to me and congratulate me all over again. Even some girls from East, ones who'd never talked to me before, came up to show their support.

"You go, lady," one of them said to me as she'd clapped my shoulder in passing between classes. "That took balls yesterday."

But none of them, none of their encouragement, could reignite the excitement that had been extinguished, unexpectedly and in one fell swoop, after the game.

I avoided the lobby in the morning in an attempt to avoid him. Hours later, I'm still sorting out my feelings in response to his *explosion*. The adrenaline crash after the game left me too worn out to even think about figuring it out, so I faked a good mood with Marcella and my parents, and then buried myself in two hours of homework as a distraction.

His cruel accusation continues to pop into my head, though.

You stole the show just because you could.

I shut my eyes against them and hurry into my English classroom. At the door, Marcella peels herself off Brian and follows me inside, taking a seat beside me.

"Hey, Superstar."

Her greeting makes me cringe. "Stop."

Superstar.

I mean, does he really *think . . .*

I push our encounter out of my head, again, and follow Marcella's gaze to the doorway. Brian's still hanging out outside our classroom, talking to a few guys from the East soccer team, laughing at something some girl is saying.

Marcella's lips come together in a tight line as she observes. But she doesn't say anything, she just keeps her eye on him until he wanders away with the rest of the guys and the girl walks into our room.

Mrs. Jabrowski appears in the door as the bell rings, Pepsi can in hand, and makes her way to her desk. "Okay, people," she calls over our chattering, "so I don't forget, I'm going to collect your *Crucible* pre-reading assignment first thing."

On all sides of me, classmates bend over backpacks or open folders to retrieve packets for the new unit. I sit, motionless, panicking at once. The assignment isn't due today; it's due tomorrow. I'm certain of it. So why does everyone else have theirs?

I flip to the syllabus page in my binder. Right there! It's due March 16, just like I thought. I recognize the packets they're all pulling out—I completed half of mine last night before nearly falling asleep at my desk. But I'd planned to finish it tonight. The night before *it's due*.

Mrs. Jabrowski approaches our corner. She waves her hand impatiently above my desk while reaching for Marcella's packet. "Eve, may I please have yours?"

"It's at home." It's hard to meet her eye, so I point to the syllabus instead. "I thought it was due tomorrow."

"It *was* due tomorrow." She turns in the direction of the white-board, where assignments for all her classes are listed. "But I updated the due date on the board yesterday at the end of class. We finished *To Kill a Mockingbird* early, and I needed to adjust our schedule."

Now I meet her eye, shaking my head. I missed the last fifteen minutes of class due to our early dismissal to get changed for the game. And she knows it. "But I left early. I wasn't aware of the change. And you didn't send out an e-blast through the system."

She stares at me, silent for a few seconds, because she knows I have her on this point. It's a requirement for teachers to formalize syllabus changes through the school's e-blast announcement system. Yet my calling her out on it seems to make her huffy, and she refuses to stay on the matter at hand.

Mrs. Jabrowski's hands go to her hips. "Eve, you left my class fifteen minutes early to do nothing more important than change into your uniform and sneakers," she starts.

Cleats, I'm tempted to say.

"Now, I don't fault students for participating in extracurricular activities. But sometimes there are consequences to missing portions of class. Like the zero you'll receive for this assignment." She turns her back, as if the discussion is over.

As if.

And suddenly I'm on my feet. "But that's not fair!"

She slowly looks over her shoulder, voice cold as she raises one eyebrow in my direction. *"Excuse me?"*

"It's not fair," I repeat, my voice strong and even. "I had permission to leave class early; I was hardly 'skipping' anything. My assignment is almost finished and definitely would've been with me tomorrow. And you didn't send an e-blast." I shake my head. "It's not right that I get a zero for the assignment. It's harsh, and unfair, and . . . just not right."

Marcella tugs at the bottom of my shirt. "Eve. Sit down," she hisses.

But I won't. I can't swallow the injustice.

The classroom is mostly silent, with the exception of a few boys who are snickering in the back. Mrs. Jabrowski is practically sneering. "I'm in charge of this classroom and can make decisions as I see fit. I know you think you're something special, but I can assure you, this classroom is not a playing field. And you're not getting any special treatment from me."

"I'm not asking for special treatment. I'm just asking you to be fair."

"I would like to move on with class now." She actually

points at me. "One more protest and you can spend the rest of the period in the detention room instead of disrupting mine." Mrs. Jabrowski turns her back on me for a second time.

I glance down at Marcella, her wide eyes full of warning. I'm sure most people would give it up, sit down, understand the meaning of "pick your battles." I mean, the assignment only counts for twenty points.

But I'm too filled with indignation, and after riding the roller coaster of emotions I've been on for the past twenty-four hours, I'm not in the best place for making smart decisions. And so my mouth ends up opening one more time of its own accord.

"Yes, it was partly my responsibility, but it was partly yours, too. You didn't send the e-blast. It's policy, and you know it."

Mrs. Jabrowski whirls around, arm extended toward the door. "You're finished in my room for today, Miss Marshall." She hurriedly fills out a detention slip and thrusts it in my direction. "So you can head to detention now. Or if you'd like to continue making your argument, you can stop at the office and take it up with the principal."

I accept the pass and grab my things. "Bullshit," I murmur under my breath as I storm out of the room.

But once I'm in the hallway, I come to a sudden stop. I have no idea where the detention room is. Not at this school and not at my last school.

I glance over my shoulder. *That wretched woman.* I feel so stupid, standing there, needing to ask *directions* to the detention room.

Wearily, I trudge toward the main office, cheeks pink as I ask the secretary for the location of the detention room. She directs me to room 116, which is located in a dark, creepy corner near the rarely used elevator and janitor's closet. Could this be any more stereotypical? And now that its reality is upon me, I feel kind of queasy, because I'm unsure of how it all works, if my parents or coach will be notified that I ended up here.

I nudge open the door, sort of expecting to find a prison riot in process behind it, but instead it's just . . . crickets. The tiny room is oppressively hot and silent, occupied by a few derelict types with their heads on the desks, sleeping. I can't quite tell if the monitor is reading a magazine behind a desk or sleeping, too. Only a couple of boys are awake, chins tucked, discreetly playing on their phones. Most of them are hiding out in their hoodies. None of the delinquents even bother to turn their heads in my direction.

None of the delinquents . . . but one.

And if I thought this day couldn't get any worse, *boom*, there it goes, getting worse, exponentially.

Jamie's in detention, too. Fan-freakin'-tastic.

I didn't realize it was him at first, the way he fits right in with the rest of them, in a gray, zip-up Pirates hoodie, the hood pulled up over his head, earbuds shoved into his ears. And although his face offers no sign of recognition, I catch the way he fake-casually removes his earbuds so he can find out what's going on.

The monitor finally glances up at me, bored. "Whose room are you coming from?"

I clear my throat, the noise loud and kind of embarrassing in this quiet coffin of a room. "Mrs. Jabrowski's."

I hear it at once from across the room. An obnoxious snort. A murmur. "Told you so."

And until that moment, I'd forgotten about his little warning, his assertion regarding Jabrowski's mistreatment of student athletes. I remember how dismissive she was of my reason for leaving class, how her comments felt unnecessarily personal. But to hell if I'll acknowledge that he's possibly right about her.

I walk forward, giving my slip to the monitor. "You're in here for an hour," he informs me, before returning to his magazine.

I glance up at the clock, confused. "But it's two o'clock now. School ends at two forty."

"You take the late bus," he informs me without looking up. He chuckles once. "Guess it's your first time at the rodeo."

"I have practice at three."

"Well, I guess you'll be late."

The satisfaction oozing out of Jamie is so palpable, it nearly slithers across the floor and covers my feet.

My stomach drops and suddenly I want to cry. It wasn't worth it. Twenty points wasn't worth it. *She* wasn't worth it. Not for this. Slinking across the room, I drop into the only empty seat in the minuscule space, diagonal from Jamie. Seriously. If she wanted to punish me, consider it done. I'm definitely being punished.

I hear him making a *tsk-tsk* noise behind me. "Would never have expected to see you down here. Talk about disappointing your coach."

I flick a braid over my shoulder and don't bother to turn around. "And look at you, making him so proud."

He laughs quietly. "Coach knows what to expect from me. But you . . . this . . . they'll be *appalled*."

That's it. My head whirls around so fast I'm momentarily worried I strained a nerve in my neck. "Shut up, Jamie," I snap.

Those blue eyes light up, like he's getting a kick out of this.

He lifts his chin in my direction. "You get mouthy like that with Jabrowski? Is that how you ended up down here?"

I grip the corners of the scarred wooden desk. I can admit to the tendency to get mouthy, or I can admit that he was right, that it seemed like she was being unnecessarily hard on me simply because of my devotion to sports.

Or I can just sit here and try to ignore him.

From the corner of my eye, I see him settle back against his chair, crossing his hands behind his head languidly. "You can just say it. I was right."

The monitor looks up, irritated. "Guys. Enough."

We both ignore him.

"You weren't right," I mutter.

Jamie laughs again, all smooth and arrogant. "Too stubborn for your own good. Seriously. Whatever."

A moment later, I glance back at him once. Then again.

God, he is infuriating, probably the most infuriating person I've ever met. I mean, why does he have his hood up in the middle of detention, anyway? This lack of concern, this bad-boy persona . . . it's not like any other girls are in here to appreciate it. He thinks he's such hot shit, those full lips smiling arrogantly, those blue eyes alight at my misfortune.

I huff. I don't know *why* I keep staring anyway.

I shake my head, refocusing, finally turning all the way toward him. "I don't know what you're smiling about. You weren't right." A new wave of anger . . . and hurt . . . and embarrassment crests within me. "You weren't right about anything."

"You two." The monitor raises his voice, clearly annoyed that he's being bothered to discipline us. "This is supposed to be a silent room."

But I ignore him, again, because hell, I'm already in detention and going to be late for practice. And because it's time Jamie Abrams hears these things from me, once and for all.

"I'm not out to get attention like some people, and I didn't 'steal the spotlight' because I enjoy being there," I inform him, arms folded over my chest. "For your information, I'd do just about anything to avoid being there if I could just play the game and leave it at that."

"You seemed pretty damn smiley in that magazine feature. Didn't seem to mind the spotlight then."

"That feature was a huge letdown." Suddenly I'm admitting something to him I haven't admitted to anyone else. "I thought they were actually going to include the interview, which they used all of two sentences from. They used me for an angle, used the pictures of me in a pink jersey with a baseball glove as a selling point. They didn't really care about what I do on the field anyway."

This shuts him up for a second and I look him right in the eye, because I'm tired of this, of all this, and I refuse to be scared of him, regardless of how his anger scared me yesterday.

"I have one more season, maybe two, but who knows? You can go to college and play, you can play in work leagues, hell, you can coach your son's Little League team someday if you want to."

My throat tightens unexpectedly and I have to swallow, hard, because I would *never* let Jamie Abrams catch me being weak.

"I play, and pitch, because I love to play and pitch. I love being out there, I love every minute of it, I love every part of it, probably the exact same way you do when you're actually caught up in the moment and not worried about being 'Ace' or worried about what I may or may not be stealing from you." I have to pause, and swallow, one more time. "And knowing what I do, accepting my physical limitations and biomechanics, accepting that no, I won't be able to keep up with the boys forever, knowing what it feels like to see a limit to my time on the field approaching . . ." My eyes suddenly feel watery, but I'm too wrapped up in my speech to even care anymore. "To hell if I would ever actively try to take that feeling away from someone else for the sake of being in a freakin' *spotlight*."

My voice rises as I make one final point. "And maybe if you'd pull your head out of your ass and stop feeling so personally offended by everything I do, you'd see that. You'd see that I love the game every bit as much as you do and deserve to be out there, too."

The monitor slams his magazine down on his desk. "All right. It's just ridiculous now."

I whirl around and throw my hands in the air. "Oh, what you are going to do, send me to detention?"

The monitor looks a bit shocked. I'm kind of shocked at myself. And in that moment I wish I had my own hoodie—Bulldogs, Pirates, or otherwise—because more than anything I wish I had something to burrow inside, strings to pull tight, something dark and comforting to block out this remarkably *awful* afternoon.

Chapter 10

March 17

Jamie

I hate working Friday nights.

I hate working Friday nights, especially when they come right off an away win. It means I have to hustle to get to work on time, and the celebratory mood I leave behind, a mood that only increased in intensity on the long ride home, is something I desperately want to keep going. I know what my teammates do once they get off the bus—they linger in the parking lot, make plans to meet up later, check in to see who has beer or where the girls are going to be hanging out. They always try to include me as I dash off, because none of them really get it. I don't let them get it.

"Abrams, what the hell, man?" Matt asks. "George was a Pirate back in the day, and you've worked there forever. How come he always puts you on the schedule on Friday nights?"

Because the tips are best on Friday nights. Because George pays me time and a half because no one else wants to be there on Fridays and because George is decent.

"I like to have Saturdays off better," I lie. I cover it with a grin. "No practice, no games . . . more time to focus on other things . . ."

They get my drift and snort in response to this, and Matt says, "All right, Ace, well, text me when you get off. We might still be out."

"Yeah. I will."

I quickly duck inside my Jeep and close the door. God, I hate working Friday nights, and I'd give anything to stay with my friends, to celebrate, to *chill*. But there are things in life I hate even more than working Fridays.

I stare at the center of the steering wheel.

I'd walked in on her crying over a pile of envelopes the other afternoon. I'd asked her what was wrong, which was a dumb question. What's wrong *now*? What bills can't we pay *now*? Which collection agency is threatening *now*?

My mom had trouble meeting my eye when she answered. "The calculations just never work out the way they're supposed to. There's always something. Every time I find a way to save some money, something comes up that sucks it right back out of the bank. If I work more hours to bring in more income, we lose SNAP benefits like that, and the difference in my paychecks after taxes wouldn't make up for the loss."

My hands tighten around the outside of the steering wheel as I remember what she said next.

"Maybe I should've just dealt with him," she muttered. "What was the point of making him leave if things were still going to be so hard? It was hard before, but at least we could pay the bills."

My disbelief must've been obvious, because she was quick to add, "Not for me, but so I could take care of you guys. Things you need."

"That's not right," I said.

"It's something they don't tell you beforehand," she whispered, "the sad, messed-up thing about becoming a mom. Your happiness means more to me than my own."

Screw that. Screw even considering Doug again.

My foot slams the brake to the floor as I shift gears, and the Jeep bucks out of my parking spot. There are plenty of things I hate more than working Friday nights, so I'll be behind the counter at the Burger Barn as quickly as humanly possible.

I fly across town, running a few stop signs, and park in the rear of the already crowded lot. Daryl asks me if we won, nods in approval when I tell him we did, and then fires me up a burger on the house. I wolf it down, tie on my apron, and manage one deep breath before heading out behind the counter.

There are plenty of kids from East hanging out in the restaurant and at the counter. Kids I've known my whole life and kids I recognize now as South transplants. It doesn't bother me, constantly having my classmates where I work—plenty of my friends work—but some nights it's tougher to keep up the image than others. Tonight, I'm beat and I don't feel like it. Don't feel like playing to the girls. The freshman girls, whispering and giggling, deciding who has the nerve to approach me at the counter and pay their bill. The girls from the local Catholic school, one of whom I'm pretty sure I hooked up with last summer, talking behind their hands while blatantly staring with their eyes.

It's a relief when Naomi comes sauntering in and sidles up to the counter. Naomi's an easy game to play. We've been friends with benefits for a while. And friends even longer than that—since the summer after eighth grade, the night of the Fourth of July fireworks at the park. I'd stumbled upon her sitting in a bed of pine needles away from the crowd, drinking stolen peach schnapps years before most of us were drinking. She'd opened up to me about her shitty home life, which sounded a lot like mine. It was the first time we kissed, and some sort of bond formed that night that had lasted over the years.

Elbows on the counter, I lean down in front of her, catching a breath about an hour into the shift. "Hey, baby."

"Hey, Jamie."

She shrugs out of her jacket, showing off a tank top too skimpy for March. The weather doesn't stop Naomi. Never has.

"You eating?"

"Nah. Can you grab me a Diet Coke with lemon, though?"

"Sure."

"Thanks," she says when I set the tall vintage Coke glass down in front of her. "How'd the game go?"

"We won."

"You start?"

"Nah, Coach let Marshall have the start."

Naomi rolls her eyes. "How'd that work out?"

"Pretty much like watching a train wreck."

"Well, good," she says. "Maybe it won't take your coach too many games to come to terms with how stupid he's being." She takes a long pull on her straw, looking up at me, waiting for me to agree.

"Yeah . . . ," I start.

Then I stop, sort of surprising myself, wipe down the counter with a clean rag, and change the subject.

I lift my chin in her direction. "Where's everybody else tonight?"

Naomi groans. "Ugh, we were all hanging out at Becky's, trying to figure out what we wanted to do. But Meg is going to get back with Hayden; I know it. You can feel her crumbling, and it's the most pathetic thing ever to watch. So I told her, I don't feel like hanging out here tonight if you're just going to sit here, texting him back, being a moron."

I chuckle. "Fair enough. No point in being subtle."

"Right?" Then she stares off into the distance. "Dipshit Dan is having his poker game at the house tonight. His friends are pigs."

Dipshit Dan is Naomi's stepdad. From the stories she's told me, he's on a par with some of the winners my mom has dated.

"So I just drove here instead of going home; saw your car in the parking lot."

Then she gives me the look, *that* look, the smallest corner of her mouth upturned, her eyes narrowed like a cat's. "You just going home after?" she asks.

"Yeah."

"You shower after the game?"

"Yes!"

"Come over after, then. Basement door." Her smile grows. "They'll all be drunk by then and no one will even notice. We can hang out . . . or something."

Like I said, no point in being subtle.

"Okay."

She finishes her soda, hops off the stool, and reaches across the counter to tickle my wrist. "See you then."

"Don't forget to unlock the door this time."

She giggles as she goes. I watch her walk out the door, because it's always worth it, watching Naomi walk away, but once she's gone, my shoulders drop. I rub at my neck. I'm tired and my muscles are stiff, and all I really want to do is go home and sleep. But . . . when a girl like Naomi pretty much throws herself at you, well, you don't look *that* gift horse in the mouth.

Before the door can even close behind her, it's being opened again, the three guys walking through it taking their sweet time to look over their shoulders and check her out. I recognize all three of them from the Spring Falls varsity team. Especially since I struck out two of them less than four hours ago.

The sight of them reinvigorates me some. I lift my arms up and smile smugly. "Really, boys? You're going to subject yourselves to my pretty face two times in one day? After the way we shut you down?"

"Suck a dick, Abrams," one of them says, pulling a chair out from the nearest table and sitting down. He shrugs. "There might be a few pussies on our JV squad, but at least no one on our team has an actual, ya know, pussy."

The girls who followed them into the restaurant giggle like he's the most hilarious thing they've ever encountered.

"That's pretty fucking lame, Johanssen," I tell him.

He shrugs again. "Whatever. It's true." Then he turns his back on me.

They're a big group, too big to fit at the counter, so I'm spared having to actually wait on them. They stay for a ridiculously long time, though, because apparently no one from Spring Falls has anything better to do with their weekends than hang out where I'm getting *paid* to be. Losers.

I ignore them, going back to the counter crowd, which finally starts to thin out around eight thirty. Dinner's pretty much over, and the nine o'clock movie crowd is on its way out. I'm changing out the register drawer when the bells on the door clatter and I look up.

Eve Marshall walks in with Marcella. She's in sweats, and the first thing I notice is that she looks as tired as I feel. Marcella's holding on to her arm, talking close to her ear, a mile a minute. Does that girl ever *stop* talking?

I watch Eve's face as she nods, feeling . . . nothing.

For the first time, ever, I feel nothing.

No rush of resentment, fury, loathing.

Tonight, nothing happens when Eve walks in the door, and maybe I'm just that tired, not getting worked up over her existence like I usually do.

I'm not sure if they even notice me as they head toward a corner booth, but I'm still observing them from the corner of my eye, trying to make sense of it.

Before, any time Eve appeared on the scene, it felt like a match was automatically lit inside of me, dangerously close to something flammable. But then that day I blew up at her, told her the truth about why I resented her so much . . . some of the pressure inside of me got released, and it just hadn't built all the way back up afterward.

Even when she unleashed on me.

Plenty of girls have yelled at me. But never like that. No one's ever left me speechless.

Then there was the game we won, together, without either of us blowing up, something of a miracle.

And then there was today. Today was rough. She had a lousy-ass start and got pulled from the game way earlier than anyone had expected. Any guy I knew would have been behind the dugout, head in his hands, kicking the cement or throwing helmets. She sat there, chin up, revealing nothing. She didn't come close to *crying* or anything. She congratulated me on the win before getting back on the bus. And I didn't even feel like gloating or saying something smart.

It was weird.

I stare at them another minute, and then I realize I'm not the only one staring toward Eve and Marcella's booth. I notice the staring, and then I'm aware of the change in the tension in the room. The guys from Spring Falls: they definitely recognize her, too, and they're nudging each other, making comments under their breath that I can't quite catch.

Eve doesn't notice any of it. She and Marcella are huddled into that booth, faces serious.

I glance back at the Spring Falls table. They're quieter, much quieter than they were before, and instinct tells me I should alert her to their presence, but . . . guess that's not my place. And I mean, they're not even doing anything really.

I turn my back on all of them, find the broom, and start sweeping the floor behind the counter. There are at least a hundred french fries back here. People are disgusting.

I take a tub of glasses to the dishwasher and refill the ice bins for the late-night crowd. I'm finishing up when someone impatiently clears her throat at the register.

It's one of the girls from Spring Falls, and when I glance toward her table, I realize most of them have left. But she's clearly raided the freezer by the door—she's got a few quarts of ice cream, cans of whipped topping, and a jar of cherries on the counter.

"We decided not to order dessert here," she explains, even though I don't ask her to. "We're going to have it at home." Her eyes are sparkling as she grins at me, and for a second there, I think she might be offering some sort of lewd proposition.

But finally I just shrug. "That's cool."

Across the restaurant, Marcella stands up, reaches across the booth to give Eve a big hug, and then takes off out the side door.

Eve stands, too, but instead of following her out, drags herself to the counter instead.

I look at her sweats again. What does she *do* on a normal Friday night, anyway? Who does she hang out with? I know Scott was hanging out with the team tonight, and Marcella, she's constantly doing the PDA thing with that dude from South.

She drops down onto a stool and looks over at me, unsmiling. "Hey," she says.

It's obvious she's too tired to get herself all riled up over nothing. Which isn't a terrible thing. I'm almost too tired to fight back if the situation called for it.

"Hey."

"My mom wants me to bring her a sundae back. A CMP."

"A what?"

"Sorry. That's chocolate-marshmallow-peanuts. Not a big seller, I guess." She rolls her eyes. "And I'm almost embarrassed to say this out loud, but she made a big thing about making sure the peanuts are crushed. She knows it's usually just whole peanuts here, and apparently, that ruins the whole thing. I don't even know. She just asked me to ask if someone could crush a few peanuts."

"She must be as big a pain in the ass as you are."

It slips out automatically, but I'm half smiling as I say it.

But she doesn't react; she doesn't fire off a zinger in return, not up for our usual banter.

The smile quickly fades, my gaze dropping to the floor as I stand there, confused. When did it become banter, anyway?

When I glance back up, Eve's staring at me. "Can you just put the order in?"

"Okay." I shrug. "I'm going."

"Thank you," she says. Begrudgingly.

I pin the order up at the ice cream station and go into the kitchen to chop the damn peanuts myself. I take a handful of whole peanuts and bash them to bits with the bottom of a metal shake tumbler.

When the sundae's ready, I dump the exquisitely crushed peanuts over the whipped cream and put the plastic lid back on, then hand deliver the bag to Eve. She thanks me one more time and drags herself off the stool.

When I turn around, I notice that the trash can is overflowing. Again.

It makes me angry. Without singling anyone out, I call to Jenn and Laura, who are working the counter with me. "Nobody else capable of taking the trash out?"

Laura actually has the nerve to be leaning against the counter, playing on her phone. "You're a *guy*, Jamie. Help us out."

"Whatever," I mumble under my breath. "I'll do it. Again."

I carry the heavy bag out the kitchen door, into the parking lot, and stop in my tracks.

Just a few steps behind where Eve has stopped in her tracks. She's frozen now, paper bag dangling from her hand, staring in confusion at the hood of what must be her car.

The words are artistically spelled out in whipped cream and even decorated with rainbow sprinkles.

Dyke in Spikes.

They're huge, covering the entire hood, except for the space they left next to them. There, boobs are sculpted out of mounds of whipped cream, complete with cherry nipples. There's a smiley face below them.

It's immediately obvious to me who was responsible—the douchebags from Spring Falls; the girl they had do their dirty work. But Eve is still confused, because she doesn't know who the enemy is; she didn't recognize them inside. For a second, I wonder if she thinks there's any way *I* was responsible.

Eve hasn't moved a muscle. She hasn't turned around to find me behind her.

I leave the trash bag at my feet and turn back to the store. I grab a couple of clean rags from the pile and return to the parking lot.

She's moved now; she's attempting to wipe off her car with one of those little tissue-packet things grandmothers always have in their purses.

I walk up beside her, swiping the boobs away and onto the pavement with the rags. "Those tissues aren't going to do shit."

She ignores me. She keeps going about her business, going through her tissue pack, even though they practically disintegrate upon contact. But she keeps trying.

"I got this," she finally says out the side of her mouth. Her expression is blank but her voice is strained in some way, sort of breathless as she still attempts to ream me out. She blows a strand of loose hair out of her mouth. "I don't really do the whole knight-in-shining-armor thing, but thanks."

I just shrug and wipe at some more whipped cream. "Good. Neither do I," I inform her.

She doesn't make any further attempt to send me on my way, so we finish the job in silence. Then I duck inside to get a bucket of water to rinse the whole mess away so her parents don't see any trace of it in the morning. I mean . . . something about that would just make it suck even more.

Eve finally stands up and takes in a huge breath of air as the water rains down off her car. She stares at her car as she says it. "Don't be nice to me just because I had a shit game."

"What?"

"You know what I mean," she says tersely. "When you see me as an actual threat, you hate me. It's only when I have a lousy game that you'll consider being somewhat human to me." She shakes her head. "I don't need that." She lifts her chin. "It's demeaning."

I stare at her, eyes narrowed. *What?* I was being nice because when it comes to other teams, it's us versus them, and in this case, it was *us* versus those jackasses who were too weak to even harass her to her face.

I wasn't being nice because she had a lousy game. I was being nice because she took it without so much as a tear, because she took this crap without a tear, and it was pretty damn impressive, coming from a girl.

Or . . . anyone.

But apparently that's not how she sees it.

Her whole body sort of collapses, and she tells me wearily, "You win today. Okay, Jamie? You win."

Really?

I mean, I hadn't even felt like battling today.

But I'm sure there's no point trying to convince her of that.

I throw my hands up instead. "Fine." I gather the dirty rags and the empty bucket. "Let me know if you need anything else to clean up."

She's out there another ten minutes. During which it occurs to me to grind up some more damn peanuts and make another sundae, because the one she has is clearly ruined. And I didn't go to all that effort to remove traces of the incident only to have a melted sundae give it away.

I'm not sure she even notices when I switch the bags.

She's on her way after that, and I clock out fifteen minutes later. I change my shirt, douse myself in some body spray, and try to muster up the energy to go see Naomi.

Chapter 11

March 17

Eve

As soon as I give my mom her sundae—which appears miraculously intact considering my holdup at the restaurant—my parents let me escape up to my room. They only talk briefly with me in soft voices, avoiding words like *baseball*, *pitching*, and *game* altogether. They know the drill after bad games and let me go to brood in peace.

I walk upstairs, close my bedroom door behind me, and stand before it, staring at myself in the full-length mirror screwed to the back of it. I look past my image, reflecting on the week instead. The missed *Crucible* assignment and lost points. The resulting fight with Jabrowski. Being sent to detention. Being sent to detention with *Jamie*. This afternoon's loss. And, the literal "cherry on top," the defacement of my car.

I screw up my face. *At least next week can't possibly be any worse*. I manage to laugh out loud for about five seconds before my laughing turns to crying and my face goes into my hands and my body folds up on the carpet. I cry for a few minutes, as silently as possible, before wiping my snotty nose on the back of my hand. What a shitty week. The fact that *Jamie Abrams* found me pathetic enough to be nice to me . . . I shake my head . . . that right there illustrates exactly how crappy everything was.

I sniffle a final time as I get myself back together.

He was so decent.

Not, for the record, that I was on the verge of crying when I found my car covered in obscenities and whipped cream, which I assumed was the handiwork of someone from Spring Falls. Their words didn't hurt me. But their actions made me angry. Not angry that they did it, but *pissed the hell off* that I'd had such a lousy game. If I'd had a good game, at least I'd have given them a reason to attack me. This felt like a sucker punch, harassing someone who'd performed as poorly as I did. I'd feel better about the whole thing if I'd given them a reason.

I'll give them a reason next time, that's for damn sure.

Using the corner of my bed, I pull myself back up to standing and dig my phone out of my back pocket. The text message from Scott is the first on the list.

You want to Netflix and chill? Ya know, for real?

This brings a small smile as my fingers tap in reply. *Thanks, but I think I'm in for the night.*

Don't wallow. I'll make cheese fries.

Thanks, but I'm good. Not wallowing.

A second later, another text comes in. *Crap, now I have no reason to make cheese fries. We running tomorrow morning?*

Scott and I often run together on Saturday mornings, long,

lazy runs on the river trail, and I'm halfway done confirming when and where we're meeting up when I remember something.

I have to take a rain check.

How come?

I stare down at the screen for a minute, totally clueless as to how to respond. Certainly not with the truth. I end up ignoring his question and go back to the index of messages instead. Jasmine's also been in touch.

Hey. My brother's band is playing at O'Brien's. If we go before ten we can get in.

I picture the scene—a loud, crowded restaurant-slash-bar jam-packed with college kids spilling beer.

I'm not in the mood for a scene.

You're not used to not being on top of your game, my basketball cocaptain teases with a winky-face emoticon. *Come out! You'll feel better.*

Nah. I repeat what I told Scott. *Thanks for the invite, but I think I'm in for the night.*

I put my phone away, before Scott or Jasmine can follow up. I change into my pajamas and sit atop my bed. Then, out of habit, I stare across the driveway. Marcella's window is dark. My stomach sinks and suddenly I feel uncomfortable in my skin.

I stare into the darkness. Tonight her window seems farther away than it used to, like there's some new distance between us.

....

She made me go get dinner with her, even though I tried to turn her down. She'd been waiting for me, hair looking uncharacteristically unkempt, limbs jittery, outside the girls' locker room. I'd taken a long time getting changed after the game, because I'd wanted to avoid as many people as possible. But apparently, Marcella was insistent on finding me.

She practically pounced when I emerged. "I need to talk to you, Eve."

My shoulders slumped. "Is it something that can wait? I have to warn you, I'm in a lethal mood right now."

"Please."

Marcella said the word quietly, flatly. She wasn't begging me, but there was some kind of panic in her eyes I was entirely unused to seeing. Just like that, I was less concerned with my problems and more concerned with hers. She grabbed my arm. "Dinner. We can go to dinner. My treat." Then her eyes went to the ground. "I mean . . . I need my best friend right now."

"Okay," I answered immediately. "Of course."

"I have to babysit the Lindemans till eight. Meet me at the Burger Barn. Like, eight thirty," she said, immediately whirling on her heel before I could rethink it.

With a sigh, I nodded. A few hours later, I found Marcella in the parking lot, pacing, but for someone who was visibly upset, she greeted me with talk about the unusually starry sky, the seasonal ice cream being advertised in the window, and the near accident she'd witnessed on her way there. Even as we walked inside, as she held on to me, she was yakking in my ear, still talking a mile a minute.

I barely even noticed Jamie behind the counter.

She led me to a corner booth and hid behind her menu while waiting for the server to appear and take our order. Then, after she did, Marcella went right back to it. "I mean, I think I'm being a wonderful sport, all things considered, but the class president can't fight me on everything just to make a point. We started prom planning way before they did, apparently, and this whole fashion thing is actually going to be fun, and useful, so I'm really not understanding the pushback and why—"

"Marcella."

She looked up in surprise.

I sighed loudly. "Girlfriend, you know I love you with all my heart, but it was a bad week, all right? Did you honestly lure me out to vent about bullshit prom politics, or at some point before my food digests are you going to get around to telling me whatever it is you wanted to tell me?"

"I might have had sex with Brian."

My stomach turned cold at once, something akin to fear settling there, but I managed to chuckle anyway. "Umm, not speaking from experience or anything, but I'm pretty sure that's a yes-or-no situation, not a maybe."

Her head fell forward, long hair covering her face. "It's a yes," she mumbled.

I had a million feelings I didn't quite understand swirling about, but after a minute of silence, all I could do was state the obvious.

"That wasn't part of your plan," I pointed out, raising an eyebrow. "You, deviating from the plan . . . wow."

I know Marcella's timeline. She's spelled it out for me on several occasions. Married by twenty-four, kids by twenty-six, because she wants at least three of them. Sex wouldn't happen until college, at least, if I remember correctly, something about "wanting to feel like an adult first" so it didn't seem dirty. Under her parents' roof would feel dirty.

"I didn't change the plan," she said. "It just happened. Last night we were just doing . . . stuff . . . in his basement. And he didn't stop me, because, well, he never has. And last night . . . I didn't stop him." Marcella gave a tiny shrug. "In the moment, it felt okay, I guess."

"You sure about that?" I asked flatly. "The look on your face . . . doesn't look all that okay."

Abruptly, she sat up straight and even folded her hands on the table. This time, she nodded assuredly. "No. It is. Okay. It felt like the time was right. It just was, and I had to ask myself: Why am I applying all these rules? What am I waiting for, really?" Marcella smoothed her hair and looked me in the eye. "We've been together for three years, and it's time for our relationship to actually develop."

"Uh, okay. If you're sure."

At that moment, our waitress returned and delivered our food. There was a double cheeseburger and fries on my plate. A house salad on hers. I watched as she barely picked at it. Then I put my burger down and looked at her again.

Her eyes dropped back to the tabletop. "Anyway . . . what I just told you . . . that's not really what the . . . big . . . problem is."

"What's the big problem?"

"Well, as I said . . ." She shredded a piece of romaine into bits. "It wasn't exactly planned, and . . ."

She couldn't finish her sentence, her cheeks turning bright red.

I was confused for a minute. Then my eyes almost popped out of my head.

"Marcella! Are you kidding me?! You, of all people, had sex without protection?"

Her head whipped from left to right and all the way behind her. "Shh, okay?" she hissed. She swallowed hard. "At first, I didn't think it was really happening, and then everything got carried away, and then it *was*, and everything was happening really fast, and it was sort of over before I could even really . . . and I don't know . . ."

The bright red drained from her cheeks entirely, and suddenly she looked pale enough to puke.

"I don't want to feel like I made a mistake with this, but this part of it . . . ," she whispered. "I'm scared to death, Eve. I have to *fix* this."

I was about to lecture her that it wasn't really an action that could be fixed, or undone, but then I remembered something. "Aren't there, like, pills? Isn't there something you can take?"

She started gnawing on her nails. "I've been too scared to look. I'm afraid it's too late for that."

I shook my head as I felt around for my phone. Apparently my best friend lost her virginity and her good sense in one fell swoop. The Marcella I'd known for over a decade would have immediately googled it and promptly *handled* it by now. "I'll look," I said, swiping my screen.

"I think you have up to seventy-two hours. They probably carry this pill at the CVS on Maple Ave."

"No, look for one farther away," she said. "What if we run into someone?"

"Who's *we*? You and Brian?"

"No, umm . . ." She took a long drink of her water. "Me and you."

I laughed out loud.

"Please, Eve! I can't do this by myself. I can't look someone in the eye and ask for the *morning-after* pill."

I wanted to point out that if she was ready for sex, she might as well be ready to say those words aloud to a pharmacist. Except I'd sound way too much like our health teacher, and not like her best friend.

And why *wasn't* Brian going with her?

I didn't say anything about that, either.

"It's going to make you really sick," I informed her, still scrolling through the sites. "Like headaches and nausea and vomiting sick."

Her shoulders collapsed as she nodded miserably.

I shook my head, struggling to understand how any of it was worth such awful side effects. Looking at the expression on Marcella's face, I decided she didn't seem convinced, either.

So I leaned forward. "Marcella, what's wrong? For real?"

She looked into my eyes for a long moment before retreating again, pulling herself together. "Nothing. Nothing's wrong. I just need to get this taken care of, and then I'll feel one hundred percent better about this. And I'll always be smart going forward."

It was clear right then she wasn't going to tell me the truth of what was eating her, what *else* was eating her, regardless of how many truth bombs she'd just dropped on me.

But Marcella is my best friend, so all I did before she left was tell her when I'd pick her up and give her a big hug.

"Get some sleep," I told her. "You'll deal with it tomorrow."

Then I watched her walk toward her car, leaving me with the

uncomfortable feeling that she was somehow walking away from *me*, on some scale larger than the Burger Barn parking lot.

....

I stare at her window some more, hands twisting uneasily in my bedspread, wondering if she's at home, asleep, or if she went over to Brian's.

The thing with my car, the interaction with Jamie . . . the truth is they fazed me way less than they probably should have.

This thing with Marcella is what's really shaken me.

She and Brian are closer than ever. And even though she came to me for help and support, suddenly it feels like there's this huge gap between us. She's on one side and I'm on the other, and the truth is, I have no interest in crossing over to hers. Marcella feels like someone different, someone I don't fully know.

It's just sex, Eve.

It is just sex, and lots of people have sex. Marcella hasn't turned into an alien.

But . . .

. . . this is Marcella. And for all the ways we're different, it was one way we were alike that is now gone.

She's having sex and tracking down the morning-after pill.

And me, I'm taping my boobs down.

I close my eyes, swallowing over the lump in my throat, forcing myself to confront the question in my mind head-on.

What are you scared of?

It takes me a minute to answer myself. I squeeze my eyes tighter shut, forcing myself to face it, in the hopes that I'll stop feeling so bothered and finally be able to get some sleep.

I'm scared of it changing.

All of it.

My body. My place on the team. My friendship with Marcella.

Because if it all changes . . . will I even know who I am anymore? Will there even be a place where I fit?

Chapter 12

March 27

Eve

Before I run back onto Linville's field, I take a final glance at the scoreboard, even though I'm well aware of the score and know when and how every run was scored. We're up 6–4, with a lead we've maintained from the second inning.

Now, with two innings to go, it's my job to hold on to things, keep it together, so we can take home another win. Jamie started off strong and probably could've kept going, but Coach wanted to save him for a particular opponent later in the week. He put me in at the bottom of the fourth, and I'm trying to stave off the fatigue that's starting to settle over me.

Scott lumbers toward the infield, adjusting his chest protector, hesitating when he sees me lingering behind the fence. "All good?"

I take a deep breath, steeling my body and narrowing my eyes toward the mound. "All good." I wipe my hands on my lucky bandanna and tuck it away. "Just want to get through these last two and out of here."

He steps toward me and extends his fist for a pound. "Let's do that, then."

"Let's do it."

I take a final deep breath, locking my line of vision dead ahead, doing everything in my power to keep my eyes off the home bench, the set of bleachers behind it.

Some teams, some towns are just worse than others; that's the way it's always been. There's an invisible animosity in the air surrounding the field, and without even so much as glancing in their direction, I can feel the weight of the crowd's stares. It's something I realized over time, that stares have a weight about them, and here at Linville, I feel their hostile presence on my back.

I take my place on the mound and grind my cleats into the dirt. *I have two X chromosomes, losers. Get over it.*

I stare into Scott's eyes before winding up. Seconds later, a perfect curveball smacks his glove, which is centered perfectly within the strike zone.

I hide my smile behind my glove. Stares have a weight about them, sure. Sometimes they can also be as motivating as hell.

. . . .

It's a quick inning with a couple of hits but no runs scored, and ten minutes later I'm tugging on a batting helmet and stepping up to the plate. It's our last at bat, and we'd all feel more comfortable adding a run or two before Linville gets their last chance to take the victory.

Their pitcher is tall, almost gangly, but has a mean fastball.

His first pitch is a strike, but I get a piece of the second one, sending a pop fly into foul ball territory behind me.

I grind my molars together, frustrated with the 0–2 count, feeling the pressure building in my chest. It's a tough hole to dig myself out of, and my resulting grip on the bat is painfully tight.

The pitcher takes his sweet time before throwing the next pitch. He takes an extra second to look me in the eye and smile cruelly. Then he's whipping his arm around the side of his body, windmill style, lobbing the ball toward the plate the way a soft-ball pitcher would.

I'm too stunned to think about swinging as the ball zips past me. I'm too stunned to react at all.

Luckily, the plate umpire is not. He stands, pushing up his face mask with a heavy sigh, turning toward the home team's dugout. "Coach, pull your player from the game or I will."

I look at Linville's coach. Even from a distance, I can tell his face is already red with fury, his lip curled up like he's snarling. He beckons for his player with some angry gesturing, and even though the idiot pitcher takes his time jogging over to his coach, there's no avoiding the reaming-out that awaits him. We don't get the pleasure of hearing it, but from the way the coach takes his arm and jerks him behind the dugout, we get a sense of what's in store.

There's another moment of stunned silence, but before one of their assistant coaches can call another pitcher in, before the umpire can say "play ball," someone stands in the second row of the home-team bleachers, shielding his eyes against the sun.

"Hey, ump, can't we have a sense of humor?" he calls. "He technically didn't do anything illegal."

He's tall and gangly, too. Must be the idiot's dad. Father Idiot.

The umpire doesn't even bother to turn in his direction. "My call," he shouts in response. "Poor sportsmanship."

"It was just some good-natured heckling," Father Idiot protests. "He didn't say anything demeaning or nothing." He gestures toward the scoreboard. "How is it poor sportsmanship? We don't even have the lead."

Glancing over my shoulder, I notice the umpire finally turning toward him, squinting in confusion. "Really?"

"Really. Charlie's coming up to bat, and he could still bring this home," the man continues. "You can't throw him out of the game."

The umpire's growing sense of irritation is evident, anger finally revealing itself in his voice. "Actually, I can. And I can ask you to leave as well."

"Well, that would just be par for the course, wouldn't it?" Father Idiot directs his question toward the other Linville fans. He climbs down off the bleachers, but instead of turning toward the parking lot, he makes his way down to the fence, directly behind me. My limbs twitch when he grabs the fence. I'm mad at myself when I realize it, how his close proximity intimidates me. I freeze, sort of like a rabbit when a predator comes into its peripheral view.

"Eve. Get in here."

It's Coach Parsons who calls my name, and I finally have the wherewithal to trot toward the dugout and join my team, the players who have collectively jumped to their feet and are watching the scene unfold.

"If I'm going to go, might as well say my piece first," the man rants from behind the fence. He sticks a finger through it, pointing toward our dugout while unloading on the umpire. "This team has an unfair advantage in the conference. Those coaches over there got to cherry-pick players from two already strong teams. It's bullshit that they got away with it."

Coach Jackson makes a move to step forward. "We should put a stop to this," he mutters.

But Coach Karlson extends an arm, blocking him from going any farther. "Let the umpire handle it," he says, looking unruffled.

"It's going to be a farce if this team wins the conference. If they're allowed to go on to districts," he continues.

Around me, I can sense my teammates growing angry, tension radiating from their bodies, a few of them spitting toward the dirt.

I'm right there with them. *None of this was our fault!* I want to shout. *We sure as hell didn't ask for this!*

Then Father Idiot has to go ahead and make it personal.

He presses his face against the fence, twisting his neck so he can scan the dugout, his gaze finally coming to rest on me. "And then there's their little secret weapon."

He shakes his head with a chuckle, glancing over his shoulder toward the other Linville supporters. "Great tactic, right? Throw the other teams off-kilter, stick a *girl* out there on the mound as a novelty."

My ears pick up on a few people actually applauding him.

The sound of it makes me see red when I blink.

The umpire steps toward the man and stands face-to-face with him, glaring at him through the chain link. "It's time for you to go. Don't make me say it a third time."

"Whatever." The man rattles the fence. "This season's a joke." He steps away, but not before pointing in my direction. *"You're a joke."*

And just like that, I go from rabbit to mountain lion, launching my body in his direction without ever actively deciding to move.

But hands grab my shoulders before I gain any momentum. I whip around, flinging them off, but it's Scott's steady face I find behind me, and it snaps me out of attack mode at once.

"Don't stoop to his level, Eve. Don't give him the satisfaction."

I pause, take a breath.

"You've dealt with this before," he reminds me. "Don't you dare give him the satisfaction of a reaction."

He's right, of course, even though it takes me by surprise every time, how so many parents at rec sports are the most infantile individuals on the scene. They've always been more dismissive, more derisive, than the other coaches or opposing players. They all believe each of their precious little snowflakes is a star; they're so upset when I shut them down.

Scott puts his arm around my shoulder. "Come on. Sit down."

"Don't let them get to you, Eve."

I turn toward the voice, surprised to hear that it's Greg, one of the original Pirates.

"Yeah, Eve. Forget that guy."

This time it's Brendan giving the encouragement.

Looking around the dugout, I'm so stunned at the realization that my team seems to have my back, my entire team, I actually manage to keep from charging toward the fence. My eyes end up meeting Jamie's last, pausing there for a moment, trying to read his expression. I guess I sort of expect to find him gloating, enjoying this spectacle, but he isn't. He just seems to be studying me in equal measure, his reaction inscrutable.

I look down, peeling my batting gloves off, waiting for my heart rate to decrease.

And then I have to wait some more. Wait for the ranting father to finally leave the field, wait for the other bench to settle down, wait for a replacement pitcher to warm up. Scott approaches me again, once I've calmed down, and makes a big deal of keeping my arm loose, jostling my shoulders and trying to make me laugh.

"I'll be fine," I assure him. "He's gone. It's not that big of a deal."

But it sort of is. I still have a 0–2 count, and now there's no way in *hell* I can let them strike me out.

Luckily, the new pitcher isn't nearly as strong as the jackass who got tossed, and on my first swing I send a solid line drive between the shortstop and third and safely make my way to first base. He walks the next two batters, and then a ground ball from Scott sends me home.

And after the inning closes, when I run back onto the field, glove in hand, to put this game to bed once and for all, I do it with the sense that my team's behind me. I hear their voices as I go.

"You got this, Marshall."

"One more to go."

"Make them eat their words."

That last one's from Scott.

I think it's the first time that the sense of us versus them is stronger than the feeling of us versus us in our dugout.

My muscles feel invigorated as I trot toward the mound, and with my team behind me, I close out the game, shutting the door on our 8–5 win.

Thank God this game didn't slip away, I think as I line up with my teammates to slap hands.

We line up on the first baseline, walking toward the plate and the line of red-and-blue uniforms. The pitcher who decided to get cute has apparently been forced to join his teammates, but when he reaches me, it's abundantly clear that he hasn't learned his lesson. Evidently, he has his father's blessing to be an asshole, because when he walks past me, he withdraws his hand at the last second, refusing to touch mine.

Chris Jamison, in line behind me, calls him out immediately. "Slap her hand, dude."

He shrugs. "No."

"Slap her hand."

I'm done being riled. I pull Chris forward. "Not worth forcing the issue. I'm not interested in slapping his hand, either."

Jackson's in line behind Chris, so he witnesses the snub, too. And so after we gather our equipment, lining up to make our way back to the bus, he nudges one of the cocaptains. "She closed this game out after all that," he says. "Let's show a little support." He puts his right arm in the air, extending his index finger. "One team."

Scott, being Scott, is quick to pick up on the gesture. He puts his hand in the air. "One team."

And down the line it goes, as more and more guys pick up on it, putting their right arms in the air as they walk, repeating the words. "One team."

Irritated as I am, my heart warms at their show of support, started by a Pirate and everything. And for whatever reason, I can't help myself. I scan my teammates, looking for Jamie, curious if he's playing along. But he's hanging back, talking to Coach about something, and so I head for the bus unsure if he's buying into the sentiment or not.

As soon as I collapse into a seat in the middle of the aisle, exhaustion settles over me like a parachute that's lost its wind. I didn't let it show on the field, but now the stress and tension of it all gets to me, leaving me depleted, devoid of the energy that fills the bus after an away win.

When Scott drops into the seat beside me, I ask if I can borrow his phone to listen to music, because when I open my bag, I realize I've forgotten mine back at school. He finds my favorite playlist and hands over the headphones, and I promptly check out, closing my eyes to the chatter and chaos around me.

When we get back to the school, we shuffle off the bus, me heading toward my locker room, the rest of them heading toward theirs. I peel off my uniform, unwrap the disgustingly sweaty Ace bandage . . . and only then realize I've forgotten my towel. I stand there for a second, wondering what *else* I've managed to forget today.

Screw it, I think. *I'll shower at home.*

With a long, tired sigh, I pull on a pair of sweats and an old Bulldogs T-shirt, jamming my Pirates hat back on over my braids because my hair is a laughable disaster. I'm eager to get home, but when I glance down at the bench one last time, I see Scott's phone sitting there.

I sigh a second time. Scott takes longer than any girl getting changed, because he spends so damn long socializing and joking around before bothering to shower. And I'm simply too tired and too spent to wait around outside for him. His energy supply may be bottomless, but today, mine is not.

I swing my duffel bag onto my shoulder, pick up his phone, and make my way across the hallway from the girls' locker room to the boys'. I knock once and get no response. I hear the showers running inside, loud comments being tossed back and forth over the din of locker doors slamming.

I can hardly storm in there. Rolling my eyes, I raise my fist a second time and start pounding. I pound for a solid thirty seconds and am still pounding away when the door finally opens, sending me off balance.

When I realize it's Jamie Abrams standing behind the door, when I realize the state he's in, I almost lose my footing entirely.

He appears entirely unfazed. He leans against the doorjamb, tilting his face to assess me, realizing I haven't really gotten cleaned up yet.

Then he raises one eyebrow. "You're really taking this 'one team' thing to heart, huh?"

I glare at him, forcing my eyes to stay locked on to his.

Which is *hard*, damn it.

He's still got his cleats on, still got his stirrups on. He's still got his white uniform pants on, too, except they're now sitting low on his hips. He'd gotten as far as taking his jersey off, so he's standing inches away, bare-chested, the slight sheen from sweat highlighting some rather defined muscles. *Look him in the eye. Do not look down. Do not even* think *about looking at his half-naked torso!*

I swallow hard, keenly aware of that strangely intoxicating postgame guy scent coming off him, and close my hand around Scott's phone. "Shut up. I just have something I need to give to Scott."

He extends his hand, and I retreat, thwarting the possibility of his body coming any closer to mine.

Don't look down!

"I can give it to him," he offers.

I fold my arms across my chest, keeping the phone from his grasp. "Thanks, but I'll wait."

Jamie makes no move to leave. He's still leaning against the doorjamb, narrowing his eyes as he studies me, but I refuse to look at him anymore. I stare into the safe space beyond his left shoulder.

"Have I done something to piss you off?" he asks. "I mean, something new?"

I chance a quick glance at his face. "Your locker room joke wasn't funny. And . . ." I hesitate for a second. "Didn't exactly hear any words of support coming from my pitching squad out there, and I didn't see your hand in the air, so . . ." I shrug.

Jamie shakes his head. "You confuse me, Marshall." He looks me in the eye, raising an eyebrow in challenge. "Thought you didn't *do* the whole knight-in-shining-armor thing."

"I don't, but . . ."

"Then don't give a guy shit if he thinks there are things you can handle on your own, without needing some over-the-top show of support." He pauses, voice softening some. "I knew you had it under control."

I stumble to formulate a response, but he's caught me off guard, and before I can come up with anything, he rolls off the door frame, the heavy locker room door closing slowly behind him.

And accidentally, I do it, damn it. I give in to the temptation. I stare at his naked back and admire his sculpted shoulders as he disappears from sight, feeling the flush—which I'm pretty sure has nothing to do with my temper flare-up or the steam escaping the locker room—creep over my chest.

Chapter 13

March 31

Jamie

Every spring, apparently, the administration subjects the junior and senior class to some boring and uptight Power-Point presentation about prom fashion guidelines. It's for the girls more than the guys—tuxes are tuxes—but everyone has to go so their lecture doesn't seem sexist, I guess.

This year, though, with Marcella leading the charge, the newly combined student council for our class managed to talk the principal and PTO president into getting rid of the PowerPoint. She talked them into replacing it with a live version of the rule book, a fashion show where kids would actually model what exactly you could get away with at prom and what you couldn't.

When Naomi asked me about being in the show a few weeks ago, I said, "Prom stuff? Already?"

She gave me a look of disbelief. "Prom is less than two months away, Jamie."

"Yeah. That's a long time."

Then she got really exasperated, throwing her hands in the air. "Sure. Okay."

"What is this thing again?"

"It's like a fashion show."

"No thanks," I answered quickly, turning back to shove something in my locker.

Naomi wrapped both hands around my biceps until I twisted back around. "Come *on*," she groaned. "We need guys to do it, too. It's stupid if there are just girls up there. Guys will make it funny." Then she smirked at me. "Don't play hard to get with this. We all know there's nothing you'd enjoy more than strutting across the stage with a few hundred people staring at you. And you get to miss fourth block that Friday to get ready."

I made her wait a minute. "Guess if you're going to make someone put on a tux and get up there, you might as well do it right. . . ."

Naomi smiled knowingly. "Knew you'd give in. It'll be fun."

She was right, for a while there anyway. I happily handed Jabrowski the pass to miss her class and got ready backstage with a bunch of guys I knew, some of my boys from the team. When some of the girls came out, gushing all over us, I didn't mind checking them out, especially some of the girls in the "no" dresses that were particularly short or low-cut. And I didn't mind walking across the stage, two senior girls on my arm, while "24K Magic" played, the crowd cheering and hooting, all eyes on me.

Naomi does know me pretty well.

But then, during the short intermission when the girls were changing their dresses, I stopped having a good time with it.

Nate was nearby, reading from one of the prom flyers he'd

grabbed. "Seventy-five dollars per ticket, that's ridiculous. I heard the food's always terrible anyway, and it's just some lousy DJ. And Kayla thinks that I should buy both tickets because girls spend so much more on their dresses."

"Tell her to buy a cheaper dress, then," another senior named Mark advised him.

"It doesn't even add up like she says," Nate continued, glancing over his shoulder to make sure Kayla, one of the models, wasn't anywhere nearby. "So maybe their dresses cost more, but we have to rent the tux, buy the flowers, find someone to get beer and pay them for it, and usually pay for the limo, too."

A buddy of ours named Sean stepped over and chimed in. "Yeah, and did you hear Billy's parents just decided we can't use their shore house for the weekend? The girls still want to go, so now we have to pay for some crappy hotel that's going to jack their rates up because they know we're in high school. My brother told me that he ended up spending almost seven hundred dollars that weekend between prom itself and the weekend after."

Suddenly my mouth felt desert dry and I was struggling to swallow. Seven hundred dollars? Seriously?

"Such bullshit," Nate muttered. Then he grinned and slapped my chest. "But we'll pay it, because we're suckers, right?"

I managed to laugh, but my mind was elsewhere. Naomi probably assumed we were going together, and if we did, she would definitely have high expectations and plan on going to the beach weekend. With her date.

Not that she was the girl I was concerned with letting down. Instantly, I thought of my mom.

We could scrape together the money; I could pick up some extra shifts. My mom would do what she had to do, convinced she had to find a way to sacrifice so I didn't go without. But just talking about prom had already left me with a sick feeling in my stomach; I highly doubted it would go away the night of prom, knowing what a waste it is, knowing that we actually had the lights turned off while I sailed out the door, where a fucking limo was waiting, wearing a tux.

I started feeling trapped backstage, the feeling only increasing as I tried to make my way through the thick, dark curtains to escape the room for a minute and get some air. I kept pushing the fabric aside, only finding more of it, feeling like I was never going to get out of there. When I finally made my way through, the hallway didn't seem good enough.

I kept going. I pushed on through the double doors leading to the courtyard and made my way down to the grass, not looking back.

. . . .

Ten minutes later, I'm still sitting on top of a picnic table, head in my hands. I've loosened the tie that came with the stupid tux and unbuttoned the top buttons on my shirt. I can't seem to make myself go back in there. And F it, I don't want to. The girls have plenty of guys to walk them across the stage. I'm done for today.

I'm staring down at my knees, but my head jerks up when I hear the doors open, assuming it's Naomi, on a mission to find me and drag my ass back inside.

I do a double take when I realize it's Eve.

She doesn't see me at first, either. Her brows are drawn, and she's staring at the ground as she walks away from the building, feet stomping against the ground. It's only when she's about twenty yards away from me that she realizes she's not alone in the courtyard. She comes to an abrupt stop, and I can tell her instinct is to turn around and pretend she didn't see me there.

Except she's a few seconds too late to ignore me entirely. She stares at me, questions me like *I'm* the one who interrupted *her*. "What are you doing?"

I look past her, staring toward the road that runs in front of the school. "Too hot backstage," I mumble. "I needed some air."

"You looked like you were having a good time up there."

Sure. It had been a nice ego boost, until the conversation backstage had knocked me right back down. I just shrug, too distracted to get into anything with Eve Marshall.

She stands there another few seconds, then pivots abruptly. "Well, sorry to interrupt your solitude."

She makes her way back to the door, even opens it. I can hear the pulsing beat from the sound system, make out strains of "Girls Just Want to Have Fun." Eve drops the bar on the door like she's just scalded her hands and steps back and away. She just stands there, staring at the door.

"What's wrong?"

She shakes her head slowly, not turning to look at me. "I *really* don't want to go back in there. I wanted some air, too."

"So don't go back in." I draw a wide circle in the air around me with my hand. "Air. It's sort of in abundance out here."

"Smart-ass."

"Takes one to know one," I respond coolly.

But she doesn't fire off another quip, and she doesn't make another attempt to go back inside. Instead, she walks toward my table. Climbs up the bench and sits down next to me. Well, I don't really know if you could call it next to me. She's so far away I'm pretty sure she's on the verge of falling off the other end.

Then it's quiet, for a really long time. Which is good, because I really didn't want to talk to anyone anyway. I fiddle with the borrowed cuff links, eventually pulling them out of the sleeves and shoving them in a pocket. Eve sits with her elbows resting on her knees. One braid is covering her cheek, making it hard for me to see her face.

Then we both start talking at the exact same time.

"Are you—"

"Did you—"

I gesture in her direction. "Go ahead."

"You a Phillies fan?"

She doesn't look at me when she asks the question, so I don't look at her when I answer.

"Yeah. Of course."

Half a minute passes.

"Opening day next week. What do you think?"

"About their chances?"

"Yeah."

I shrug. "I dunno. Everyone's always said 2015 and 2016 were the rebuilding years, and this year we could actually be contenders again. I'm not sold yet."

"Me neither," she agrees. "It's great that Mackanin has that much faith in the farm teams, but"—Eve shakes her head—"that can't be the be-all and end-all. And there just wasn't that much elite talent up for grabs in the off-season. Not with it being so entirely unappealing to come to Philly right now."

"Bullpen's decent, though. Pitching staff can start off strong. If Nola stays healthy."

"That's a pretty big *if*. It's just been a lousy couple of years. My family makes it to about half as many games as we used to."

"How many games did you go to before?"

"A lot. Well, because we've had season tickets forever."

I feel that muscle in my jaw twitch. Of course they have season tickets. Of course she does.

"Anyway, I don't miss it so much; I don't get all that into Citizens Bank Park." Eve finally flips the braid over her shoulder and I can see her profile again. "I like watching games up at Reading better."

"Me too."

The surprise in my voice is evident. But I've never heard someone acknowledge this opinion, which I happen to share. I'd been downtown—only a few times because of the astronomical ticket, parking, and food costs—and I still prefer my family's trips to Reading.

"The hot dogs, right? Way better."

I feel a smile pushing at my lips. "For sure. And"—I pause for a second, feeling sort of dumb—"the smell of the park. It smells like a game in some way the city can't match. I don't know."

"I do." She nods. "I know exactly what you mean. It's just less commercial. More authentic. You want to be a Phillies fan, go to Citizens Park. You want to watch a baseball game, Reading's where it's at."

I'm nodding right along with her. "Word."

"My parents have always let me miss school for opening day, but . . . I don't think I'm going to go this year. I have a math test on Wednesday, first mock trial meeting, and we have practice."

"It's just practice. You could miss it."

"You'd like that, wouldn't you?" She studies me, a sarcastic smirk appearing on her face. "So the start the next day is automatically yours?"

"Do you only talk about baseball?"

She bristles. "No."

I hadn't meant the question to come out as an insult; I was actually kinda curious. But since she'd opened her mouth till now . . . only baseball had come out.

Eve snorts. "Just seemed like the safest topic of conversation," she tells me. "Best way to avoid an argument."

"We don't argue about baseball?"

She turns her face, but I can still see the way her cheek lifts, how my pointing this out makes her smile. "Touché."

Now I'm grinning, because I'm pretty sure the unmovable Eve Marshall just conceded a point to me.

Then her mouth turns down as I watch. "And I pretty much wanted to talk about anything but what's going on in there," she says, pointing toward the school. "So . . . baseball was a better choice."

"You're bagging on Marcella's show? You two are together all the time. I thought you were tight."

"We are tight. She's like . . . more of a sister than a friend." Her expression shifts, revealing something I can't quite read, something she covers up again. She lifts her chin. "But she knows better than to ask me to play dress-up with her. She gave up on that years ago." Eve shakes her head toward the ground, finishing kind of quietly. "I'm not going to put on some sequins and try to walk in heels just to get a laugh."

Another minute of quiet passes, and then Eve turns back

toward me, shifting the focus, looking me over in my tux. "Of course *you* didn't say no."

"Nothing wrong with having a laugh." I sit up, straighten my shoulders. "And I looked good up there, sweetheart, you might as well admit it."

She throws her head back and laughs, loudly, like she really thinks I'm ridiculous. "You're so arrogant."

"Confident."

"Whatever. I'm fine with you being the sole representative of Pirates pitching up there."

I glance at her from the corner of my eye. In leggings, a Pirates Windbreaker, and messy braids, for whatever reason, she looks strangely more appealing than the girls inside. I mean, a cute girl in a Pirates Windbreaker . . . definitely works for me. And she's not even trying.

Out here, where I can breathe, far away from the stage, I hear myself sharing that opinion.

"I don't really think I'd get a kick out of seeing you done up like that anyway. I like you better like this."

She chuckles, just once. "Since when do you *like* me?"

This makes me laugh. "I don't. Not really."

Eve shrugs. "Yeah, well. The feeling's mutual."

"Wouldn't expect anything less."

"Then you've got it."

"Is there a particular reason you need the last word?"

"People who ask that question are inevitably trying to get the last word them—"

The door opens again and loud heels, loud enough to make me think the Budweiser Clydesdales are approaching, are suddenly clomping down the concrete stairs. Naomi appears before us, in something strapless and gold, stopping when she sees me, hands going to her hips. She doesn't look surprised to see Eve beside me. She doesn't even bother to acknowledge her.

"Dude. What are you doing? Why'd you bail at intermission?"

"Just stepped outside for a minute."

She tilts her head and beckons impatiently, looking like a bird with ruffled feathers. "Well, get *in* here for the end. I walked around the entire second floor looking for you."

"Okay." I sigh, easing myself off the table, buttoning my jacket again. But before I go, I look at Eve a few seconds longer, realizing I don't know how to say good-bye to her. I don't know if I have ever said good-bye to her before, like, nicely. But Naomi is standing there, and it's awkward.

"Well. See you at practice."

"See you."

Naomi waits until I reach her before she smiles again, taking my arm and leading me back inside. She doesn't say a word to Eve as we leave, and she doesn't bother to mention her or ask about her as we rejoin the crowd. Eve is entirely irrelevant to Naomi, even though I've heard Naomi give scathing commentary on most other girls she sees me with.

She found me in time for us to line up with our friends for the big finale of the show, when all of us are supposed to walk out together and amp up the energy, get people excited about going out and buying dresses and renting tuxes and getting prom tickets. My friends are pumped, the music's loud, and the crowd is cheering as we walk across the stage. Naomi's dancing toward the stage, tugging on my hand.

I take one last wistful glance in the direction of the

courtyard before forcing a smile on my face and pumping my fist in the air. But for the first time I can remember, there's somewhere I'd rather be than center stage. I'm struggling more than usual to get caught up in the act, still holding on to how good it felt to drop it, for a few minutes there, atop the picnic table.

Chapter 14

April 2

Eve

I'm getting dressed for church, which means khakis, a cardigan, and a *dressier* pair of sneakers, when I hear someone knock on our front door, then open it one second later without waiting for anyone inside to answer. Feet come prancing up the stairs, and Marcella opens my door without even bothering to knock.

"Hey." She's holding a pink cardboard box. "My dad got Sunday doughnuts. Nabbed you the chocolate glazed that was left."

My eyes light up at the sight of my favorite doughnut. "Thanks. You're the best." I take a huge bite. "Well, your dad's the best, anyway."

Her hand goes to her hip. "Umm, I'm the one who thought to get it for *you*."

I shrug, not bothering to apologize.

The truth is, I'm feeling a little salty toward Marcella. Last weekend I endured the uncomfortable and mortifying task of standing beside her at the pharmacy counter to get the morning-after pill, and she barely bothered to say thank you. She practically jumped out of my moving car to get inside and take the thing, but still. She didn't call me after to tell me if she started throwing up or anything. She didn't call me at all. She went from crisis mode to planning mode almost overnight. By Monday, she'd thrown herself into final preparations for the fashion show and talked about little else the whole week, like it was the most important thing in town, if not the entire world.

And as it turns out, she's still talking about it. She's plopped down onto my bed, directly in front of my closet. "So you know that fuchsia dress I wore last in the show? I was thinking of buying it from the store that lent them to us. I mean, it's a bummer that Brian's already seen it, but it fit so perfectly. And I could wear it in the pageant, too."

"Nope. Didn't see it." My voice is tight when I answer her.

Marcella looks up in surprise. "You weren't watching?"

I bend down, retying my right shoe. "To be honest, I wasn't even there."

She doesn't say anything, but when I stand up, the hurt's written all over her face, and I find myself backtracking. "I mean, I saw the first part, but after a while . . . it was just more of the same." I grimace. "All the prettiest girls, all the girls who naturally look good in dresses . . . I doubt there was anyone up there who's above a size four."

"I *asked* for volunteers," Marcella replies. "I would've taken anyone who wanted to do it."

"Right, but at the end of the day, you know the girls who feel confident enough to get up there are the ones who get the most compliments on a daily basis, and it's not like you made any effort to round out the group. To ask . . . other people."

Marcella stares at me for a long minute, until I have to look away. "Eve?"

"What?"

"Are you mad I didn't ask *you* to be in the show?"

I recoil in horror. "No."

But she keeps staring. "You are! Who are you and what have you done with my best friend? Did you get beaned or something?"

Marcella using the term "beaned" breaks my funk for a second and actually makes me laugh. I finally turn and look her in the eye. "Did you really just ask me if I got beaned? How do you even *know* that expression?"

"I've picked things up," she says indignantly.

"No, I didn't get beaned, and I'm not mad you didn't ask me to be in the show, because, obviously, I would've said no. But only seeing all the girly girls up there onstage"—I shake my head—"it's just annoying."

Marcella gets to her feet. Her hands are back on her hips, an incredulous expression on her face. "Eve. It's not like I didn't ask you just because you don't like pink or own a pair of high heels. You know I think you're gorgeous, and I would've loved to see you up there rocking a dress that fit your personality. I didn't ask you because you never would've let yourself get up there and . . . I don't know." She waves her arms in the air. "Let loose. Have fun with it. Because, by the way, the whole thing was sort of a joke anyway. All of us having fun with something that would've been super boring."

"I have fun with things!"

"You have fun *winning*," she says. "If you're not competing, well . . . you don't really get out there and just have *fun* being part of a group."

"That's not true. Every sport I play is a team sport."

Marcella cocks her head and makes a face. "Always the captain. Always winning the trophy." She points toward the net from states. "The person taking home the net. All these team sports, but you're not much of a team player for the sake of it, just sayin'."

It's one of those rare times where I find myself struggling to make an argument.

I square my shoulders and lift my chin. "Well, anyway, you could've asked me. Just so I could have had the pleasure of telling you no."

She shakes her head wearily. "You're out of your mind." Then she comes over and gives me a hug anyway. "And you're lucky I love you."

"Eve!" My dad taps on the door. "Leaving in five."

"I'm on my way, too," Marcella says, stepping back and adjusting her ponytail. "I'm meeting Brian at Starbucks to study for trig. Call me later."

She's out the door as quick as she entered, but her perfume lingers and I can still feel the warmth of her hug, tempering my irritation about everything that's been going on with her. It's a good feeling, that my best friend still understands me. Maybe sometimes even better than I understand myself.

. . . .

Every week after church, I tag along with my parents for grocery shopping at Giant. Something about it makes me feel like I'm five years old—maybe it's my mom, asking what I want in my lunch this week, or my dad trying to lure me into cart races—but it's not worth driving separately to church. Plus, I'm the last one at home, and I get the sense having me go grocery shopping with them actually means something to them.

My mom waits in line at the deli counter while my dad and I start down the aisles. "You sure you want to pass up opening day?"

"I don't want to—I have to. Besides practice, I have a test that day and the first mock trial meeting. Isn't Ethan taking the train down from New York to meet you?"

"He is, but we still have four tickets."

"It's okay. I'll wait for the game on Sunday."

"You're a responsible kid." My dad squeezes my shoulder, then grabs a jar of Ragú from the shelf.

"I know, right?"

"It's pretty sad when your own father is trying to talk you into playing hooky."

We round the corner, starting down aisle four, which is empty except for a lone figure at the opposite end. I freeze, and stare.

It's Jamie.

He's wearing his Pirates hat, Windbreaker, and loose charcoal sweats. Staring intently at the canned vegetables shelf. Definitely Jamie.

I glance at my father, considering my options. He's not what you'd call quick on the uptake. If I try to nudge him discreetly, direct the cart elsewhere, he'll loudly ask why. But if I do nothing, we're on a crash course with Jamie.

My heart is fluttering like the wings of a moth trapped in a child's hands, and for the life of me I don't know why. I mean, I've already had a million and one awkward, unpleasant, and hostile exchanges with Jamie Abrams. I could go *pro* in awkward, unpleasant, and hostile exchanges with him.

And he was . . . totally civil on Friday.

Friday.

I still didn't understand it—how I, prom fashion show defector, ended up sharing a picnic table with Jamie. Moments earlier, he'd looked like he was having a blast up there. But he'd looked pissed off when I found him, and Lord knows I have a knack for pissing him off, so instinct told me to walk away rather than make things worse.

But somehow . . . we'd talked, and after a while, when he opened his mouth, it wasn't for the sake of being argumentative. We were just talking for the sake of talking, and I'm pretty sure we both might've smiled a couple of times.

I suppose crazier things have happened.

Slowly, half hiding behind my father, I make my way down the aisle, continuing to study him.

He's at the store by himself, it seems, lost in concentration as he carefully consults a list, checking labels and sizes before putting items into his cart. He looks like he's doing the grocery shopping for his family. Interesting. Surprising.

My dad drops a large can into our cart, and the noise causes Jamie's head to jerk up. His eyes meet mine at once. He stares for a second before murmuring, "Hey."

I lift one hand in greeting, trying to be discreet so our conversation doesn't become a whole family event. "Hey."

But the two-word exchange doesn't escape my dad's attention, of *course*, and he feels the need to join it, eyes going to Jamie's jacket.

"Hi there!" he greets him enthusiastically. "You must play ball with Eve!"

Jamie looks back and forth between us. "Uh, yeah, I do."

"Right. You're a fellow member of the all-star Pirates pitching staff." I avert my face and cringe, while my dad thrusts his hand forward to shake Jamie's. "Real good to meet you. I'm the proud father."

It takes Jamie a second to respond. "Nice to meet you, too."

My mom appears around the corner. And just when I think this little meet and greet couldn't get more embarrassing, I notice that she has a box of tampons in her hand. "You had these on the list, right?"

I feel an inferno beneath my cheeks, wondering what the chances are that an undiscovered fault line is beneath our feet, one that might open and send an avalanche of cans of peas to bury both my parents.

Jamie takes advantage of my mom's appearance to pass by without saying good-bye, which I'm perfectly fine with. I grab the box from my mother, stuff it beneath some nonperishables, and say a quick prayer that I can survive this day without *any more mortification.*

I take my sweet time in aisle four, making sure to give Jamie a solid head start, ensuring we don't run into him again as we make our way up and down the remaining aisles. I don't catch sight of him again until we're ready to check out, as he's unloading his cart in the last row. Without hesitation, I lead my father to the next checkout kiosk.

He gives me a strange look as I line up behind two other carts, even though there's no one behind Jamie. "What are you doing?" He directs the cart back in the other direction. "This looks much quicker."

But not less painful.

And so, against my will, we end up behind Jamie, who's carefully separating his groceries into two piles, leaving me to wonder if he's also shopping for a grandparent or something. I pluck a magazine off the rack, pretending to be utterly fascinated with celebrity gossip, in an attempt to avoid any further embarrassment.

"No."

My eyes fly upward at the impatient-sounding exclamation from the cashier.

She's shaking her head at Jamie, her lips pressed together as she points at a couple of items in the first of his groups on the belt. "You can't pay for those with the SNAP account," she tells him. "Those items aren't eligible."

"I'm sorry," he mumbles quietly. "Still figuring out the system."

I put the magazine back in front of my face, realizing she's referencing a government assistance program.

I try my best not to pay attention. I hang back as my parents unload our groceries, trying to keep my distance. I try to ignore all of it, how after completing one transaction with the SNAP card, Jamie doesn't have enough cash left to cover the rest of the items and has to select some to put back.

The cashier dumps them into an empty basket with an annoyed sigh before finishing processing his order.

Finally he's done, and as he puts the last plastic bag into the cart, my father has to open his big mouth again. "We'll see you down at the field this week, Jamie."

Mentally, I curse my father. *Why are you oblivious?*

And Jamie's forced to look back at us, to abandon the pretense that we haven't been standing there, observing all this. He tersely says good-bye, his cheeks flaming, his eyes every bit as stormy as I remember them looking a couple of months ago.

But . . .

I stare at his back as he walks away.

I don't think he's angry, not really. I think anger tends to mask a lot of other emotions with Jamie Abrams.

And I think this morning, he's embarrassed.

I look down, feeling sort of embarrassed myself, realizing for the first time that the life he leaves at home to breezily walk into the lobby as the cocky all-star might not be so simple. That when he yelled at me about how much he needed baseball, he maybe meant it.

When I finally look up, certain he's left the store, I can see him through the windows, carefully transferring his bags of necessities into the back of his Jeep. I keep staring.

I thought I had him pegged. Always brimming with bravado, needing to be seen. The guy I saw today—handling the grocery shopping for his family and paying for their food with a government-issued card—would've liked to be invisible.

My dad has to nudge me to move the cart forward to start filling it up, our bags full of Voss water and organic deli meat. I'm standing there like a robot, still staring.

There was also the person who helped me clean up my car without a word about what had happened, who apparently never told anyone else about it, either. A person who actually said he liked me "better like this" in my Windbreaker and ratty sweats when there was an auditorium full of girls in tight dresses just inside the doors.

I watch him walk around to his door, climb inside with his shoulders slightly hunched.

What's he like? I wonder. *That person in the middle?*

Chapter 15

April 6

Eve

Even though it's pouring on Thursday afternoon when practice starts, forcing us into the gym, spirits are high among my teammates as we gather and await our coaches, who are unusually late. Some people are loudly rehashing yesterday's victory, talking about our standing within the district. Someone's turned on the speaker system, Justin Timberlake's echoing off the walls, and a couple of the guys are executing some pretty ridiculous dance moves in the lower section of the bleachers. I notice a group of seniors from East whispering in a corner, quieter than the rest of the group. I'm sitting on the wood floor next to Scott, stretching my hamstrings.

I glance over my shoulder, noticing Jamie stretching with a few of his buddies from East. His gaze meets mine, and I quickly bow my head and deepen my stretch. I don't know if I should smile or what, unsure what "normal" looks like for the two of us now, given the time we spent together in the courtyard and the run-in at Giant.

Thirty seconds later, I find myself staring at him again. He's back to being "Ace," giving Nathan a hard time about something or other, and I can't seem to make myself stop watching them, trying to figure him out, trying to better understand where Ace ends and Jamie begins.

It's annoying.

I force my attention back to Scott. "Did you catch how yesterday—"

The double doors to the gym slam shut, making me jump, and the music abruptly cuts off. Coach Karlson, with the rest of the coaching staff on his heels, comes striding into the gym, a stormy look on his face. The guys in the bleachers look like they're caught in a game of freeze dance, and Coach looks at them, then pointedly stares at the gym floor. "Stop goofing around and sit your asses down."

Coach's voice is full of barely suppressed anger, and my heart starts pounding at once, nervous system on immediate edge. The instantaneous change in mood is obvious to everyone in the room, and in seconds the gym becomes pin-drop quiet, Coach's footsteps echoing in the silence as he stalks across the floor and positions himself in front of us. I scoot a bit closer to Scott.

What the hell's going on?

Yesterday was a key victory for our positioning within the district, and we all know of Coach's friendly rivalry with our opponents' head coach, that we'd earned him points by getting the W yesterday. I have no idea what happened between yesterday and now to bring about such evident fury.

Coach stands in front of us, his assistants behind him, forming a triangle, staring wordlessly. He stays like that a long time, too long, looking each of us in the eye, one at a time. Even with no idea what he's searching for, I suddenly find myself racking my brain, trying to recall any misstep or error I might have committed that he is aware of and I am not. When he trains his penetrating glare on me, my face heats and I start sweating, even if I know I did nothing wrong.

When he's finally done with the silent interrogation, he speaks. "I'm not disappointed. I'm furious." He lets this single statement sink in for a few more torturous moments before continuing. "You've embarrassed yourselves, your team, and me personally, and that's not something I take lightly."

Scott turns his head, ever so slightly, and meets my eye, his expression confused and concerned. So it's not just me; he has no idea what's going on, either.

Coach reaches back and snaps at Coach Parsons, who hands him an iPad. He holds it up before us, and I have to lean forward and squint to figure out what exactly he's showing us. My heart sinks when I recognize the huge ram statue outside Westdale High School, the site of yesterday's victory. Its snout is covered in lipstick, it's dressed in a bra and panties, and two unfurled condoms encase its curly horns.

"I don't tolerate sore losers," Coach says, his voice hard, "but sore winners I absolutely despise."

Nathan, brave idiot that he is, calls out without bothering to raise his hand. "Coach, why do you think it was us?"

"Don't waste my time with asinine questions, Furman," Coach retorts. He swipes at the screen, producing a second image, this time from a security camera. The screen is dark and the image is blurry, but I can still make out the figure in a Pirates Windbreaker adorning the statue.

Shit.

"Now, you may feel fortunate that the camera wasn't close enough to provide us with a face or the name on that Windbreaker, but that puts whoever did this in a very unfortunate scenario, as it turns out. Because now you can go ahead and admit your stupidity in front of your entire team."

I look around. All my teammates are doing the same. No one looks ready to speak up, and no one is hanging his head in shame.

"Don't make this difficult, people," Coach says. "Someone knows *something* about disgracing my entire team, someone knows *something* about making me look like a jackass to one of my oldest friends and a respected colleague."

Even though he's trying to keep his voice even, Coach's face is getting redder and redder, and I see a vein pulsing in his neck.

"If you think I'm impressed by your loyalty to each other, then you're sorely mistaken. Your choice." He releases his clipboard, which slams against the wooden floor with a metallic bang. Then he nods over his shoulder to his staff. "Set up the stations," he instructs them, voice menacing.

I'm suddenly picturing medieval torture chambers, and my worry turns to fear.

"On your feet," Coach Parson snaps.

Coach is setting up some cones now. "We're coming off a win. Today should've been an easy practice, maybe even some fun." He glances back at us with a tight, forced smile. "Now you can look forward to it being anything but.

"This is your last chance while the other coaches set up the drills," he tells us. "We'll be doing interval sprints around the gym, for fifteen minutes, or until someone decides they're man or woman enough to speak up."

My mouth falls open at the word "woman," even though I'm wise enough to clamp it shut. I can't help but feel appalled that Coach included it in his rant. Does he really believe it's possible that a "woman," the only woman, was responsible?

But a few seconds later, as I'm lining up in single file with my teammates, I decide I can't fault him for using the differential terms. Why should he exclude me from his list of potential suspects? What would that be saying? And as embarrassing as it is to feel singled out by his terminology, I have to admit it's only fair that he acknowledge me as a possible perpetrator.

He blows his whistle and we all start jogging, the person at the front of the line wisely setting a nice and easy pace, and the last person in line sprints from his spot to the front, setting off a chain reaction, the new caboose starting off on a sprint as soon as the last sprinter's reached the front. I don't like the drill, I don't like the individual attention on me as I take my turns sprinting, but I'm well-conditioned from running back and forth across the gym during basketball season, and I can run.

Still, it's not what I'd call fun.

About ten minutes in, when it's getting old, when it's sinking in that we still have what's likely a grueling workout before us, the captains start calling out. I hear Jamie's voice among them.

"Yo, someone man up."

"I'm going to kick whoever's ass is responsible for this."

"Somebody put a stop to this shit."

But no one speaks up, and Coach blows his whistle when fifteen minutes comes to an end. I fall forward in a mass of limp limbs, feeling a bit light-headed. It's incredibly humid in the gym, and our water break is so quick it can barely be considered a "break." My sense of dread grows as Coach describes each station. Bleacher sprints. Mountain climbers and squat jumps. Pull-ups and push-ups. And the Terrible Twenties.

I sneak a look at the clock. It's only three forty-five, which means we still have over an hour to go. And I'm scared. I don't want to admit it to myself, but I am. Conditioning-wise, I can hang with most of the guys. But some of these drills call for brute strength, and I'm worried I'm going to embarrass myself. Fall. Collapse. Clearly, Coach has no intention of making things easier for me, and there's no way I can ask for any type of special treatment.

Scott, standing next to me, looks scared, too. I try to remind myself I'm probably not alone in that feeling.

Mentally repeating every mind-over-matter, you-got-this-girl mantra I know, I prepare myself for the rotations, at the same time silently cursing the dumb-ass who got us into this situation. We should be celebrating our victory, not being drilled to the death inside a humid gym.

And it's pretty much as awful as I anticipated. People trip and fall on the bleachers. During the Terrible Twenties, Scott has to stop to throw up in a trash can before getting himself back in the game. With this, warning bells start firing in my head, and I can see other people are ready to beg for mercy. Finally, Coach allows a water break and five-minute rest.

"One last chance for someone to speak up, put an end to this," he calls to us as we stand there in various stages of collapse.

When no one does, he blows his whistle and we drag our-selves back into rotation.

I'm at the pull-up and push-up station with fifteen minutes left in practice. My positioning was purposeful, because I know I'll struggle here most, and if I'd come here early, the potential mental defeat might have crippled me at the other stations. Coming here last means I'm utterly wiped, but most of my team-mates seem to be in the same boat, and this bolsters me some-how. I mean, I'm surviving. I haven't dropped yet.

The expectation at the station is that while one individual completes eight pull-ups, the others in the group do push-ups on the ground beneath him. The faster he is, the fewer push-ups have to be done before there's a one-minute break as we switch positions.

When it's my turn to get off the ground and grip the bar, I feel Coach grab my elbow.

"Flexed arm hang for you, Marshall."

" 'Scuse me?" I pant.

"Flexed arm hang." He meets my eye briefly. "Willing to make an adjustment on this one."

But . . .

. . . I'm not. I can't. Not today, when we're all suffering together. I can't expect any allowances on my behalf, not ones that highlight my physical differences, not ones that give any indication that Coach believes it wasn't me involved in the vandalism.

As miserable and grueling as they are, it's days like these that build a team, and if I want to be part of that team, I have to get through today. All of it. "No thank you."

"What?"

I inhale quickly. "No thank you. I'll do the pull-ups."

I don't know if my body can deliver. In gym class, we've always done the flexed arm hang during gym tests, and I'm not confident that I can do pull-up after pull-up.

All the same, I hear myself rejecting Coach's offer.

He's irritated and impatient now. "Suit yourself, Marshall."

I grab the bar and hang there. How hard can it be? It's just another case where mind has to triumph over matter. I mean, I've always crushed the flexed arm hang in comparison to my classmates, and I can crush this, too. Eight times. That's all. I can do this.

Below me, members of the group start in with push-ups. I summon all the willpower in my body, I channel it into my arms and shoulders, and . . . nothing happens. It's like trying to push lead, and I've got nothing left behind my effort. I'm shaking just hanging there.

I picture my teammates below me, still doing push-ups, possibly forever. They're unable to look up and actually witness this debacle, but it will soon dawn on them that they've been doing more push-ups this time than any other. I try to use this humiliation to propel myself upward. But it doesn't amount to much in terms of actual output, and I hang there like a cat from a limb, useless and weak, hating my body for letting me down for about the first time in forever.

"Eve," Coach says quietly. I think it's the first time he's ever said my first name. "Wise up and take my offer."

With tears in my eyes, I let myself fall. I turn around and grip the bar from the other direction.

"Fifteen seconds is the equivalent," Coach tells me, looking at his watch.

I tremble like a leaf in a hurricane the entire time, but I make the fifteen-second mark before dropping onto the ground, landing heavily on my butt.

Jamie is doing bleacher sprints, and he's watching me on his descent. I close my eyes so it's impossible for him to see the tears lingering there.

And at last, we're done. The torture wraps.

We lie on the mats, struggling for air, dripping with sweat, several people laid out on their backs, staring vacantly toward the ceiling.

"Next time any of you think it's a good idea to gloat, I want you to remember how your bodies feel at this moment," Coach chimes in. "And for damn sure, you better rethink your decisions. We'll move forward, but it's not forgotten."

The coaches leave, but no one makes any attempt to move. We all lie there for a long time, trying to recover, before people start extending hands to help others up, patting each other on the back. There's no further grief given about who's responsible for the actions that got us here; I think everyone's too wiped to even care anymore.

Today, I'm actually grateful to have a locker room to myself. I struggle inside, peel my sweaty clothes off, and collapse on the floor in my underwear under the warm spray of the shower. I sit like that a long time, limbs still quivering, feeling nausea as I sit there, then actual pain when I attempt to stand up again.

I slowly dress in my sweats, noticing that even my fingers are shaking as I try to tie my sneakers. When I look in the mirror, exhaustion reveals itself on my face, my damp, matted braids pressed against my head like a doll that's been left out in the rain.

When I finally emerge, the hallways are quiet and semi-dark. But the gym doors are open, its lights still on, and that damn bar is directly in my line of vision. It's silently mocking me, I swear, looking all superior from its spot high up on the wall.

Nothing has ever defeated me so wholly and utterly before. Let alone a stupid horizontal piece of metal.

I have to whip it into submission.

As utterly incapacitated as my body feels at this moment, my mind is resolute. I have to whip it, and I have to whip it *today*.

I drop my bag and stride across the gym, eyes focused on the bar.

Fuck you.

Anger propels me forward, and I feel confident and renewed as I grab the bar and hang there.

And I'm immediately crushed all over again. I hang there, and it's evident as I attempt to move my arms that absolutely nothing has changed.

"For God's sake, why are you back inside this gym?"

Startled, I lose my grip and drop like a brick. It happens so fast it takes my breath away, and I whirl around to find Jamie leaning against the door frame.

"Why are *you* still here?" I turn my back on him, looking up at the bar. "Go home."

But he doesn't. Instead I hear him walking toward me. "I was already in my car and out of the parking lot when I realized I forgot my math book, and I can't get another zero for homework. I'm staying on top of things this semester."

Jamie drops his backpack on the ground, and then walks around so that he's standing in front of me, his back against the wall, arms folded across his chest. "Girls aren't expected to do pull-ups," he tells me, so matter-of-factly I want to smack him. But when he starts up again, his voice really isn't all that smug. "Look, Marshall, I *get* that you're used to proving everyone wrong, overpowering physical limitations and all that jazz, but there are some things that just won't work." He shrugs. "Before you bite my head off or rip me a new one . . . that's not a personal insult. It's not meant to be demeaning. It's an anatomical fact that guys have greater upper body strength, more muscle mass." I see a flicker of a smile. "It's not God flipping you off. It's just nature."

"Women have to do them in the Marines."

"What?"

I won't meet his eye. I'm still staring at the bar. "Women have to pass a pull-ups test in the Marines. If it were impossible, the test wouldn't exist."

"How the hell do you know that?"

"My second-oldest brother is in the Marines. I know stuff."

"Are *you* planning on joining the Marines?" he asks.

"No."

"So let it go already."

"No." I stare at him, my position mirroring his as I fold my arms across my chest. "No, we're not naturally inclined to do pull-ups, but partly because we're not expected to. We're not conditioned to; we're not taught. But we *are* physically capable, and I'm going to get myself above that damn bar. Once."

Jamie doesn't look amused. "Have I told you that you're too stubborn for your own good?"

"Once or twice."

"Then let's make it three. This is ridiculous."

"Whatever," I mutter, stepping toward the bar again. "I told you to go home."

"Whatever," he echoes, grabbing his bag, starting across the gym without a good-bye.

When I'm sure he's gone, I jump up and grab the bar again.

I hang there, and seconds later, I hear the voice from the doorway.

"Your elbows are too wide. And you're holding your body too straight and rigid."

I look over my shoulder, finding that he hasn't gone any-where, that he's walking back toward me again.

"Huh?"

"Your body's too straight. There has to be some give."

I try to act on his instructions, tucking my elbows closer to my body.

"You can't be like a board," I hear from below. Then, out of nowhere, his hands are on my body, on the small of my back, nudging it forward, forcing it to soften.

My hands slide off the bar and I fall, him steadying me as I come to the ground, ending up with my body nearly pressed against Jamie's.

"Whoa," he exclaims.

I turn around without meaning to, finding myself face-to-face with him, his skin smelling shower fresh, his hair still damp and darker than usual. His eyes looking right into mine.

I swallow hard, realizing his hands are still on my hips.

Blushing, I take a step back and away. "I slipped." I wipe my hands on my sweats, even though in truth they're bone-dry.

Jamie studies me. "Come on. You're actually shaking. Why don't you conquer Everest another day? We're all fucking beat."

"Today," I insist.

He shakes his head with a resigned sigh. "How many do the Marines have to do?"

"Three."

"Please, God, tell me we're not going to stay here till you do three."

When did this become a group activity?

"You don't have to stay anywhere," I say. "And I just want to do one. To prove to myself that I can."

Looking at the expression of defeat on Jamie's face, it occurs to me that dealing with me might be more exhausting for him than the last two hours were. This makes me smile a little bit.

"Make sure I'm aligned the right way," I call over my shoulder as I grab on to the bar again.

Jamie guides me through one pull-up, using his strength to lift me as he comments on adjustments that need to be made in order for me to do it by myself.

"Now you know how it feels when you're positioned correctly." Gently, he releases his grip on my legs. "I'm gonna let you go now."

This time, shaking with adrenaline more than weakness, all the while feeling like I'm grinding every gear in my body, forcing my muscles in a way they're not meant to be forced, I move. I strain, and push, and demand . . . and I get my damn chin above that bar.

I release the bar, throwing my hands up in victory, and with a burst of renewed energy, take a victory lap around the half-court.

Jamie's expression is perplexed when I return. He has his

backpack on again and shakes his head. "You're the weirdest girl I've ever met. Are you done now?"

I walk toward the door, collecting my things. "Yes."

Now ready, willing, and able to leave the gym behind me, I immediately begin making my way down the dark hallway toward the parking lot, Jamie beside me, nodding in the direction of the janitor, who is likely the only other person still in the building.

We step outside, and once we're in the parking lot, Jamie glances toward me. "You know what I heard?"

I shake my head.

"In the locker room . . . I got the sense that the thing with the mascot last night, it was someone from South. One of the guys who had personal issues with someone from Westdale." He looks me in the eye. "Someone who hasn't been with Coach as long, someone who doesn't care as much about respecting the Pirate name."

I feel my hackles start to go up, and I open my mouth to protest, but Jamie keeps going.

"Which sort of sucks. Because it was kind of starting to feel like we actually were one team."

He's right, I think, feeling surprised. *It kind of was.*

"It wasn't me. And I don't know anything about it," I say.

"Wasn't me, either. And neither do I. Besides what I told you."

"I know that."

"Anyways . . . just sucks."

I don't say anything in response, because I happen to agree with him. For once.

Jamie reaches his car first and nods in my direction. "Later. Go eat a banana."

"What?"

"You're gonna be sore as shit tomorrow. The potassium helps."

"You're gonna be sore, too," I retort. "So . . . you eat a banana, too."

I think he might be smiling in the dark. "All right. Later."

"Later."

I climb into my car—it hurts—and drive home. Climbing the steps to my room hurts, too, but I need to lie down for fifteen minutes before dinner, and I very much want my bed.

When I open my door, it's obvious the cleaner was here today: vacuum lines on my carpet, clutter arranged into a pile at the foot of my bed. Atop it sits the mailing envelope from *Sports Illustrated*, the one they'd sent me the copy of the magazine including my feature in, along with a personalized letter. And a very nice check. I'd forgotten it was still here.

I pick up the check for about the hundredth time, holding it away in disdain. I hadn't been able to bring myself to cash it, because it felt like selling out after the way the photo shoot had turned out. All that pink clothing they'd brought and made me wear. Some with sequins spelling out the word *phenom*. Vomit.

But if I don't take it to the bank soon, it's going to become void. Might as well make a run to the drive-through ATM and get it over with. So it's out of my room once and for all. The desire to be rid of it is stronger than my desire to rest, even though I have no plans for the money. I drag myself back downstairs, find my parents in the kitchen, and tell them where I'm going.

Catching sight of a bunch of bananas in the fruit bowl, I remember Jamie's words and grab it as I go.

Chapter 16

April 7

Jamie

It's silent in the locker room, and when I shut my locker, the noise is unnaturally loud. Once the door closes, I catch my reflection in the mirror at the end of the row. My expression darkens at the sight of my pale blue button-down and khaki pants, and I shove both hands in my pockets, trying to make the stiff pants more comfortable.

Did I say I hated working Friday nights? Because right now I'd kill to be on my way to the Burger Barn, about to walk into a tiring five-hour shift. But Jenn asked me to switch with her because of some last-minute plans with some guy, begging me to take her Saturday shift instead. And when I realized there was somewhere else I should really be tonight . . .

I glower toward the mirror. *Screw you, William Shakespeare.*

I failed the test on *Hamlet*. Jabrowski hasn't handed them back yet, but I know it. SparkNotes didn't help at all, and there were a few short-answer questions I left blank because I had no idea how to respond. All that iambic-whatever and quotes that didn't make any sense. Why can't authors just say what they mean and tell the story, damn it?

I hadn't gotten the story when we'd discussed it in class, and I couldn't bring myself to sign up for a tutoring session if Coach didn't do it for me. Even if working with Eve might've helped me pass the *Mockingbird* test.

As we left class yesterday, Jabrowski stood at the door, handing out flyers for an extra-credit opportunity. Like she was *counting* on some of us failing or something. She'd arranged for a bus to take interested students to a local college production of *The Taming of the Shrew* tonight. To hell if I'm an interested student. But the extra-credit points will bring my grade back up to passing and ensure that I'm not benched next week. In all my other classes, I'm doing enough work to hang in there, but English keeps kicking my ass.

I took my sweet time getting changed, goofing around with the guys, acting like I had nowhere to be since I had the night off. No way was I letting them see where I was actually headed tonight; it's bad enough I have to give Jabrowski the satisfaction of showing up. It's six fifteen before I leave the locker room, heading away from the gym wing and down the long hallway toward the opposite end of the school and the auditorium where we're supposed to meet.

I'm not surprised by the small group of kids I find waiting there—some faces I recognize from drama club assemblies and a few overachievers who have nowhere better to be on a Friday night. I lean against the wall, Pirates hat still in hand, squeezing and unsqueezing the brim, wishing I was anywhere else.

Jabrowski starts calling us together, and I'm trying to force myself to join them, but I do a double take, rooted in place when someone rounds the corner, one final overachiever I'd forgotten to consider.

Eve.

Her damp hair is pulled back in a low ponytail. She's wearing a casual dress and shoes that aren't sneakers for I think the first time ever. Considering the no-jeans-no-T-shirts-no-sneakers dress code Jabrowski dictated on the flyer, I have a bad feeling we have the same Friday night plans. *Why in God's name is she here?*

I don't think she even recognizes me at first, but she actually stops in her tracks when she does. I watch as she pulls herself together, smoothing her hair and lifting her chin before sauntering over to me.

"Jamie Abrams." She sounds sort of haughty, actually. "Secret fan of the fine arts. Who knew?"

I give her a dead stare in return, but she keeps pressing.

"Didn't know you had this sensitive side."

I exhale loudly. "You know exactly why I'm here, and that it has everything to do with baseball and jack shit to do with the theater." I look her over head to toe. "Better question is why are *you* here? Do you actually take every single opportunity to get an extra-credit point?"

Now she's glaring at me. "No." She squares her shoulders, then turns and focuses her attention on Jabrowski. "That day I ended up in detention. She wouldn't admit she was wrong and it cost me twenty points. I'm here to get them back. I'm not giving her a reason to give me anything less than an A."

"You still haven't moved past that?"

Eve shrugs as the group starts moving toward the double doors. "Nope."

The word pops off her lips, and I turn my head before she catches me smiling.

We end up at the back of the line together. "And you do know the show is *The Taming of the Shrew*? I have to think it's like, against every single one of your principles."

"I don't think you really know all my principles," she responds coolly, "but yes, it is a misogynistic piece of garbage."

I bite back another grin.

"I'll probably just take a nap once the lights go down," she says, getting onto the bus.

She picks an empty seat near the middle, and out of habit I head toward the back. Only when I'm there do I realize I've invaded some sort of nerd territory, and they're all staring at me like I'm an alien or something. I glare at them as I plop into a seat, then stare at the back of Eve's head for the duration of the ride, her presence on the bus something familiar and oddly . . . comforting.

Jabrowski's waiting to line us up as we file off the bus, and so I'm stuck with the same group as we file into seats in the darkened auditorium. I think it would be somewhat more tolerable to sit near Eve and trade barbs once in a while.

The live-action version of the story is every bit as boring and difficult to follow as the book, and it just doesn't hold my attention. I lean my head against the top of my chair and close my eyes. An eternity later, I'm jerked back to reality by the sound of applause and the lights coming back on.

"It's over?" I mumble to the person beside me.

"No." He gives me a look, astonished to find I wasn't captivated by this nonsense. "It's intermission."

Crap. It's only *half* over.

Stepping into the lobby, I glance at the clock and realize it's eight fifteen. I notice the theater department has set up a table, selling snacks and drinks, and automatically my stomach starts rumbling. I'd forgotten about dinner, that there wouldn't be a chance to eat any. And suddenly I'm starving.

Walking over, I grab a soft pretzel and a bag of peanut M&M's. Only when I reach into my pocket to pay do I remember I left my wallet back at school, in my jeans pocket when I was changing for practice. "Oh, sorry," I tell the girl behind the table. "Just realized I don't have my wallet."

"I got you."

Glancing over my shoulder, I find Eve standing two people behind me, two pretzels from the Philly Pretzel Factory box in her hand. She steps forward and picks up a couple of bottles of water. "Want something to drink?"

When I don't answer, she shrugs and pays for all of it without a second thought. I'm too busy staring at her wallet, which is about an inch thick and stuffed with bills.

Annoyance flickers within me. She just . . . walks around with that much money on her.

And instead of saying thank you, I end up running my mouth instead, nodding toward her wallet and asking, "Wow, did you already get an endorsement deal with Lady Foot Locker or something?"

She presses her lips together, her expression darkening. "Yeah, no," she tells me, before shoving the snacks into my hands and walking off. "Enjoy the second half."

I open my mouth, wanting to take back what I said, just say thank you instead, but I don't. I find a bench away from the crowd, stuff pieces of pretzel into my mouth, and try to calculate how long the second half will be. It has to be shorter than the first, right?

I stay awake this time, counting down the minutes, occasionally staring at the back of Eve's head again. When the female lead delivers some big speech near the end, says the line "Such duty as the subject owes the prince, even such a woman oweth to her husband," Eve rolls her eyes so hard her entire torso moves.

Even I get the gist of what the actress is saying, and Eve's reaction is so predictably intense, I can't help but smile in the dark.

Another decade passes, and finally we're out of there. The show did nothing to convince me that live theater's a good use of a Friday night, and that it's a better use of my time than working. The second we step outside, I untuck my shirt, loosen the collar, and put my Pirates hat on. Jabrowski can't say shit about it now.

I wait at the end of the line to get back on the bus, deciding there's no way I'm putting up with that group in the back again. Their jokes are horrible and they're *still* talking about Harry Potter, years after they started talking about Harry Potter.

I see that Eve's reclaimed her seat in the middle. It's dark as I make my way past her, holding on to the seat backs as I go. I pause, two rows beyond her.

Then, with a frustrated sigh, I double back. I drop into the seat beside her without even glancing her way, pulling my hat low.

Given her reaction, the way she scoots as far away as

possible, drawing her limbs closer to her body, she doesn't really make me feel welcome.

"What are you doing?"

I stare straight ahead. "I don't think the group in the back will miss me too much." Then I look at her pointedly. "I'm sorry—was someone *else* sitting here?"

She shakes her head.

"Okay, then. I am."

Eve shrugs. "Okay, then."

I lean back, staring out from beneath the brim of my hat at the seat back in front of us. Both of us are silent when the bus starts moving, and we're still silent when I pick up on the sound of the wheels moving steadily over the expressway.

My body feels tense; the silence is uncomfortable. What was I expecting, anyway? What was I hoping for?

Our conversation last week. During the assembly, on the picnic table.

I guess I was hoping it would be like that.

But it's not. That was probably a fluke, anyway. I grip the seat back in front of us, thinking about standing up and leaving her in peace.

"Did you recover from yesterday?"

She's still facing away from me, and I barely catch the question. "Huh?"

Eve turns around, and if I didn't know better, I'd swear she looks kind of disappointed to find me getting ready to go. I slowly drop back into the seat, and she repeats herself. "Did you recover from yesterday?"

I nod. "I crashed at home pretty much the second I walked

in the door. Didn't even eat dinner. But my mom cooked a big breakfast today, and I felt all right by the time I got to school." I raise my eyebrows in her direction. "You?"

A wry smile appears on her face. "Didn't you see me hobbling around school today?"

My lips curve upward. I *had* noticed her going down the steps like an old woman in need of a hip replacement. "Maybe."

"I ate two bananas," Eve says. "They didn't do anything for me." She folds her arms over her chest and gives me a look, like somehow it was my fault she pushed her body past repair. "I can't lift my arms past my shoulders."

"Well, go figure. You're the one who decided to enlist in 'basic training' after that shit show at practice yesterday."

She looks away for a second, but I catch her biting her lip. When she's sure she will not, in fact, laugh at something I said, she turns back around. "Has Coach ever pulled something like that before?"

"Yes and no. Nothing that bad."

"Didn't think so. It felt unfair, and fair is the first thing I ever had him pegged as."

My eyebrows go up. "I'm sure he seems fair to you. Doesn't necessarily feel that way to everyone else."

She stares at me.

"You got your special tryout." I shrug. "Not sure how many people he would've done that for, especially when you were too busy with another sport to make his tryouts. But I guess not all of us are on the cover of *Sports Illustrated*."

Even in the dark, it's impossible to miss the anger flashing in her eyes.

"God. Everyone thinks the *Sports Illustrated* thing is something I'm so thrilled about." She shakes her head against the back of the seat. "I told you before; it wasn't like that at all. I wish those pictures didn't exist. I mean, did you see it?"

I'm stuck on how to answer her, because I can't really tell her to her face I threw it out before actually *looking* at it.

"They made me . . . Baseball Barbie." She practically spits out the words. "I thought the article was going to be the focus of the feature. Truth is, they were more interested in designing a pink jersey for me to wear and making sure my makeup was just right for the lighting." Eve sighs heavily. "It was such a fucking disappointment."

She's quiet for a minute, glancing at me out of the corner of her eye, considering something, before she starts up again, voice softer. "That's why I have all that money."

"What?"

"I don't usually walk around with so much money," she says. "But it's from my check from the shoot. I hadn't cashed the check because taking a payment for that debacle just felt dirty. I feel guilty spending it, like I'm okay with what they did."

I don't say anything, feeling kind of guilty myself. For jumping to conclusions and being smart with her when she was nice enough to buy me something to eat.

Then Eve pauses. "I don't know why the hell I'm talking about this. Should be over it by now." She rummages around in her tote bag, eventually finding what she's looking for. "Gum?" she asks.

I look down at the pouch she's extending toward me, with the purple letters and familiar slugger on the front. "Are you serious with this? You seriously walk around with a pack of Big

League Chew in your purse? Do you have Cracker Jacks and sun-flower seeds on hand at all times, too?"

She grabs the skin on my forearm and twists it.

"Ow!"

"They still sell it at the deli near my house. The grape flavor is better than Bubblicious grape. God. Do you feel compelled to give me a hard time about everything?"

I smile, looking down, still rubbing my sore arm. "I actually kind of enjoy your reaction, when it's not directed toward me. How you go from zero to sixty in about two seconds flat."

She's biting her cheek, again fighting her smile, and I get the impression she likes this idea, that she considers it a compli-ment or something.

"So you want gum or not?"

"Yeah, I'll take some gum."

Who doesn't like Big League Chew?

I stuff a huge wad into my cheek, then grin around it, feeling satisfied. Most of the time, she's scowling. The smiles are rare; you end up feeling rewarded when you've earned one.

I end up staring at her mouth, the shape of her lips in the dark-ness, way longer than I should. I raise my eyes to hers, before I get caught staring. And still, I feel like some weird guilt must be written all over my face.

"What?" she asks.

"Nothing," I mumble. I tug the brim of my hat down again, feel-ing some sort of unease I can't really figure out. "It's nothing."

. . . .

The bus pulls up right in front of the auditorium to drop us off. Eve and I are quiet as we walk the length of the sidewalk in front of the school, back to the other parking lot, where we both left our cars outside the locker rooms. It's late, and she doesn't stifle a loud yawn as we make our way down the path.

Before she ducks inside the girls' locker room, she raises one hand wearily, and I do the same. I guess that's good night, and I walk inside to grab the rest of my stuff. When I step back out into the parking lot a few minutes later, making my way to my Jeep, I feel some strange sense of relief when I see that Eve's car is still in the parking lot.

Why? Why are you glad she's still here? You said good night already.

I linger at my door, watching as she walks to her car, pushing the annoying question out of my mind, irritated and restless and undecided. Then, after watching her unlock her car, right before she climbs inside, suddenly I'm jogging in her direction, backpack bumping against my back, gym bag jostling against my hip.

"Hey!" I call to her before she can close the door.

She pauses, looks around in confusion, then waits beside her car as I come running up.

I close the distance, coming up to her, taking a step closer than typical parameters for personal space would dictate. I can't seem to help it, that extra step.

Eve ends up caught between me and the car door, and to be honest, she looks every bit as uncomfortable as the time I turned on her in the parking lot, when I blew up at her. So I talk quickly, because I'd kind of like to erase that memory.

"I didn't say thank you," I blurt out.

"What?

"For dinner . . . the pretzel . . . whatever."

She stares at me a minute, then shrugs. "It was no big deal."

"Well, I was starving, so it kind of was. And I should've said thank you at least." I give her a little smile, wink at her. "Manners. I sometimes have them."

Then I extend my hand. If Eve were a guy, I'd shake his hand. A girl? I don't know, but I do know that Eve doesn't strike me as particularly huggable.

She stares down at my hand for a few seconds before reaching forward to join hers with mine. When she does, our eyes meet, and she swallows hard. "You're welcome," she says quietly.

Our hands stay connected as we stand there in silence a few seconds longer.

Then Eve pulls away. "Well." She gives me the quickest flash of a smile. "Guess I'll see you Monday."

"Yeah. Catch you then."

I turn around and walk toward my car, refusing to look back. It's only when I'm inside, when I'm sure she can't see me, that I glance back in her direction, watching as the lights go on, as she drives toward the exit, and eventually out of sight.

Monday.

I lean back against my seat, an uncomfortable sensation in my gut rising and creating this weird pressure in my chest.

Monday . . . suddenly feels like it's really far off.

I close my eyes, fingers closing in a fist around my keys.

Oh . . . fuck.

Chapter 17

April 12

Eve

Yesterday's win was one for my personal record book. Pat had a lousy start and couldn't get it together, and by the fourth inning we were down 6–0. It took me half as many innings to get things back on track, and I made sure no additional runs were scored. My team responded to the change in momentum and started hitting, Jamie sent a grand slam over the fence the next inning, and we ended up winning 7–6.

Definitely one of my best games.

There was also talk that someone had personally apologized to Coach for the Westdale incident, and that a punishment was being dealt with privately. I guess after running us into the ground, Coach didn't want to reveal the identity of the person responsible out of concern for what our response might do to team morale. I didn't love his thinking, but I understood the rationale behind it.

Most importantly, Coach seemed like himself again—pleasant and calm—and last night the team got an e-mail from him, with the brief message that in lieu of practicing Wednesday, we'd be participating in a team-building activity off campus.

My phone rang as I was reading the e-mail. It was Scott. "Hello?"

"Hey."

"Guess you're calling me about this e-mail?"

"Yeah. Got any guesses?"

"Nah, still processing," I told him. "Trying to decide if it's a good thing or a bad thing."

"Considering his last 'team-building' exercise made me puke," Scott answered, "I'm not overly optimistic."

"Well, it can't possibly be as torturous as that, whatever it is," I told him.

We discussed the cryptic e-mail for a few more minutes before hanging up.

Guess I could ask Jamie.

The thought popped into my head and was instantly unwelcome there. I dropped my phone onto my desk like a hot potato, balling my hands into fists, like I'd found myself doing all weekend.

You are not actually going to ask Jamie. There is no reason why Jamie popped into your head as someone to ask.

I turned off my light and crawled beneath my covers, pulling them up over my head for good measure.

. . . .

I meet up with the team outside the locker rooms at three o'clock, as the e-mail directed. From a distance, I assess Jamie.

He's wearing a tight black T-shirt and a pair of black Pirate-issue sweats, and looking around, I notice a couple of the other guys are dressed in head-to-toe black also.

What is going on? All that black isn't really reassuring.

The coaches appear a minute later, and Coach Karlson claps his hands together, grinning. "Welcome to our annual team-building exercise," he greets us. "I wanted to wait a while until you all got comfortable with each other, but . . . I think we're getting there." Then he stands, silent, letting the anticipation build.

We look from Pirate to Pirate, trying to figure it out, waiting to see if anyone is going to chime in, but no one does. Until Brendan finally calls out, impatient, "Come on. Where are we going this year, Coach?"

Coach is quiet one more minute. Then, "RUSH laser tag arena."

A few guys throw their hands in the air, and even more break out in hoots and hollers. I stand there, feeding on the excitement, feeling it in my stomach, a slow grin spreading across my face. I've had some epic laser tag battles with my brothers, and I'm not at all worried about heading into the arena.

"What are we playing for?" Jake asks.

Coach puts both hands up before him. "Just bragging rights, got it? Nothing that constitutes harassing the losing team."

His response is greeted with loud booing, but he just waves it off. "I'm teaming you up a little differently this year." He extends his left arm. "Catchers and infielders, over here." He points with his right hand. "Pitchers and outfielders, over here."

Scott grins at me before jogging off to join his team. "Watch your back, baby."

We regroup ourselves, the catcher-infielder team boarding

the bus first, the rest of us lingering behind. I turn around and realize Jamie's now standing right behind me, and when my heart starts pounding, I fold my arms across my chest, like I'm trying to keep it in check or something.

Narrowing my eyes at him, I nod in the direction of his clothing. "Pretty coincidental you and your buddies showed up in all black today. What kind of unfair advantage do the captains get anyway?"

"Heard a rumor this might have something to do with laser tag," he answers. "Those black lights pick up on any white you've got on." Jamie takes one step closer, leaning toward me. "Don't know what you're complaining about. I'm on your team. You won't be complaining when I save you with my skills."

My head falls back on my neck and I groan. "Save me, my ass. If I were you, I'd watch out for friendly fire."

"That would be just like you."

And just like that we're sparring again. But he's grinning, and I'm grinning, and shit, we're grinning together. I clench my fists again, nails digging into my palms, trying to get all the smiling under control.

....

Once we get to RUSH, it feels like forever before we're actually allowed inside the arena. First we're ushered into the vesting room, where my team is suited with green vests and Scott's team given orange vests. We're equipped with our holsters and guns.

The coordinators make a big deal out of leading us into the briefing room, their faces stern, ominous music pumping through the speakers, smoke coming out of the vents when the doors open. It's all an illusion, but now that we're armed and huddled together with our teams, it's transformative, my nervous system instantly on high alert, anxious sweat making a trail down my spine.

They're all business as they review the rules for inside the arena, where our main goal will be to find and deactivate the sensors at the other team's base camp while suffering the least number of hits to the sensors on our shoulders, chests, and foreheads. They remind us how long our weapons will be deactivated after getting hit, how many shots we can fire before needing to return to our home base for recharging purposes.

We're given a few minutes to confer with our teams, and my fellow pitchers and outfielders hurriedly divvy up roles—who will be responsible for defending our base camp, who will be responsible for destroying theirs.

"We need more people going for their base," Jamie says, pointing to the scoring system hanging on the wall atop the airbrushed murals of a cityscape. "We get more points for hitting targets than we lose for getting hit ourselves."

I adjust my gun in its holster. It's an offensive strategy rather than defensive. I'm good with that. There's no sense in playing if you're just going to hide out in the back of the arena, which I have no intention of doing.

Then the thirty-second countdown timer starts flashing red above our heads, a robotic voice saying the numbers aloud. We all fall silent as the room goes almost black, my eyes finding Jamie's—wide and almost silvery in the darkness—as we wait. Adrenaline courses through my body, amping up my heart rate before the doors even open.

"Three . . . two . . . one . . ."

The doors open with such force they practically ricochet, and I launch myself forward, intent on distancing myself from the group as quickly as possible. In my peripheral vision, I assess the multilevel arena as I run, trying to take note of landmarks, the murals on the walls designed to look like an abandoned city. There are tons of panels with shoot-through spaces, glowing in the black light. I run toward the back right corner, turning only once to shoot when I see someone on the other side of a panel.

And just like that, I hit the sensor on Scott's left shoulder, the rest of his sensors going dim when I make contact.

"Marshall, what the *hell*?" he cries as I take off.

When I reach the back of the room, I sprint up the stairs. It's risky, that kind of exposure, but I'm banking on the fact that everyone is still getting their bearings and I can make it up the tall, narrow set of stairs before they realize where I am. If I can find a good spot upstairs, close enough to our base camp, I'll have the ultimate vantage point, able to take my opponents out like a sniper would as they approach our territory.

I select one tall panel nearest the railing, crouching behind it and positioning my weapon within the shoot-through space, and wait, my breath sounding like a freight train in the silence, running in overdrive.

I close my eyes to get a better sense of what direction the footsteps are coming from in the darkness, and when they're finally close enough, I aim my gun downward, shooting in a sweeping motion from left to right the way Evan taught me years ago, hitting more sensors than I would if I just aim and fire.

When one of them realizes where the shots are coming from, he points, calling to some of his teammates who aren't too far away, whose sensors are still active. "Up there! He's up there!"

I grin in the darkness. They have no idea who is shooting at them; there's not even a thought of taking it easy on me because I'm the only girl in the arena. It's lights-out, and it's a level playing field.

One that I'm currently commanding.

I duck down, weaving through a few more panels, eventually reaching a point where I need to dash across an open space to get the best cover and viewpoint.

"He's on the move!" I hear a voice below me. "Follow the black light. It's picking up the swoosh on his sneakers!"

Shit!

When I hear them making their way up the stairs, I double back, positioning myself to meet them head-on, and when three guys round the corner and come bounding up, I take the whole group out before they even see me up there. They shoot back, making contact with a sensor on my shoulder and one on my knee, but I refuse to drop back, knowing if I hold my ground and keep shooting, I'll do more damage than is being inflicted on me. I'm right, and eventually they're forced to head back to base to recharge.

The upper tier is quiet again. In fact, all noise is moving away from my end of the arena, back toward the entrance point, so I drop to the ground and crawl across the open floor, back toward the action, waiting for my weapon to reactivate. I glance around before standing up, making sure it's all clear, then jump to my feet and brush myself off.

An arm shoots out from behind a panel, grabs me, and pulls me behind it. Before my scream can even leave my mouth, a hand is covering it. At first all I can make out in the darkness is a matching green vest. Then, looking up, an all-too-familiar pair of icy blue eyes.

I start to push him off, but he shakes his head at me, covering his mouth with one finger. He waits for me to calm down, then grabs my arm, pulling me close enough to whisper in my ear.

"They're only leaving one person to guard their base," he tells me, sending shivers down my spine. "The rest of them are splitting up to both stairwells. They're amassing the whole team to take out the sniper."

I nod, swallowing hard as I try to catch my breath, and then it escapes me all over again as Jamie pulls me close a second time, shifting his head to whisper in my other ear. "Should've known it was you." I can hear him grinning. "They actually think you're hiding out somewhere."

As if.

"We need to get down to their base when they come up," he says. "But they're charging both directions, so we have to be careful."

I look left and right. "The far stairwell," I whisper. "They have to be almost recharged by now. We can't get to the other one in time."

Jamie positions his body, ready to move, along the edge of the panel. "Watch my back," he instructs me.

He sprints to the nearest panel, hiding behind it, checking around him, and then gesturing with his weapon that it's clear for me to go.

We make our way across the floor like that, covering for each other, hiding behind panels until it's safe to move again. He grabs me by the waist when I'm about to step out one time when he hears noise from below, pulling me back behind a panel that's tucked in a particularly dark corner, our heavy breathing echoing in the space as we wait to move again. His body is only inches from mine, something I'm acutely aware of, the heat radiating from it as I squeeze in behind him, the tension in his muscles as he holds his gun at the ready.

We stare at each other in the darkness, waiting, exhaling in rhythm, the noise sounding loud in the silence. Maybe it's the eye contact we can't seem to break, how our mouths are only inches apart, or the way my heart is thumping anew, but for whatever reason, in the middle of a war scene, I'm imagining what would happen if he took one step closer.

The idea makes my stomach drop to my feet, and I jerk back and away from him, clenching my eyes shut to shake the image.

"I don't know where their base is," I whisper quickly.

It takes him a beat to respond; he's still staring at me. "It's at about three o'clock once you reach the bottom of the stairs. We've just gotta go hard. I'll hold them off. You hit the target."

"Why can't I hold them off if you know exactly where it is? I'm a good shooter and you're faster."

"Do we need to argue about this? We only have seconds to get moving and you're—"

"Because if we do this, we might as well do it in a way that makes—"

Loud footsteps interrupt us. Jamie throws his arms up. "Fine. I'm going in. Do what you need to do."

We pound down the stairs like we're leading some type of stampede, Jamie jumping from the fourth one, almost getting launched onto his face, but regaining his footing at the last second and sprinting toward the base camp, gun blazing.

I root myself into the ground between the approaching orange team and their base, firing with reckless abandon until my gun gives out, then bracing myself for the inevitable assault as the remaining active members of the orange team barrel toward me.

But in that last second before I get annihilated, a loud, piercing alarm starts sounding on repeat and the lights in the arena go on, nearly blinding me.

Jamie must've made it to the target, and round one is over.

I whirl around to find him running back toward me, a wide grin spreading across his face, our palms meeting with a loud smack of satisfaction.

I'm smiling so hard in return it almost hurts, and then out of instinct I'm curling my fists again, trying to keep my smile in check, trying to turn off the obnoxious combination of pleasure and heartache that courses through me when our hands touch.

....

Back at school two hours later, I'm suffering an epic adrenaline crash, feeling twice as exhausted as I do after extra innings, my ears still ringing from the loud, enthusiastic recap of the match on the bus and the buzzers and alarms we left back in the arena.

I end up waiting in the front lobby, standing next to the huge trophy case, so I can see my mom pull up. A few of my teammates, those taking the late bus home, file past, still giving me crap about being the sniper, or slapping my hand if they happened to be on my team.

I watch the bus pull away. I listen to the silence, which feels almost oppressive after so much noise and activity.

Then I hear a final voice behind me.

"Still hanging around, Marshall?"

I know who it is without turning, and I do so slowly, trying to put some kind of shield up as he approaches. He's still wearing that tight black T-shirt, damn it, his face still lit up with exhilaration.

My gaze drops to the ground. "Yeah, waiting for my mom. Her car was getting inspected, so she has mine today."

"Do you need a ride?" he asks.

He asks like it's no big deal, like it wouldn't be a big deal, sitting in a car with him, alone. I bet the interior of his car smells just like him, the way he smells right after he showers. I wonder what radio station is on; I wonder how he'd position his hands on the wheel.

"No," I say at once, shaking my head adamantly, my words coming out in a rush. "She's already on her way, so . . . she'll be here any second."

I turn robotically, staring into the trophy case like there's some reason to do so.

But it doesn't shake him, and he comes and stands beside me.

"I see what you're looking at in there, you know."

"Huh?"

Jamie points toward the tall Cy Young trophy, nestled among district championship trophies and other award plaques. It's engraved with the names of past recipients. He raises an eyebrow as he turns to look at me. "We might get along okay these days, Marshall, but that trophy still has my name written all over it."

I lean forward, squinting. "Huh. I see the 2017, but I don't see any name next to it." I straighten, turn toward him, and shrug innocently. "Looks like it's still up for the taking. And do I need to remind you what happened yesterday?"

He chuckles and shakes his head slowly. "Too bad it's not about one game, right?"

"We're neck and neck and you know it."

From the corner of my eye, I see him swallow hard. He has nothing to say. There's no rebuttal because I'm right.

A moment later, he adjusts the shoulder strap on his bag. "Well. Gonna take off. Sure you don't need a ride?"

"I'm good."

He starts walking away, then turns back once more. "Nice job today. Pretty badass."

Jamie lingers, looking at me, eyes questioning, lips slightly parted. Then, finally, he turns and leaves for good, and I breathe again, my brain instantly retracting its words, turning down the offer of a ride.

Don't go.

It feels like I just lost something precious and rare, the opportunity to sit beside him in his car. My stomach drops, leaving me feeling queasy.

When I see my mom, driving my car, appearing in the fire lane, I dash out to meet her.

"Hey, baby!" she greets me cheerfully. She reaches over to tug on one braid, but I shrug away from her, still distracted. "So what was the big mystery today?"

I answer her succinctly, but she's in a chatty mood, asking a lot of questions. But even though I *was* pretty badass in the arena and enjoyed every second of it, I hear myself giving her one-word answers, secretly wishing she'd be quiet because it's taking so much energy to focus on what she's saying. My hands are at my side, but no matter how hard I clench them . . . it does nothing. It doesn't cut off the feelings the way I want it to.

And if I'm being at all honest with myself, nothing I tried over the weekend kept them from tormenting me, either. I still ended up . . . time after time . . . reliving the conversation on the bus with him, replaying his words. Remembering how . . . okay, how *good* he looked all dressed up like that, how he looked even better when he untucked his shirt and turned his hat around. Like an MLB player getting off the bus from a road trip, which is pretty much the height of hotness.

Replaying that moment in the parking lot, when our hands touched, when he winked at me. Sure, it's probably a practiced move of his, but yet . . . it didn't seem like Jamie was putting something on with me.

I stare out the window and swallow hard. I draw my fist up to my mouth and end up biting down on a knuckle, knowing that after today there will be even more moments to replay, more sensations to squelch. After being pressed into that dark corner with him, his body making contact with mine, conjuring thoughts of kissing.

Suddenly, I'm full-on nauseous, because as hard as I try, I can't keep the feelings at bay, and I can't play dumb, either.

I know what that obnoxious combination of pleasure and heartache is . . . I know it's a crush.

My shoulders collapse as I finally acknowledge it, my eyes going skyward toward the clouds that pass in a blur.

Dear Lord, please spare me the indignity of having a crush on Jamie Abrams.

Chapter 18

April 14

Jamie

As practice is ending, cars start pulling into the parking lot and taking the spots nearest the cafeteria. My teammates and I file past the lunchroom, its windows open, the scent of garlic wafting out. The girls' lacrosse team is having its yearly spaghetti dinner fund-raiser tonight.

Coach encouraged all of us to go, support the team and their event, make sure the female athletes knew they're recognized here at school beyond Title IX. I hadn't felt like paying twelve dollars for lunch-lady noodles and watered-down sauce, but Naomi had slipped me a ticket "on the house."

Pitchers were working together at the end of practice, and everyone else cleared out ahead of us. I'm walking next to Eve as we head to the locker rooms, and I sneak a glance at her. I clear my throat. "You staying for the thing tonight?"

"Uh, yeah."

She glances over to meet my eye, then quickly looks away again, but not before I see irritation, or anger, flicker across her expression. It's happened a bunch of times these past few days, and I don't understand it. I don't think I've pissed her off again, but that's how she looks. Pissed.

"I was going to go later, with some of my friends from the basketball team, but . . ." She shrugs, then reaches for the door of the girls' locker room. "Here now, so might as well stay."

"Cool," I say. "Save me a bread stick."

Eve gives me a weird look and ducks inside.

I stand in place, squinting into the distance, feeling like a dumb-ass.

Save me a bread stick? What the hell was that?

I open the door, head to my locker, and peel off my sweaty clothes. I take an extra-long time showering and getting myself together, to the point that most of the other guys have left the locker room before I'm done. I get dressed in an old gold-and-white tee, my jeans, and gray New Balances. I brush my teeth for five minutes. When I'm done, I check the mirror once . . . smooth my hair down . . . check again.

I look myself in the eye in the mirror, asking why I'm taking so long getting ready. I turn around before I have to answer.

When I make my way down the long hallway from the gym to the lobby that leads down into the cafeteria, I find Naomi, Colleen, and Erika manning the money box. As I hand her my ticket, Naomi slides down in her seat and nudges my foot under the table. "Hey you."

"Hey."

"Stick around when you're done, okay? We all did prep work and have the first lobby shift, but then I'm done. I'll find you."

I'm already looking past her, down into the crowded cafeteria. "Yeah, okay."

I take my time walking down the steps, scouting out the scene, finding that most of my teammates have already been through the line and claimed a table. None of them took as long getting ready as I did.

Shit, even Eve didn't take as long getting changed as I did. She's with them, now wearing a zip-up hoodie and running leggings. She turns to look for a table, and I try not to stare at her ass.

All right, I don't really try that hard.

The line's longer now, and I start feeling frustrated as I wait behind lacrosse team parents and siblings, chatting with the girls behind the counter. I'm not here for the food, and I'd wish they'd dole it out faster.

I strain my neck, glancing toward the seating area of the cafeteria, lips pressed together in irritation. What *am* I here for, anyway?

What feels like four hours later, I finally have some spaghetti and a can of Coke on my tray, and I walk toward the table where my team is sitting together. Eve is sitting with them, out of a sense of obligation, I guess, even though I see that the majority of the girls' basketball team is here now. She's doing her own thing, though, reading from a textbook, flipping its pages with one hand while she holds her fork in the other. There's a blank worksheet beside her.

I consider the seating options. The table's crowded, and I only see one chair at the other end, next to some of the seniors who came over from South. Otherwise, the only open chair with the team is the one directly across from Eve's. No big deal. I set my tray down across from hers and sit down.

Apparently, it isn't a big deal. She doesn't even look up.

Pat's to my right, and I end up talking to him for a few minutes. But periodically I look over at her, kind of amazed at the level of concentration she's able to maintain in a loud cafeteria at a table full of loud guys. How is she capable of blocking everything out so entirely? Her sitting there, doing that, is actually distracting *me*.

And after about ten minutes of being ignored completely, irritation gets the better of me. I lean forward, nudging the back of her hand with mine, causing her eyes to fly upward. It startles her, and her cheeks turn pink, like she's been caught doing . . . I don't know what.

"It's rude to read at the table," I say. "Didn't your parents ever teach you that?"

She rolls her eyes. "What? Yours did? I highly doubt you were ever caught *reading* at the dinner table."

I can't help but laugh.

"Anyway." Eve turns another page. "I'm not reading. I have to put this worksheet in my teacher's mailbox before the weekend. He already let me take till tonight."

"Working on a Friday is overrated." I stab a meatball with my fork, pop it into my mouth, and smirk at her.

She tilts her head and purses her lips at me. "Says the boy who spent Friday night watching Shakespeare. Are your grades really that solid one week later?"

I nod, wiping my hands on my napkin. "I'm not even close to the ineligibility list," I tell her. I wink at her. "So don't get your hopes up."

She bows out of the exchange, looking back down at the equations on the page.

I spear another meatball, bring it to my mouth, and take a bite of it. I chew, shaking my head. "Man. These meatballs are garbage."

Eve doesn't respond.

"I'm going to guess the ratio of bread crumbs to meat is about eighty–twenty. Should be the other way around."

With a sigh, she finally looks back up. There's a small, wry smile trying to hide at the corner of her lips. "You're not going to give me any peace and quiet, are you?"

"Nah, I don't think so."

"And what the hell are you talking about, anyway? Meatball ratios?"

"Yeah. My nana's one hundred percent Sicilian. I know some stuff." I put my fork down and tick the points off on my fingers. "It's about ingredient ratio. It's about brand. From the Italian specialty store, not Giant. And it's about density. You don't compress them enough, they fall apart in the gravy. You compress them too much, they taste like golf balls."

"What do you mean, gravy?"

I shrug. "Sunday gravy. When she lived nearby, Nana used to make Sunday gravy."

"It's sauce."

"Do you even have any Italian blood?"

Eve hesitates. "No."

I lean toward her slightly. "Didn't think so. It's *gravy*."

A chair screeches as someone backs it away from the table. I turn toward the sound, see Nathan rising from his seat, getting ready to take his empty tray over to the trash. He does a double take when he sees me. He stares for about ten seconds. And then his mouth slowly widens into an obnoxious grin.

"Aww. You guys are really cute down there."

My response is instantaneous as I spear my last meatball with more force than necessary. "Shut up, Nathan."

But he doesn't.

"Didn't even know you were here." He raises his eyebrow toward us. "Looks like you're in your own world down there."

Neither Eve nor I bother responding.

"Brendan, looks like they're in their own world, doesn't it?"

"Yeah, gotta say . . . looks like it," he says.

"Grow up." I stand suddenly, striding toward the condiments, getting napkins that I don't really need. I take my time, first getting too many, neatly putting the extra back on the pile, and by the time I return to the table, my jackass friends have moved on to something else.

But something else has happened in that time as well. And it's evident when I casually ask her if she's ready for the game on Monday.

Her eyes are flat when she looks up this time. They look far away, and her face is practically grim.

"I really should"—Eve gestures toward her paper—"ya know, finish this. Like I said. So . . ." She trails off, gaze returning to her text. Shutting down. Shutting me out.

I don't like the way it feels.

I feel my internal temperature drop a few degrees. My tone turns nasty, and the muscle in my jaw twitches. "Whatever."

There's nothing but silence between us anymore, but it feels different from when I first sat down. It feels heavy and cold.

But three minutes later, a warm pair of hands covers my eyes and there's a voice in my ear. "Guess who?"

I don't have to guess—I know her voice and the smell of the perfume at her wrists.

I shift around to find a smiling Naomi behind me. Her smile falters some as she assesses my tablemates, one in particular, but it's Naomi, and she always bounces back quickly.

"I'm done with my shift now." She looks toward my table again. "Do you *have* to sit with the team?"

"No. Not at all."

She tugs on my hand. "Come sit with me, then." Naomi points across the room toward some half-empty tables, where her friends are already camped out.

I let her pull me to my feet. "Yeah, sure."

Eve doesn't even look up as I gather my tray, napkins, and plastic utensils.

"I'll be over in a sec," I tell Naomi. "Let me get rid of this."

As I walk away, I only glance back toward the baseball table once. What am I doing sitting down there at the end, anyway? I could've squeezed a chair in somewhere near Nathan or Brendan. Why didn't I sit with my friends?

What am I *doing* here?

I empty my tray and roll my neck before heading over to Naomi.

Deciding on a path that will not take me back past Eve.

She pisses me off.

Sure, sometimes I like talking to her, more than I like talking to other girls.

More than I like talking to most people.

And I think about her. A lot.

And somewhere over the course of things, I've gone from rooting against her to rooting *for* her, from hating her to . . .

But what?

What was I thinking was going to happen here, anyway?

Clearly, she's not one of my girls. It wouldn't be like it is with them. It wouldn't be easy; there wouldn't be this understanding.

With Eve, things would be different. More. And I don't know shit about any of that.

I chuckle and shake my head. Not like she cares anyway. This past week, it felt like things had changed somehow. But she was pretty blunt tonight about a complete lack of interest in even talking to me, so again, whatever. I don't need this. I don't need her.

I settle into a chair beside Naomi, and she promptly slides her tray over, hops into my lap.

I have Naomi. It's simple.

She takes her time winding some spaghetti around her fork before bringing it to her mouth and taking a dainty bite. "What's up with you and that girl?" she asks breezily, concentrating on her spaghetti.

"What girl?"

Naomi chortles. "Umm, the only girl who was sitting with you guys. You *know* who I mean."

I feel myself tensing beneath her, but I refuse to give her a reaction. "Nothing," I say coolly.

Now she looks at me, one eyebrow raised, eyes challenging. "You sure about that?"

"Damn sure."

Then I laugh, like the idea is as completely ridiculous as it sounds coming out of Naomi's mouth.

She smiles in satisfaction at my response. "Good. 'Cause I want you to drive me home tonight." She bends her head toward mine, the ends of her hair scratching my cheek, mouth right over my ear. "Let's go the back way. I'll get my car later."

From the distant corner of my eye, I see Eve stand up at the end of her table. I'm not sure, but I swear I can feel her eyes on me. So I smile back at Naomi, just in case. "Absolutely."

We leave the cafeteria together ten minutes later, going back the way I came, down the long hallway toward the locker room so I can pick up my stuff. As we approach the gym, Naomi grabs my arm, pulling me into the dark alcove in front of the boiler room.

In the semidarkness, I can see her biting her lip. "Screw the car," she says. She nods toward the supply room where team equipment is stashed during the off-season. Then her hands are on the back of my head, pulling me in for a kiss.

But before my lips can even meet hers, I'm distracted by the sound of footsteps, and I glance over my shoulder in the direction they're coming from.

The person pauses, and I stand as still as stone, not certain she can see me, hoping she can't.

Because I can see her, even in the dim light of the hallway after hours, and I swear, before she even recognizes who it is inside the alcove, she looks upset. Then recognition must dawn, because I hear this little surprised, embarrassed gasp. That's it before she turns on her heel and disappears. The footsteps sound faster than when they approached. She's running away.

When your team's up to bat . . . when you're at the plate . . . you have seconds to process, to make a decision between the time the pitcher releases the ball and when you start to swing. There's no conscious decision made; your mind is made up before you even actively consider the choice.

And just like that, I hear myself saying something to Naomi before I even process the thought. "I can't take you home tonight."

Naomi's face goes from confused . . . to shocked . . . to angry. The transformation happens in record time, her voice coming out cold and steely. "What the fuck?"

"I forgot," I say lamely. "Something I had to do."

Then I'm running down the hallway, too. I don't look back.

....

Eve

I dart outside and end up leaning against the brick wall around the corner from the locker room, trying to get ahold of myself. The tears that started stinging my eyes the second I saw them turned from sad to angry in a flash. I actually bat at them, hard enough for it to hurt.

Do not cry. For Christ's sake, do not cry. You don't want this. You don't want any of this. And you will not disgrace yourself by crying over Jamie Abrams!

I don't want any of this. Lord knows I don't.

A shudder shakes my body as the vision of them cozied up in the dark corner flashes across my mind.

I don't want him. But apparently, I really, really don't like seeing him with Naomi, either.

What was the big surprise, anyway? Batting at my eyes again, I consider. She's been there all along. The two of them have always had a thing. Why, when, did I start thinking that had changed?

And it hurts, actually stumbling on the fact that it hasn't. It hurt when he left with her, regardless of how I was acting toward him. Regardless of how much I don't want it to hurt, regardless of how hard I'm actively pushing him away, it still hurt watching him go.

Despite my battling them back, two tears spill over onto my cheeks. *Damn it.*

Shaking my hands at my sides, I try to distract my body with some other physical sensation so that I'll stop crying. I hate crying, hate everything that goes along with it, the snotty nose and that gaping feeling in your chest.

"What's wrong?"

I'm so startled, my hand goes to my heart and my entire body flinches. When I calm down enough to realize it's Jamie who's found me there, Jamie who's actively come looking, I turn my back on him at once, desperate to hide my tear-streaked face. Which will require an explanation I *really* don't want to give.

"Go away, Jamie," I mumble over my shoulder. I discreetly wipe at my eyes and nose. "What are you doing out here, anyway?"

He doesn't answer for a few seconds. "That was my question for you."

I turn only my head to look at him, to offer up a weary look. "I don't feel like playing tonight."

"Okay." He nods. "I'll answer you, then."

Jamie comes around, so that he's leaning against the wall beside me in the direction I'm facing. I'm tempted to turn my back again, except I'll look like a toddler. And because I guess I'm more tempted to hear his answer.

"You were upset. I could tell. So I followed you."

He turns his face toward mine, only inches away. He looks genuinely confused, like he doesn't even fully understand the answer he's just given me.

And I snap back into snark mode.

"That was big of you," I say, my voice sharp. "Considering Naomi's hand was halfway down your pants."

But Jamie doesn't snark back. He just stares into my eyes, this look of pleading in his. "Eve," he whispers. "Stop. Okay?" He spreads his hands before him. "My weapons are down. Maybe you could drop yours, too."

My head hangs. I don't make some retort. It's the best I can do right then.

"Why did you look sad?" he asks quietly. "When you saw us?"

I try to lift my chin. "I wasn't sad."

"Yes, you were."

"No."

"Yes. You were."

His voice is insistent this last time, increasing in pitch and frustration, and the words explode from me before I have any chance to wrangle them back inside.

"I like you, okay?"

I throw my hands up when I say it, but I need them back, right away, to cover my face. Jamie must be stunned into silence, and I end up continuing on through my fingers. "I hate you. I think I really hate you, except"—my voice goes quiet for a second—"except I don't. And so I'm pissed off, and confused, and sad, and . . ."

My hands fall back to my sides as I stare at him, looking more appealing than ever in that worn baseball tee. "And how many of those damn shirts do you own?"

"What?"

"Nothing."

I take another glance at him. He's smirking. "You like me?"

I try not to notice the way those beautiful blue eyes light up when he asks the question. Otherwise, I'd want to smile, too. "Stop mocking me," I murmur.

He shakes his head. "I'm not mocking you." Jamie inches closer to me. "So maybe I know what it feels like to . . . like someone against my will, too. Sucks, doesn't it?" he whispers. I close my eyes. I don't see his hand gently capture mine, but I feel it. In every single cell of my body, I feel it.

He doesn't wait for me to answer. Jamie kisses me instead.

His lips touch mine, and this kiss is the last thing I'd ever expect from the legendary Jamie Abrams. It's soft, and gentle, his fingers closing infinitesimally tighter around mine when he finds my mouth with his. My eyes pop open, just for a second, instantly seeing how his are clenched, like he's tentative. Almost like he's scared to look.

It's this alone that does me in, and as I let my eyes fall back shut, my hand goes to his chest. I feel him stiffen in response, probably anticipating my pushing him away, but my fingers twist in the soft cotton of that shirt instead, pulling him closer. Pulling him all the way against me, feeling the warmth and firmness of his torso against mine as I deepen the kiss.

Jamie's free hand goes to my hip, steadying me, keeping me close, before cupping my jaw, keeping my face close to his as he kisses me back. And for every imaginable thing that Jamie and I have argued about, there's some kind of natural agreement in our kissing. We find our rhythm easily, without bumping, or awkwardness, or hesitancy.

Jamie lets me kiss him for a long time, and I let him kiss me. It's only when I hear the echo of him chuckling from inside my mouth that I pull back, ever so slightly, seeing some new person whom I've never seen before in front of my face.

"What?"

He's grinning like the cat that ate the canary. "Just making sure this is okay. That you're not on the verge of kneeing me in the groin or anything."

I'm grinning right back, grabbing a breath, letting my forehead fall against his. "Don't give me reason to."

And then we're kissing again, urgently, like both of us regret breaking it off in the first place. We kiss for so long that my muscles feel stiff from standing up straight, and I end up pressed against the brick wall, Jamie's body against mine, both hands on my lower back, dropping dangerously close to my butt.

When I open my eyes, it's completely dark. I have no idea how much time has passed. My parents are probably starting to wonder where I am.

So after letting myself enjoy the feel of his lips for ten more seconds, maybe fifteen, I pull away, taking a quick gasp of air, trying to focus. I take a step away. I tuck a strand of hair that's escaped from a braid behind my ear. "I should go home," I exhale.

Jamie plants one last, slow kiss on my jaw. "Do you need a ride?"

"No. I have my car."

Now that they're no longer attached to him, I don't know where to put my hands. They flounder awhile before coming to rest on my thighs. They feel damp with sweat.

I start looking left, then right, making sure no one is possibly around.

I mean . . . what if someone was? What would happen? What would that be like?

I frown, thinking about it, because . . . how does something this private translate into something public? When it's me . . . and *Jamie Abrams*.

I poke one finger into his chest. "Don't ever talk about this," I warn him.

He raises his eyebrows. "No deal." But he's smiling, a little bit. "That was pretty good; you have to admit it."

I cross my arms. I bite my lip. "No, I don't."

But I make the mistake of looking at him. The impish nature of his smile is irresistible, and before I know it, a smile blooms in spite of me, revealing everything.

As soon as it appears, he kisses it, like he was waiting for it to make an appearance. "Those smiles are so worth it," he whispers.

Never in a million years would I tell him so, but maybe so were those kisses. Maybe I'd endure it all over again—the warring, the confusion, the heartache—for a first kiss like that.

Chapter 19

April 15

Eve

I'm groggy when I wake up, my thoughts confused and hazy, feeling like I've been startled out of a dream. One of those good ones, full of moments and feelings and characters that have no place in your actual universe. The kind that makes you wish that the alternate universe within your head is somewhere you could actually stay.

My fingers go to my lips as consciousness fully dawns. The pressure on them last night was real. The admissions they made . . . also real. The herd of butterflies in my stomach might as well be real.

There is a warm glow alive within me, like I swallowed the sun. Because Jamie kissed me last night. He left her, to track me down. To kiss me.

Barely managing to contain a squeal, I jump out of bed, flip on the light, my reflection appearing suddenly in the mirror on the back of my door. Questioning me at once.

Do you not see the million issues inherent in that equation? my brain berates me. *That five minutes before he kissed you he was ready to go for it on school grounds with another girl?*

I stare at myself in the mirror.

God, look at you. You look downright smitten.

This is Jamie Abrams, player extraordinaire, we're talking about here. You've seen him with half a million girls. He does more scoring off the field than on.

Why do you feel special?

And what would Scott say?

Good God, what would Marcella say? When she suggested you let loose every once in a while, getting down and dirty against a brick wall with Jamie Abrams was hardly what she had in mind.

What would your parents . . . your teammates . . . everyone say?

A cold pebble of futility announces itself in the pit of my stomach, growing in size by the second, weighing down the butterflies until I can't feel them at all. I don't like how it feels when they're gone. I don't like the way my brain obliterated the light, breezy, *happy* feeling I'd awoken with.

So I turn my back on my reflection. I straighten my shoulders, talk back to my brain.

I don't care, I decide. *For at least a few hours . . . I'm not gonna care.*

I grab my towel and go shower in the hallway bathroom. Afterward, I don't like the clean smell of my skin, how it seems to punctuate the ending of yesterday and the beginning of today. But when I bring my discarded shirt up to my nose, I make the amazing discovery that it still smells like him around the collar. I'm grinning like an idiot again, and I pull it back over my head.

I braid my hair quickly and skip downstairs, finding my mom in the kitchen.

"Hey," I call to her breezily, opening the fridge, grabbing the eggs, a bag of cheese, and milk.

"I'll cook," she tells me, reaching for the ingredients in my full hands.

But I shrug her off. "That's okay. I feel like doing it."

Glancing through the small window above the sink, I notice the sun's already shining, notice a few buds on the Japanese cherry tree have actually blossomed. Spring might truly be here.

I crack two eggs into the bowl and add some milk. I whisk, then dump the whole mess into a small frying pan, keeping an eye on the edges, occasionally nudging it with my fork.

I don't even notice my mom come stand beside me or feel her eyes on my face as she stares. Not until her voice interrupts my whistling.

"What are you smiling about?"

I turn toward her, finding her smiling, too, her eyes narrowed and pensive.

Crap. I didn't even know I was smiling, and I work quickly to wipe it off my face. What if my mom is one of those sitcom moms who can *tell*? Who knows exactly what I was up to last night?

"I'm not," I insist, staring down at the pan with renewed concentration, willing my eggs to cook faster so I can busy my mouth with eating and keep less of a close eye on what it might be up to when I'm not paying attention.

....

Besides all the random smiling, it's a pretty typical Saturday. I'm supposed to meet up with Marcella around four, after she's done with one pageant rehearsal or another, and I fill my hours the same way I always do, with schoolwork, school activities, and sports. I drive to the bank to make a deposit for honor society and stop at the store to buy ingredients for the flan I promised to make for Spanish Club. Then I sit down at my desk and get as far as opening my backpack. But my mom must've snuck in and opened my bedroom window, and I can actually hear the birds chirping and feel a gentle, warm breeze reach me after it ruffles my curtains.

I sigh. There's no sense in trying to focus on something as boring as *On Walden Pond* on a spring day as nice as this one. Seconds later I'm pushing my chair back, tying on my sneakers, and grabbing a decently inflated basketball I find lying around my room.

There's a backboard mounted above the garage, one I spend quality time with on pretty much a daily basis. Even during soccer season, even during baseball season. On the weekends, I'm doing something with the future in mind, whether it's running, hitting the gym, or shooting hoops. Hundreds of them, relishing the fluid, automatic feel of my arm motions, the consistent *swish* of the ball through the net. I've spent days of my life, weeks maybe, shooting in my driveway, and it's easy to get lost in the zone, let my mind go blank, and enjoy the way the sun warms my skin as it creeps toward noon.

I've made seventeen consecutive three-point shots when I hear my phone ringing from where I tossed it in the grass. Frowning at the interruption, I cradle the ball in my elbow and jog over to grab it. I'm annoyed that I broke my streak to go get it—the number flashing across its front isn't one I recognize.

I quickly swipe the screen. "Hello?" I don't bother to try to hide the annoyance that reveals itself when I speak.

The voice at the other end is substantially warmer. "Hey." It's a single-word response, but somehow it's still slow . . . liquidy . . . like warm honey.

"Who is this?"

The resulting chuckle is familiar. "I'm insulted, Marshall. I mean, I thought I made an impression last night."

Instantaneously, my heart starts pounding like a jackhammer. Apparently destroying my mental filter as it goes. "How did you get my number?"

"Jeez, treat me like a telemarketer?" he says. "It's on the roster."

I consider this, feeling stupid. And never in a million years would it have crossed my mind to look his up. To *use* it. But he looked mine up.

Just like that I'm smiling again.

I'm happy you called.

The words flash across my consciousness, naturally. But they don't make it any further. Nowhere near the tip of my tongue. I just can't seem to say them.

"Oh," is all I manage. Stunning conversationalist that I am.

But Jamie doesn't seem offended. "So anyway . . ."

"So anyway . . ."

I glance around. Both of my parents are gone. I drop the ball into the soft grass and settle down beside it.

"I was lying in bed," Jamie continues.

A mental image flashes through my mind, making my cheeks flush.

"And I found myself really, really curious about how you spend your weekends."

I tuck a strand of hair behind one ear, trying to stop picturing him between the sheets. "Is that so?"

"Yeah."

There's a moment of silence.

"Sooooo?"

"So?"

"So what do you do?"

"Oh." I consider. "I do my homework and other school stuff. I hang out with Marcella, Scott, or some of my friends from basketball. And I practice."

"Are you practicing right now?" he asks. "It's so early."

"It's almost noon! And yes . . . I am . . . sort of. Just shooting some hoops."

His follow-up question is immediate. "Can I come over?"

I'm stunned. I sit there, mouth open and useless for several seconds. "What?"

"Can I come over?" he repeats. "You know . . . school you. On the court, just like on the field."

My eyes almost roll out of my head.

Then I sit there, thinking. I'm astounded by his brazen invitation, his lack of hesitancy in calling me, suggesting we get together. *Never in a million years . . .*

It sends me so far off-kilter, it takes me a while to actually consider. I've never had a guy invite himself over to my house before, besides Scott anyway, and I don't know the protocol, or house rules, or anything.

My parents aren't here. I can't ask them if it's okay.

Then again . . .

My parents aren't here. Neither of them is due back for several hours.

Isn't that what girls do? Girls who make out with guys against brick walls? Let them come over when their parents aren't home?

It's not like he's proposing holing up in my bedroom. I'm out here playing basketball; it all sounds very innocent.

"You're not going to beat me," I say.

Now I can hear the smile in his voice. "That sounds like a challenge. Be there in twenty."

Then, to my extreme irritation, he hangs up without saying good-bye.

Ten second later, my phone rings again. "Yes?"

"Hey, what's your address?"

"Go look that up, too."

Then, with extreme satisfaction, I hit the red button on my screen and end the call.

. . . .

My three-point shots in the twenty minutes that follow are significantly less accurate than the ones I took before the call came in. Probably because of the way my hands are shaking, ever so slightly, and the way I keep glancing at the curb from the corner of my eye.

I consider for a minute what it would've been like if a guy I'd ever really liked had shown up for a game. *It would've been awful*, I decide, shaking my head. *If my focus was shot to shit like this.*

And did I really just refer to Jamie as a guy I really liked?

He's prompt, at least, putting me out of my misery. The Jeep pulls up in front of my house twenty-one minutes after the call ended, almost visibly pulsating from the loud bass of his sound system. His door opens. I suck in one final deep breath, steeling myself.

And there he is, coming around the front of his car. In high-top Nikes, loose sweats, and a tight T-shirt. He's got his Pirates hat on backward, ever-present sunglasses in place. He removes them as he approaches, swaggering toward me. One eyebrow goes up as he glances toward the backboard, then assesses the faded white lines my dad painted on the driveway ages ago. "So this is where the magic happens, huh?"

That final deep breath did jack shit to steady me. Not as he makes his way toward me, looking as handsome and cocky as ever, effectively trapping me between himself and the garage. In a last-ditch attempt to buy myself some distance, I end up cradling the basketball against my chest, thinking of it as a shield.

Is he going to try to kiss me again?

Would that be a good thing or a bad thing?

Before I can figure out the answer, Jamie's standing in front of me. "What's up, Marshall?" he greets me casually, swiping the ball out of my grasp, running toward the net, and making an easy layup.

He rebounds his ball and returns to the top of the circle. "You should know," he begins, dribbling three times, narrowing his eyes at the net in concentration, and firing off a shot . . . nothing but net. Jamie grins. "I used to play basketball, too. Before I decided to focus all my attention on baseball. You know, the way an athlete *truly* committed to their sport would do."

"Please." I push off the wall, dashing to get the ball before he can get his hands on it again. "If you're talented enough, that kind of focus is unnecessary." I jog back to what would be about half-court, firing off the shot my brothers and I mastered after years of practice. I don't even watch the ball go in, turning to cock an eyebrow at Jamie instead. "And middle school JV doesn't really count as playing ball, anyway."

He throws his head back and laughs, then looks at me and shakes his head slowly, an amused smile still on his face. "You're a piece of work. And who said anything about middle school JV?" Jamie crooks his index finger toward me, eyes sparkling with competitive flair and lingering laughter. "Bring it, sweetheart."

I lean forward at once, ready to go, dribbling the ball before me, feeling its rhythm. "Play to eleven? Best of three?"

"Sure."

"You have a quarter?"

"Damn, this is all business." Jamie puts his hands into his pockets. "Not on me, but probably in my Jeep."

I watch as he jogs smoothly to his car, roots around inside for a few seconds, and returns, triumphantly clutching a quarter in his fist. "Call it."

"Tails."

He pushes the coin off his thumb, and we watch it turn in the air. Jamie catches it, turns it over, and smacks it onto the back of his hand. "Heads. My ball." He snatches the basketball out of my grasp for the second time today.

Jamie runs the ball back behind the free-throw line, and I switch instinctively into defense mode, light on the balls of my feet, arms stretched to either side. *There is no way in hell you will let him score this point*, I say to myself. *There is no way in hell you will give him the satisfaction of beating you at your own game.*

It doesn't take long for me to realize it's not going to be as easy as repeating a mental mantra. Jamie doesn't have much on me in height, but Lord knows he's naturally athletic—quick and agile, conditioned for endurance. He makes the first three points, then has the nerve to heckle me.

"Middle school JV, my ass. There's only one of us who should be talking about middle school JV."

I grit my teeth, not wanting to show that it's actually taking any kind of *effort* to keep up with him, and double my efforts. It's my ball now, and the lead is mine for the taking.

I take the lead at five points and never give it back. We make it to game point before he's even scored his eighth, and the feeling of triumph that results from breaking past him for a layup and sinking my eleventh basket is fairly comparable of that to securing the victory at states.

I'm tempted to throw my arms up in victory and run circles around him, pumping my fist in the air, screaming, "Yes, yes, yes, yes, yes!" except for the fact that it would let on how much I actually care about putting him in his place. So instead, I shrug nonchalantly as I pass him on the way back to the top of the court, calling out as a reminder, "Game started by the player who didn't start the last one."

"I know that," he snaps, eyes narrowed anew, as he wipes the sweat from his forehead with the back of his hand.

And now I can barely suppress the grin. I've rattled him, and it's obvious. Maybe one shouldn't feel quite so vindicated about irritating the boy she's very recently kissed, but the feeling comes quite naturally to me. *Let him get frustrated*, I think. *It'll only make this easier.*

But he keeps his cool, motivated, I guess, by the sheer force of his desire to keep me from taking the match without ever seeing a game three. It's his turn to step up his game, and it's evident from his panting and grunting that he's overexerting to keep his early lead. Which he does, by a hair, even though midway through the game I resort to a little bit of overexerting myself.

"Last chance to bow out before I embarrass you," he says as he jogs back to half-court.

"What you wouldn't give," I retort. I assess him—his T-shirt is clinging to his torso, rivulets of sweat are running down his neck, and I swear he's hobbling a little bit. "I'm not really sure you have game three in you."

"Oh, I have game three in me. Don't worry."

Game three is ugly. It's nasty, full of sharp elbows and overly aggressive body checks from both of us, and one time I (maybe) nearly trip him on purpose. After I score my ninth point, widening my lead to three, the next time the ball is in my possession, he actually grabs my free hand and pins my left arm behind my back.

"Umm, that's illegal!" I cry, coming to a stop, laughing all the while. "I mean, the fouls have been *blatant*, but come on."

His body is right behind mine, still locking my arm in place, his warm voice right in my ear. "Thought you were the all-star," he chides me. "You can't win with a handicap?"

I don't answer for a second, keenly aware, for the first time during the match, of the physical proximity of his body to mine, how I can feel the heat radiating from him, how his words reaching my eardrum make my spine tingle. Turns out there's more than one way to handicap me, and I stand there for a moment, dumbstruck, soaking up the sensation of Jamie's nearness, not wanting to move.

"Let go of me," I mumble a few seconds later, shrugging out of his grasp. "Let me put this one away."

And this time as I attempt to advance toward the net, he manages to steal the ball from me, for only the third time over the duration of the match. He scores two points in a row, way easier than he should have, again making me resent the impact a boy can have on my game. Thank goodness no guy has interfered up to now.

But I score point ten and recover the ball a minute later. I take my time back at half-court, trying to give myself that final push that will end this, that will make me the victor. I remember how I was thrust into his territory against my will, against my best efforts. How baseball season started on his turf, how uncomfortable he tried to make me there. This is my turf. This is my game, my forte, my superpower. He may be able to keep up with me because he's slightly taller, and slightly bigger, because he's a boy. But to *hell* if he's going to beat me.

I take off without warning, pushing my way past him, blocking his body with mine, spinning on a dime, and firing off a shot that I know is perfection before the ball even leaves my fingertips.

I feel it go through the net more than I really see it or hear it. And I feel my heart explode like a sunburst in my chest. I'm pretty sure there's no feeling better than winning, and winning against Jamie Abrams compounds the amazing sensation.

It's only when I turn around, when I see the actual person standing behind me, that I remember Jamie Abrams is more than a name now, that he came over here of his own free will, that he came over here to see me. And I'm shaken out of my übercompetitive trance, left questioning ever so slightly if I played this wrong, if I've potentially gone too far and pissed off the boy who followed me outside last night.

His face is blank at first, but after I retrieve the ball, I find he's standing with his arm extended, waiting to slap hands.

I approach cautiously, unsure if I'm entering a baited trap, but he only shrugs sheepishly and offers a half smile as I touch my palm to his. "Got to let you have something, right?" he pants.

I smile, relieved. "If that's what lets you sleep at night."

Using the bottom half of my T-shirt to wipe my face off, I struggle to swallow, throat dry. "You want something to drink?"

Jamie wipes his forehead on the shoulder of his shirt—we're pretty gross, the two of us—and squints toward the sun. "Yes, please."

I turn toward the open garage, then pause, causing Jamie to bump into me. "Ummm . . ."

Looking toward the dark garage again, I stare helplessly into its interior. I don't know my parents' policy on this. Boys in the house when they're not home. It's never come up. There's never been any reason for it to come up.

"Wait here," I tell him. "I'll just be right back."

I dash into the house before I can possibly read the look on his face.

I grab two bottles of water from the fridge, and then, as an afterthought, double back and get a bag of pretzel twists from the pantry. When I return, I find Jamie's settled onto the low wall at the end of the driveway. He's put his sunglasses back on and is scrolling through his phone.

But, to his credit, he puts it aside as soon as I return, and thanks for me for the water with a smile.

I stare at him while we munch on the pretzels. "Can you lose the glasses, please?"

He looks surprised. "Why?"

Using a pretzel, I gesture over my shoulder. "Because the sun's behind us. And . . . it's annoying to talk to you when I can't look you in the eye."

"Demanding," he mutters under his breath. Then, dutifully, he removes his beloved shades, folds them, and stuffs them into his pocket.

"So what's the plan for the rest of the day?" he asks. "Got any more boys lined up to lure over and embarrass?"

I smile around the pretzel stick in my mouth. "Nope, that was a privilege I reserved for you." I chew, swallow, take a swig of my water. "I promised Marcella I'd come over this afternoon. Help her make some final decisions about her pageant dresses."

Jamie turns and stares at me, an unspoken question resting on those pretty lips. He quickly glances down at my sweaty gym clothes.

"Yeah, I know." I roll my eyes. "I don't really understand what kind of help I'll be, either. After the fashion show, I may have given her the wrong impression about wanting to be involved with this stuff."

He laughs, and it's a really nice sound, when we're both laughing at the same thing.

"I have to work tonight," he tells me. "Usually I have Saturdays off, but I switched with someone so I could go to that thing last night." Jamie shrugs. "A night off sounds good in theory, until the time to make up for it comes around."

I don't say anything, and a second later, he nudges me gently with his elbow. "Guess it was sort of worth it, though."

I blush, hating myself for how easily it happens. How it mirrors exactly what I'm feeling inside.

Then, before I even have the chance to recover, a familiar blue Honda Accord rounds the corner and my spine goes ramrod straight. "Oh shit," I mutter, lips not moving, my entire body going rigid as if playing possum in the middle of the open driveway might actually work.

"What's up?"

Still my lips refuse to move. "Mrr mmm hrrr."

"What?"

"My mom's here."

To punctuate the statement, the Accord pulls into the driveway. My mom's face turns right toward us. She observes . . . tilts her head . . . smiles slowly.

"Am I here . . . illicitly?" Jamie whispers.

My mom's still taking it all in, prolonging the torture.

"No . . . it's not like that . . . it's just . . ."

What is it, just?

"It's just . . . I hadn't really planned on doing introductions today," I finally admit.

I think of the words I used to describe Jamie to my mother in early March. *Classless. Vile. Loathsome.*

I have a lot of explaining to do.

Yet beside me, Jamie visibly relaxes. "Oh. Well, don't worry. Moms love me. I got this."

My eyes shoot heavenward again as my mom's door opens. "You really give yourself way too much credit regarding your effect on the female species," I whisper.

"Sit back and observe," he says under his breath as she approaches us.

"Hi," my mom greets us. Well, greets him. Her eyes are focused on Jamie like a laser beam.

Jamie stands up. "Hi, Mrs. Marshall."

She squints her eyes and studies him some more. "I'm sorry. You look familiar, but I'm blanking." She turns her face toward me. "And Eve didn't mention that someone was coming over."

Jamie deflects the blow, extending his hand to shake hers. "Jamie Abrams. And I apologize for the damp hands. Your daughter just wiped the basketball court with me."

And just like that, three sentences, and he's made her smile. He *is* good.

Then, a second later, recognition dawns in her eyes. She shakes her head. "Wait. Jamie. Of course." She looks back toward me, confusion evident on her face.

"Hmmm . . . ," Jamie muses. "Mrs. Marshall, the look on your face tells me that you've heard my name before and"—he folds his arms across his chest—"something about that look makes me think I wasn't really talked about favorably." Jamie looks to me for explanation, eyes wide and innocent.

My mom actually giggles. I swear, she giggles.

"Well, you know what, Jamie Abrams? If you found a way to her good side, more power to you. From some of those things she said"—she raises her eyebrows at him—"it seemed like an uphill battle."

"Ah, I'm always up for a challenge," he answers her. Then he reaches out and hefts the paper shopping bags out of her arms. "Here, let me get that for you."

Her eyes, alight with something akin to amazement, never leave Jamie as she grabs the remaining bag from the car and leads him into the kitchen. I follow them, watching in wonderment as he makes small talk with her, asks her where he can set the bags, and if anything else needs to be brought in from the car.

"Thank you, Jamie, but I think I'm set," she answers. "It was . . . nice meeting you."

She stares at me, a thousand questions written all over her face, and I'm wondering how long I can extend his visit so I can put off answering them.

Jamie doesn't linger in the house, swiftly making his way to the door, but he actually stumbles over his feet and comes to a halt as he walks down the short hallway toward the front door.

I see what he's staring at and cringe.

"Holy shit," he says, pointing to the excessively large photo of me holding a rabbit, taken circa Easter 2001. "You're wearing a *dress!*"

My hand finds his back and I shove him toward the door. "Shut up."

Out in the driveway, Jamie pulls his phone from his pocket, checks the time. "I gotta go. I have to be at work soon." One corner of his mouth lifts in a half smile. "You're hard-core, Marshall. I need a nap."

"What time is it?"

"Two ten."

"Seriously?" I'm not sure where the hours went. My eyes flit to Marcella's empty driveway. She'll be home any minute.

"So, listen . . ." Jamie glances over his shoulder at me as he walks toward the shaded area beneath the edge of the roof that protrudes over the garage. "What's up?" I follow behind him, until he eventually comes to a stop at the corner, where the driveway ends and our house begins.

"I'm not gonna lie. I had an ulterior motive in coming over

here today, beyond curiosity about how you spend your Saturdays."

He's smirking at me, and I await the punch line.

"Oh yeah? What was it? Trying to wear me out . . . possibly injure me even . . . so you can ensure the next start?"

"Nah." He snaps his gum. The smirk morphs into a smile. Jamie quickly glances toward the house, then grabs my wrist and pulls me closer.

My heart bangs against my chest as my still-damp torso comes into contact with his.

Jamie's head falls forward, his forehead brushing against mine. He tilts his head, ever so slightly, allowing his mouth to graze my ear. "I wanted to kiss you again," he murmurs.

Just like that, and sudden nerves give way to wanting, and I lift my chin without any thought.

Our lips meet at the same time, and mine part at once, wanting to kiss him again like last night, wanting a new imprint on my lips to hold on to once he's gone. Jamie's hand finds my hip and he keeps me in place, taking over, kissing me like a god while somehow keeping his gum out of the way.

Man, he's good.

When he finally steps back, his eyes are kind of hazy, and a new, slow smile dawns on his face. "Yeah. Guess the ass-whupping was worth it."

Then the shades are back in place, and he's sauntering down my driveway with his patented swagger. He raises one hand, calls to me as he goes, "Later, Marshall."

I stand there, patting my lips. "Later."

I stand and watch, listen, as the ignition kicks in and the bass starts thumping again. He gives a quick honk of the horn before he pulls away, and I stand there for several minutes, both trying to make sense of the feelings that accompany his departure and trying to keep them at bay.

Plus. There's no way in hell I'm walking into the house right now.

I glance toward the discarded basketball. I should practice more. Practice is always good.

But fifteen minutes later, my mom appears at the end of the walk, one hand up to block the sun, the other hand on her hip. My shots and rebounds remain continuous; I carry on unfazed.

"You can't stay out here forever, you know," she calls. "Eventually, it's going to get dark."

I look at her and roll my eyes. "I'm not going to stay out here forever."

She holds my gaze, her eyebrows raised in a silent question.

I turn back toward the hoop and shoot. Miss an easy shot. Sighing, I turn back toward her. "It's nothing. Nothing worth talking about, okay?"

"Okay," she says evenly.

"I hang out with guys all the time," I point out. "Scott's been over here thousands of times. Not every visit from a person of the opposite sex is discussion-worthy."

She shrugs. "I was just curious. I do, for the record, remember some very unsavory things you had to say about said person of the opposite sex. But if it's nothing . . . it's nothing."

My mom turns to go back inside, and just as she disappears, the red Jetta rounds the corner and Marcella approaches, waving cheerily.

A heavy feeling weighs my shoulders down at the reality of all of it.

Maybe my mom took it easy on me. But . . . I have a feeling . . . Marcella would not. Marcella would want to gush, and poke and prod, and maybe expect me to gush, too. And there's not a snowball's chance in hell she'll ever see me act like that over a guy. Any guy. Let alone one who might still be more enemy than not, regardless of the godlike kissing.

Chapter 20

April 18

Jamie

It's a shitty, powerless feeling, being taken out of the game in the top of the first inning. New Hanover has a lousy team, and we were off to a stellar start. Bases were loaded before we were even halfway through our lineup, and I was on third base when Scott stepped up to the plate and sent a powerful ground ball right through the shortstop's legs on the first pitch. I was sprinting toward home plate . . . and then out of nowhere I wasn't.

From my point of view, it's really hard to understand how a pothole like that wasn't noticed before the game. It's really hard to understand why I'm benched so early in a game I was supposed to start, with a bag of ice bound to my swollen ankle. Maybe they blame their losing record and last-place standing on the maintenance staff's total abandonment of their shoddy field.

Or maybe they've resorted to underhanded tactics to try to level the playing field. *Jackasses.*

I'm sitting in the corner of the dugout, exhaling loud bursts of air through my nose, trying to keep my chest from exploding. There are a few discarded helmets within reach, which I pick up, one at a time, and chuck against the fence as my team warms up on the field. *"Assholes,"* I snarl.

The umpire hears me, turning and looking over his shoulder to stare me down.

"Abrams, go cool off," Coach Jackson orders, not even bothering to look at me.

I chuck the final helmet and hobble out of the dugout, rounding the corner and collapsing in the grass against its side wall. I can still make out the game in my peripheral vision, hear the ump's calls, but mostly I see a wide expanse of green grass and blue skies. The peaceful view does nothing to calm me down. Grabbing a handful of grass, I twist the blades ruthlessly and pull them out of the ground. I do it a few more times, until the need to destroy something lessens.

I stay out there through the fourth inning, having zero motivation to move. This game is over for me, and we could still beat them even if they took out half our starters. Brendan steps out once, but I shrug him off when he asks how I'm doing. Fifteen minutes later, some dumb sophomore makes the mistake of coming out, too. But my coaches know better, the majority of my teammates know better, and they leave me the hell alone.

She knows better.

I see her step outside the dugout a few times, to throw with Pat during warm-ups, to gather equipment between innings. She doesn't even look at me; she lets me suffer in solitude, which is exactly what I want right now.

I let my head fall against the cement wall of the dugout. Most girls, you throw them the smallest bit of attention, and they're all over you like butter on toast, eager to stake their claim and display it for the whole world to see. I look at Eve as she steps outside to dump out her water bottle and refill it with fresh water. I try to make eye contact, but she gives me nothing.

A new burst of frustration fills my chest. Okay. I guess if I could tolerate anyone coming out here to talk, it would be her. She'd understand. She'd be every bit as pissed off if she were in my shoes. She wouldn't try to coddle me or talk me out of my mood.

But . . . we both know that's not going to happen. Her coming out here.

The game's into the sixth inning when she trots out with Scott to warm up. Eve wasn't supposed to be in the lineup today, but from the sound of things, Matt's having the shittiest game of his life, and it's approaching the point where a loss could be a legit possibility.

When it's our turn to take the field again, I hear my teammates cheering her on, hear the clapping from the visitors' bleachers. I drag myself up, tentatively putting weight on my ankle. It's tolerable again, and I walk slowly back around to join my team inside the dugout.

I mean, it's the sixth inning. Guess it's time to stop acting like a baby. I should get my head back in the game at least.

All you, Marshall. I stare toward the mound. *Put this bullshit to bed.*

I sit up, take my hat off, scratch the top of my head, tug it back on, and pull the brim low. I'm surprised at my sudden conviction, how naturally I find myself rooting for her, when, to tell the truth, it hasn't really been the case to date. I really want to shut these fuckers down, though.

It should be an easy finish for us. But the whole game should've been an easy win, and it just seems like nothing's going right for the Farmington pitching squad today. I was done before I even started, Matt struggled, and now Eve just can't seem to find her groove. There's the mental aspect of pitching, which I thoroughly understand. She didn't expect to have the game on her shoulders today, and her mental game isn't at 100 percent. It's written all over her face, evident if you know what you're looking at.

None of us thought the bottom of the ninth inning would actually matter today. But our lead's been shrinking inning by inning, and here we are, with two outs and the tying run on third. As their batter steps up to the plate, Eve's looking at the tying run more than she should be. He's distracting her, it's distracting her, the possibility of this game getting away from us.

I lean forward, cupping my hands around my mouth. "Stop looking at him, Marshall," I holler. "Eyes on the plate. You got this."

She doesn't look in my direction. But she does square her shoulders anew, taking a deep breath as her eyes narrow in concentration, zeroing in on Scott's glove.

When I sit up, I turn and look at Brendan when I notice him staring at me.

I lightly smack the back of his head. "What, dumb-ass?"

He looks at me another few seconds but wisely just shakes his head and keeps his mouth shut.

And Eve strikes the batter out looking. I jump to my feet,

clapping my hands together once, ignoring the ache at the bottom of my leg.

This time, before running in to celebrate with Scott, she does look my way, for the quickest of seconds before she tucks her chin, the shadow created by her ball cap hiding her smile.

....

I linger at the field with the coaches after the game. Coach wants to check in on how I'm doing and has the trainer take a look. The swelling has gone down, and the trainer doesn't think it's a sprain, probably just a bad twist. He gives me instructions for tonight, estimates I'll be fine in a day or two.

Relieved, I sling my bag over my shoulder and start walking by myself toward the bus. Along the way, I consider the possibility of sitting with her or at least . . . near her. Close enough to talk to her.

I have to battle back this stupid little smile, thinking of being able to talk to her.

Eve's funny, and sarcastic, and you can pretty much count on a little bit of bite to every word that comes out of her mouth. It's not flirting, it's just . . . fun. I like how she keeps me on my toes, and I like those rare moments when I knock *her* off balance, when I see that not-so-sure part of herself that she seems loath to reveal.

I don't really think she shows it to anyone else. I've never seen her, at least.

I think back on the weekend. It was one of the best Saturdays I'd had in I don't know how long. My good mood lasted, and I made a killing in tips that night at work.

"You're in a good mood," Laura commented as she squeezed

past me with a heavy tray of dirty dishes. "Get some on your way in?"

Normally I would've had a smart-ass retort for her, given her some slightly dirty details. That probably would've been true. Probably, yeah, would've had something to do with my good mood.

But I'd only kissed Eve. Kept my hands where they belonged. And I was still full of smiles and energy behind the counter at the Barn. Go figure.

I climb onto the bus. Everyone's already inside, the last few people finding seats.

And I'm back in the real world. I remember Nathan's comments at the spaghetti dinner. Brendan looking sideways at me in the dugout.

Nah. I'm not going to sit with her.

As I make my way past her without even acknowledging her, I tell myself she wouldn't exactly welcome my presence anyway. I remember how she shut down at the dinner at Nathan's ribbing. She doesn't like that shit any more than I do, right?

In front of me, Scott finally stops running his yap to Pat and gets moving. He easily drops into the seat beside Eve.

I grit my teeth and shuffle past, keeping my eyes forward, irritation flaring in my gut.

It's not jealousy, because that would be ridiculous. I'm not jealous over the idea of it, another guy, especially Scott, sitting with her. There's nothing going on there. Nah, I'm not jealous over the idea of Scott sitting with Eve.

I'm just . . . sort of . . . miffed about the reality of it. He gets to talk with her. He gets to laugh with her.

I drop into the seat across from Nathan and Brendan, and without meaning to, my eyes meet hers.

I drop my head at once, leaning forward to look for something in my bag.

It's a purposeful maneuver, one that doesn't feel entirely good. But hey, we're all playing the same game here, right?

"How you feelin', man?" Nathan asks, swinging his arm up along the back of the seat and turning toward me.

"I'll be all right," I say. "Trainers don't think it's anything serious. Just have to keep icing it tonight."

"Good. We need you back in the game. Matty looked like shit today."

"Dude, I'm *right* here," Matt interjects.

"And I'll say it to your face. You looked like shit today," Nate says.

"You're an asshole."

Nate just shrugs. "Anyway. We need you." He lifts his chin and nods in Eve's direction. "Girlfriend barely got the job done today. Think she's wearing herself out. End of the day, girls just don't have as much stamina. And it's a long season."

"I bet she would very aptly kick your ass if she heard you say that," Brendan says.

"Whatever. Militant feminists don't scare me." Nate laughs, obviously finding himself hilarious, and reaches his hand toward mine for a high five.

My fist curls, because with the mood I'm in, I'm half tempted to punch him. But I can't. Not here, not now, maybe not ever, so instead I just shrug him off, muttering, "You're lame sometimes."

I'm grateful for the interruption when, a few rows back, Pat

Bechtel stands up, holding his phone up. "Yo, the results just showed up. Overbrook lost again today!"

A round of cheers makes it way up the bus as the news spreads.

"They're falling apart," Brendan says. "Might as well call us district champions now."

"It's a little premature for that," someone behind us comments.

Brendan turns and looks back at Pat. "How many more games do we need to clinch it?"

Pat scrolls through his phone. "Four or five, depending. Four if they get another loss. Five if they don't. I think."

"I didn't think we still needed so many," Nathan says. He points at me. "Dude, you definitely better be back at it this week."

"You have to start thinking about all the awards coming up, too," Brendan says, nodding. "All-county honors, that shiny Cy Young trophy." He laughs. "I know you'd be out on the mound in fucking traction before you'd let that slip away to League of Her Own up there."

Nathan sputters. "Marshall's not getting that trophy. Are you even serious right now? No way."

"It's definitely possible." Brendan looks toward me, and his face is serious. Brendan's always been a stats guy, even in elementary school, when he could rattle off years and years of major-league stats. "If you look at the numbers . . . sister's holding her own." He shrugs. "Not saying they'll give it to her, but they have to consider her a contender."

Brendan quickly glances at me. "Sorry, man. Just sayin'."

But I just shake my head silently, sliding over in the seat, leaning against the side of the bus and staring out the window.

Brendan doesn't need to throw the numbers in my face. I know she's holding her own, that she's keeping pace with me. I can feel it. That maybe this year, the trophy isn't just mine for the taking.

I joked with her about it that one day in the lobby . . . before anything happened . . . but the truth is, regardless of what I think about Eve these days, that trophy is still no laughing matter.

I *need* it.

I need it on so many levels, and I can't even really handle thinking about it not going home with me the night of the spring sports award banquet.

Through the small gaps between the pleather seats and the windows, I can just make out one of her braids. Just minutes ago, I was dying to sit next to her. Now, lingering resentment flares, souring my mood, turning everything on its head.

I mean, I like Eve. I do. In this separate world where we're not teammates yet not competitors, where people aren't always talking about her, making rude comments about her, or talking about . . . us.

In the real world, I prefer easy. Easy relationships, for lack of a better word, with girls I get. They know their place and I know mine. I know what to do, and everyone leaves me alone.

And in that minute, despite the smile on my face when I walked onto the bus at the mere thought of *talking* to her, I sort of wish she wasn't on this bus.

Chapter 21

April 20

Eve

In the girls' locker room after our home game against Spring Falls, I stare into the mirror before changing, feeling immensely dissatisfied. In the grand scheme of things, I know I should be happy about the outcome—we beat them, getting one step closer to districts and putting them one step further away.

But . . .

The image of my defaced car pops into my mind. I'd wanted to be the one who, personally, put them in their places. I wanted to stare each and every one of them down from the mound, not knowing who was personally responsible, but assuming they were all suspects. And take them out—one by one, strike by strike, which would be the most gratifying form of payback.

I didn't get the chance, though. Pat started the game, and Coach put Jamie in in the fourth. And Jamie was on fire today. It may have been his best game ever. There was an evident determination about him today that came through in every single pitch delivered. Spring Falls is too strong of a competitor to mess around with, and there was no way in hell Coach was going to mess with Jamie's mojo today. He got to finish the game. I didn't throw a single pitch.

So, fifteen minutes after the game wraps, I'm still utterly frustrated. Obviously there's no way I was going to go to Coach or anyone and plead my case with such a mortifying reason behind it, but I hated the fact that today of all days I was out of the game when I wanted so badly to look some of those jerks in the eye and deliver a performance to make up for the last time around.

I hear my phone vibrate in my Windbreaker pocket and unzip it to retrieve it. There's a text message waiting for me from an unnamed number. But I recognize those last four digits.

A ripple of irritation goes through me. He got something I wanted today, and it sort of makes me not feel like being very nice to him.

Then I find myself remembering what happened after discovering my defaced car. Way before we were anything close to friendly, he'd acted like he was on my side. He'd surprised me that night, not only that he bothered to help, but the way he helped, without saying much, without making a big deal about it.

I shake my head. It's not like his stealing the show today was intentional; he didn't know I wanted revenge, on my terms, from the mound. I look at the number a second time. It's flashed across my screen numerous times by now—he's texted me in the evenings sometimes, with a random comment or observation from practice that makes me laugh, and even a few times during the day, when he's obviously been less focused in his classes than I've been in mine.

Yet I haven't added him to my contacts, officially. He hasn't earned that yet. We've only very recently started kissing, and the other stuff—the other girls always hanging around him, the battles over the mound—none of it's really changed.

Sighing, I swipe my phone. *Where are you?* appears on the screen.

You know where I am. I'm right through the wall. Why are you even texting me?

Because I gave up on waiting for you. You were taking forever. #sorrynotsorry Abrams

Anyways. What are you doing later?

This time, I pause before responding. Then I find myself admitting a little bit of the truth. *I'm pissed I didn't get a chance out there today. So I'm sulking.*

No, you're not.

Yes. I am.

Here's the thing—in case you missed it, I had an awesome game today. In a celebratory mood.

And just like that, I'm fighting the temptation to strangle him again.

I hate you.

Hold on a second, Marshall. I have an idea to cheer you up.

I don't respond, waiting. And a minute later my phone lights again. *You allowed out on a school night?*

Rolling my eyes, I answer him. *I'm not a nun. Don't live in a convent.*

Pick you up at 7.

I inhale a deep breath. I don't say yes. I don't say no. And I have a feeling it doesn't really matter anyway. Suddenly a mess of nerves, I throw my things into my bag, grab my backpack from my locker, and rush out of there to get home in time to prepare myself for the inevitable reality of Jamie coming to pick me up and the also inevitable reality of having to explain this set of circumstances to my parents.

....

At six thirty, I stand in front of my closet, arms crossed over my bath towel, staring inside. I'm glowering at its contents, because it's like there's this little angel version of Marcella sitting on my shoulder, coaching me in what she hopes is a calm, nonconfrontational manner. "This is basically your first date, Eve," she coos. "A little effort, if you will?"

I swat at the air above my shoulder.

It's not a date. Jamie doesn't take girls on "dates."

She's silenced, but still I can't move, suddenly picturing the bevy of girls who show up at every home game, the way they whisper behind their hands when Jamie walks by, the way they fight to be the first to approach him, fawn over him and his performance. I see what they look like. I see how they dress. Halfheartedly, I push hangers aside, searching for something that works.

Then . . .

No.

I find some jeans, my red-and-navy Nikes, and a baseball-style Phillies tee.

As I tie my shoes, I'm keenly aware that I'm breaking some kind of girl law.

I like you better like this.

He'd said it, right? And that had to count for something. I kind of want to believe it, anyway. Since I like me like this, too.

And . . . thing is . . . when I get downstairs, and I'm standing in front of my father, who's just smiled and asked, "Where are you headed tonight?" I'm really glad I'm not wearing some ridiculously tight top or heeled shoes. It would make spitting out the answer a million times harder.

I inhale sharply. "I'm hanging out with Jamie Abrams," I confess in a single whoosh of air.

Standing beside him, my mom sips her iced tea, digesting my answer slowly. She looks at me over the glass. "Still nothing?" she inquires casually.

I sweep my hand over my body, my eyes going wide like it's obvious. "Do I look like I'm dressed up or something? No. I'm in jeans and sneakers. Exactly what I'd wear to hang out with anyone else. We're just . . . reviewing the game."

My mom steps forward. She kisses my cheek. "Sure you are," she whispers in my ear.

"We *are*," I protest. I pull away from her, grabbing my Windbreaker from the back of the couch. "And I'm going to wait outside."

"Have fun," she calls after me.

I shake my head as I leave. As if any of this is *fun*.

It certainly doesn't feel fun, not when his Jeep appears around the corner and I'm forced to actually approach it, acknowledging that I'm climbing inside and actually going somewhere with him, somewhere he has yet to mention, actually. It was okay when he was at my house, on my turf . . . his turf is infinitely more unnerving.

When I open the door to the Jeep, my senses go into

overload. "Hey, Marshall," he greets me easily, snap-snap-snapping that gum. I swallow hard, trying to stay cool as I climb inside. It smells like him, times twenty, and he looks more attractive than ever in the dim light above the rearview. Rap music is blasting, and I shake my head as I try to steady my hands enough to fasten my seat belt.

"You think you're such a badass," I say.

He just winks at me, which does nothing to help. "Pretty much." He smirks.

A roll of my eyes, and we're off.

The funny thing is . . . as he drives me across town to parts unknown, we actually *do* review the game. We talk easily and naturally now, about the remainder of the season, other players on the team, and how we think it will all pan out across the district over the course of the games remaining.

And just when I'm about to ask him where we're headed, because it seems like we've been driving for about twenty minutes, he swings the Jeep into a large, mostly vacant parking lot. About half the overhead lights aren't working, overgrown grass grows between cracks in the pavement, and a general sense of despair hangs over the whole place. A place where I spent many evenings with my parents and brothers over the years.

I turn toward Jamie. "Mitch's? Seriously?"

Mitch's Turf Farm and Putt-Putt Course is far past its prime. There's a brand-new family fun center closer to home, and it's where everyone goes these days. It's got a huge arcade, a frozen yogurt shop, and four different mini-golf courses to choose from. Half the obstacles on Mitch's fairy-tale course don't even spin anymore, like Humpty Dumpty and the Old Lady Who Lived in the Shoe have personally given up on even trying to compete. I can't remember the last time someone's thought about going to Mitch's.

Jamie shrugs. "I figure . . . Mitch's is, what? A year, if that, from being torn down." He stares through the darkness, toward the mini-golf course. "Some good memories here, and I'm gonna miss this place." Then he looks at me and grins. "Plus. I know how to get a few of the batting cages to run without tokens."

I smile, too, and follow suit when he hops out of the car.

We pass a few families playing mini golf, but on a weeknight especially, the place is deserted as we make our way down the path toward the old batting cages. No one even bothers to man the shed anymore, where they store the scarred bats and dusty batting helmets. I'm overcome with a sense of nostalgia as I select a bat and helmet. Jamie's right—there are a lot of good memories here, and I'm surprised it's something he appreciates. After I've found a metal bat I like, I turn around and make my way back toward the cages, behind Jamie, who leads me toward the stalls that are apparently rigged so you can hit for free.

"We're keeping score," he tells me as he steps inside the cage and closes the door behind him. He pounds three times on the side of the control box, and a red light starts flashing from the other end of the cage. Jamie takes his place behind the plate, eyes focused on the red light, adjusting his stance. "Three rounds again. Loser buys ice cream."

On my turns, I try to keep my head in the game, but it's infinitely harder to do so when it's just the two of us alone together in the dark night. Every time I even glance around, his face is right there, practically pressed against the wire, his voice soft and joking as he hassles me when I swing and miss. I can keep myself together in front of two teams and a crowd in the stands, but here at Mitch's, I'm distracted and self-conscious.

Tonight's victory goes to Jamie.

We return the supplies to the shed and head back toward the building that used to house a full restaurant and golf shop. Now they serve ice cream only, and the remainder of the golf supplies have been marked down 50 percent.

There is a whopping four-flavor selection left—vanilla, chocolate, strawberry, and rocky road. Jamie orders strawberry, I order a double scoop of rocky road, and, a gracious loser, I immediately pull money from my wallet to pay for the ice cream.

"Let's eat outside." Jamie gestures toward the back door with his head, and I follow him out to the old wooden bench on the side of the shop that overlooks the old chip-and-putt course. There's not a person in sight, and I can't help but consider another possible reason for choosing Mitch's—that no one would see us together here.

I catch Jamie watching me as I take a huge bite out of my huge cone, face amused, laughter in his eyes. "What?" I ask, mouth full.

He just shakes his head and bites his lip. "Nothin'."

We eat in silence, listening to the sounds of the cars passing by on the highway in front of the shop, the calls of birds in the tall pines that surround Mitch's. I consider how nervous I felt waiting for seven o'clock to arrive, but that feeling's melting with every minute that passes, like my rocky road over the side of my cone. My back relaxes against the bench, and I breathe in the crisp night air. "Man." Jamie stuffs the bottom of his cone into his mouth, wipes his lips with a napkin, and then balls it up in his palm. He leans against the back of the bench, a soft sigh escaping through his nose. "Kinda impossible to be here and not feel like a kid again. Guess that's why I'm gonna be sad to see it go." He turns, glances at me quickly, and then looks forward again. "Just something that sucks about seeing part of your childhood actually being torn down."

I stare at his profile. Any trace of a smile is gone, and Jamie actually looks really sad.

I sit there, contemplating, for a few minutes. Right now he seems approachable, but I'm not entirely convinced he won't snap shut like a clamshell if I go somewhere he doesn't want to go. But sitting here . . . next to this person I'm so curious about . . . I want to know his story. And I feel brave enough to ask, even though it might not go well.

Staring at the ground, I clear my throat. "Some of the things you've said," I start out tentatively, "make it sound like you've sort of had a hard time."

I sense him tensing beside me, but he doesn't clam up. His right shoulder lifts tiredly before falling down again. "Yeah, things weren't that great growing up," he tells me. His elbows go to his knees and he leans forward, making it impossible for me to see his face as he continues on. "Never knew my biological dad. Apparently he'd been in the military and was pretty messed up from some of the stuff he was involved in. My parents got together when my mom was still in high school, but he bailed on her as soon as he heard she was pregnant; he didn't want the responsibility of taking care of a kid. Didn't feel equipped. At least *he* was honest about it."

There's bitterness in his final words, and he pauses for a while before continuing.

"Olivia's dad, my stepfather, he came next. To say he was a

raging asshole is putting it mildly. My mom stuck around for years, and he was a fucking master at convincing everyone around him it would eventually be different." Jamie exhales a *psssh* through his mouth. "I wanted a dad so badly I always let myself believe him, too. He's the one who got me into playing ball. I think that's the only good thing I can say about the man."

There's not a trace of emotion on Jamie's face when he reveals the next part. "He was killed crossing the street four years ago."

"I'm sorry," I say automatically.

"I don't know if I am," he responds flatly. "Since then," he continues, "it's been loser after loser." Jamie shakes his head. "I don't *get* my mom. She's a smart woman, but she can't let go of this bullshit idea that she can save one of them, that she's supposed to. It's always been the focus of her life, always more important than the idea of a career, yet she's failed more times than I can count.

"The last really bad one was Doug. He had all this baggage— they always do—and she thought she was actually helping him, that kicking him out would be worse. *Helping* him, yeah. The police were at our house on pretty much a weekly basis. But when he started lashing out on Olivia, blowing up on her and saying these awful things, my mom finally, *finally* came to her senses. Got rid of him for good.

"So here we are. Before this year, my mom never gave any thought to being on her own financially. She's trying, but it's a struggle, and that's not gonna change. And when you hear all this, yeah, you can probably understand why the few really good memories of things like Mitch's . . . it sucks to see every last one of them go."

I swallow hard. I'd gotten the sense that Jamie's life was far from easy, but this . . . "I wouldn't really have guessed." I shake my head. "Seeing you at school, with your friends . . . it always seems like you don't have a care in the world."

He sits up then, regarding my face for a second before leaning against the back of the bench and laying his arm along the top of it, squeezing my shoulder gently. "I try not to feel bad for myself, because the fact of the matter is . . . sadly . . . my story's just not that interesting. Same story as thousands and thousands of kids out there, right? Families break up, money's tight. Sadly, nothing unusual about that."

It takes me a long time to figure out what I want to say. "Even if it's common, that doesn't make it easy," I say quietly, struggling to find my voice after he's shared so much with me. "Doesn't make it any more trivial."

That's all I tell him. I don't offer any more "I'm sorrys"; I don't suggest any other perspectives. But when I look down at the bench a couple of minutes later, I realize the fingers of his right hand and those of my left have somehow ended up wound together.

We sit there—I don't know for how long—lost in our own thoughts, staring up at the starry sky. Then, from the corner of my eye, I see a small smile dawn on Jamie's face, and he chuckles.

"Wait. I told you I was gonna cheer you up tonight."

"It's okay; you don't—"

"No, I mean . . ." Jamie drops my hand, turning toward me with renewed energy. "It's not entirely coincidental that we came to Mitch's tonight, that we killed enough time for it to get dark out."

I stare at him, clueless, heart pounding anyway, because I

have no idea what he's going to propose, sensing it's something dangerous.

"We're in Spring Falls territory," he reminds me. "And it's time to pay those fuckers back."

"Jam—"

"You didn't get your chance today?" He shrugs. "You've got your chance tonight."

"No. That's crazy." I shake my head. "I'm not going to do something like that. I mean . . ."

"What?"

"I mean . . . I don't even know who did it. What are we going to? Target the whole team?"

"I know who did it."

My spine stiffens. "What do you mean?"

"I saw who was at the Burger Barn that night, who left just before you did."

I stare at him. The temptation is burgeoning in my body. I feel it growing, prompting me to ask the question. "Who?"

He fires off the names. "Jeff Johanssen. Robbie Crowl. Ryan Carey. And for the record, you can find all their addresses online."

"You actually looked them up?"

"Might have."

"And what exactly did you have in mind?"

"That much I hadn't decided." Jamie looks at me, eyes narrowed. "I was thinking either Post-it notes covering their cars or plastic wrap. Post-it notes are funnier and more annoying to take off, but on the flip side, it's a more time-consuming tactic. Not sure we could get the job done."

Abruptly, a grin splits my face. He hasn't proposed anything terribly illegal or dangerous. And without another season game against Spring Falls on our schedule, my opportunities to exact revenge are dwindling.

So, without thinking, I hear myself debating the methods of attack. "Plastic wrap isn't that quick and easy, either," I point out. "I mean, how many rolls would we need to buy to cover three cars?"

Jamie pulls his phone from his back pocket. "I have an ace in the hole," he tells me, already firing off a text message. "My cousin works in the back at Home Depot. Have you ever seen an industrial-size roll of plastic wrap before?"

I laugh out loud, the noise sounding unnaturally loud in the quiet night.

Jamie looks at me again, eyebrow raised. "Does that mean you're in?" he asks, voice hopeful. He extends his fist.

I allow my fist to touch it. "I'm in. God, you're a terrible influence."

Jamie stands, smirking down at me. "Not the first time I've heard that."

After a quick pull-up to the rear of Home Depot, as Jamie drives across town toward Jake's house first, guided by the helpful voice coming from the map app on his phone, at least I retain the good sense to text my mother and check in.

I'm hoping to be home in about an hour and a half. I'm fine.

She responds almost at once.

We're going to have to discuss a curfew. For weeknights. If more "baseball discussions" are to follow.

She's joking, sort of, I think . . . but I'm really not sure. I sigh. But it's too late to turn back now, not with the hugest roll of plastic wrap I've ever seen protruding from the back of the Jeep. For better or worse, Jamie and I are in this one together.

....

It's significantly longer than an hour and a half before we're back within Farmington town limits. I anticipate a very pointed talk with both parents come morning, if not tonight, about this curfew business, and more than a few questions about the nature of my involvement with Jamie Abrams.

But as we approach my block, I'm too damn gleeful to care, riding high on the adrenaline rush that accompanied disabling Jeff's pretty Audi, Ronnie's pickup, and Ryan's Honda. Every time I picture those dumbasses walking out their front doors tomorrow morning, I start giggling all over again and can't stop. And in turn, Jamie starts laughing, too.

It's 10:40 when Jamie slows the Jeep and pulls up to the curb.

I sit up to correct him at once. "This isn't my house." I point to the next block. "It's actually . . . that one."

Jamie unfastens his seat belt. He scoots closer to me, smirking, eyes sparkling. "Yeah. I know that."

I feel my cheeks flaming to life. *Duh.* I mean, can I give away my lack of experience any more? Internally, I cringe, wishing I could stuff the words back in my mouth. I'm parked in Mr. Smooth Moves's Jeep, acting like a naive five-year-old.

But Jamie comes all the way close anyway. His hand finds my neck, snakes around and under my ponytail, lifting it gently. "So tonight was fun," he whispers into my ear.

It's hard to breathe, just like that, just with his warm breath in my ear, his hand touching my hair.

And I don't know how many girls have been in this exact position in the front seat of his Jeep, but in that moment, I understand why every single one of them was powerless to leave.

I make the mistake of looking into his eyes—they're sleepy and seductive, but also . . . they look warm and happy, and he's got the smallest little smile on his face. God, it makes me want to kiss him, and so I do, obliterating any further thought of the ghosts of Jeep girls past. Obliterating the telltale time on the digital clock, obliterating any good sense I may have had.

I really liked kissing Jamie outside of school and I really liked kissing Jamie in my driveway, but inside his car, warm and heady with the scent of him, kissing Jamie feels like the focal point of the universe, and it's all I care about.

It's how I end up letting him recline the seats, how I end up splayed against him, letting him kiss my neck, nibble on my earlobe, his hands eternally lost in my hair before demanding he kiss me again. His free hand ghosts around, coming to rest near my back pocket, guiding me closer when I start to slip away.

I can tell there's perspiration breaking out at my hairline; I sense the moisture in the car before I even notice the foggy windows. I realize Jamie's hand has found the bare expanse of skin beneath my shirt, above my jeans, and I realize how intoxicating the feeling is—skin on skin—and that I'd let him, that . . . I want him . . . to keep touching me.

I push myself up in a flash, nearly banging my head on the roof of the car.

Suddenly I'm back at the restaurant with Marcella, her confessing how it "just happened," that she hadn't really known she'd lost control of her decision making until she had.

Not that I have any intention of *that* happening, but still . . . all of it suddenly feels like a very slippery slope.

I push my mussed hair out of my face. "I better go."

"Okay," Jamie answers, voice even, pushing the button to bring his seat forward again so he can look at me. "You all right?"

I struggle to look at him. "Yeah. I just . . ." I wave my hand toward the clock. "I'm pushing my limits on the time here, and I actually care about school, so . . ."

Jamie stares at me, looking confused, almost hurt. "You didn't really need to say that. You could just say it's time to go."

I should've just kept kissing him. At least when my mouth is busy with his, I'm not saying something mean.

"Sorry. You're right. And I . . . better go."

My hand reaches for the handle. I pause, look back at him. "Hey. Thanks. Tonight *was* fun. I'm glad you texted me." I throw him a small smile. "Cheered me up."

Jamie smiles right back at me. "You're welcome." He leans back across the seat, one last time, and plants a quick, sweet kiss on my lips.

"Good night," I whisper, finally making myself climb out of the Jeep to face whatever awaits.

As I cross Marcella's front yard, through the grass, I feel disoriented. It's too late for me to be outside, and my street doesn't feel like home tonight. I feel lost, walking through the damp grass at eleven o'clock on a Thursday, lips swollen and shirt askew, feeling like a different person walking toward the door than when I walked through it to leave.

My head is sort of spinning. A few days ago, when I pulled out the win when Jamie was hurt, he'd barely even looked at me.

Today's victory was his, and I got ice cream, kisses, and the chance to put those douchebags in their place.

I glance back over my shoulder, watching the taillights of the Jeep grow smaller and smaller as he drives away. Everything about our relationship so far has been affected by our status within the team. We might be "one team" these days, but Jamie and I are definitely still competitors.

And until I figure out what's more important to him—life on the field or off—I can't bring myself to program his number into my phone, kiss him with abandon, or think about what . . . this . . . is.

Walking into my room a few minutes later, I stare at the empty space reserved for the Cy Young trophy, experiencing a sick sensation in my stomach as I touch the shelf.

How easily he's gotten into my head, shifted my focus from my game and my list of obligations, persuading me to run around town an hour after I would've been asleep. It feels like fun in the moment, but ultimately . . . he's not the only one who has to figure out what's most important.

Chapter 22

April 22

Jamie

I end up staying really late at the Barn on Friday night, reason enough to sleep in on Saturday morning. It's ten thirty before I'm out of bed, and when I lift the shade over my window, the sun is bright in the sky and I don't see any clouds on the horizon.

A wide grin breaks out on my face. I told everyone you can't trust the forecast, that the weather gods would have our backs today. No way they'd ruin this, one of the greatest parts of Pirate baseball. It's turned out to be an unseasonably warm, perfectly sunny day. As it is every year.

The lacrosse team has their spaghetti dinner fund-raiser. We have the Turn the Hoses car wash.

For years, the high school baseball team has flipped the idea of the bikini car wash on its head to raise money for new uniforms or equipment replacements. It's the guys who show up in bathing suits and board shorts in the school parking lot. After we wash the cars, the drivers have the opportunity to draw all over the Pirate of their choice with gold and black body paint, then hose him off.

The girls at school, girls at several schools, actually, eat it up, and the event is pretty much made for me. "Nothing you love more than preening for a cause," Naomi had said last year, right before smiling sweetly and dousing me with a blast of the hose. I got plenty of attention last year, most of it positive, although I have to admit that a few girls who showed up and paid for a chance to paint me were there with revenge in mind.

This year, with a whole new crop of girls at school, is definitely going to be even better than last, and noon can't come fast enough. I eat, shower quickly, and pull on a pair of red board shorts, flip-flops, and an old sleeveless gray T-shirt for the drive.

Olivia asks me to drop her off at a friend's, so by the time I get to the school, most of the guys are there already, having parked their cars and trucks on the far side of the parking lot so there's plenty of room for customers to pull in and make their way down the first row. Brendan and Nate are divvying up supplies—posters to be held up along the street, the buckets and sponges and bottles of soap, containers of body paint and brushes for its application. I start grinning again just looking at it all.

At ten of twelve, Nathan pulls the group together and goes over the plan. There are a few guys from South who still look unsure about this, but for the most part, I can tell the guys are getting into the spirit of things.

Brendan glances at his watch. "I think we're good to go." He smiles. "Ladies will be showing up in droves any minute now. Who's not here yet?"

We all look around. It's obvious, but Matty says it anyway. "Scott and Eve."

"Is Eve coming today?" someone asks.

"This is a team event," Brendan answers. "She should be."

"Sweet." One of the sophomores guffaws. "I'd kinda like to see her soaped up and topless. For a good cause, of course."

The words are out of my mouth in an instant. "Shut your mouth, asshole." I glare at him, watching him visibly shrink back into the crowd. "She'd beat your ass if she heard you say that, and you know it."

Nate shrugs. "Not like we weren't all thinking it. Defensive much?"

Wishing I could've kept my damn mouth shut, I struggle to respond. Luckily, it's at that second that we all watch Scott's car pull into the lot. The crowd goes silent, and I can't help but feel somewhat bad for her. It's easy enough to imagine how she must be feeling inside the car, even though I have no clue how she's planning to play this. Shit, Lord knows she surprised me with that little stunt during our initiation ritual.

Scott pulls up to the group to let Eve out before going to park his car. She gets out, and I swear, I see a few mouths actually fall open.

At least it's not just me.

Dear God.

I decide in that instant, if a girl could ever step directly out of my fantasies, *this* is what she would look like.

She's got the braids in. They're sticking out from under her Pirates cap, which today looks incredibly sexy given the rest of her outfit. There's not much to it. Black sports bra, cropped shiny gold yoga pants. Bare feet.

Eve looks like she's shown up to kick Jillian Michaels's ass or take on the American Ninja Warrior course or something. Like a total badass.

Although . . . it might just be the angry set to her face as she stands before us and plants her feet firmly on the concrete.

She rolls her eyes. "Whatever smart-ass comments you've been saving up, don't even bother."

My teammates are at least smart enough to keep their damn mouths shut.

She glares specifically at Nathan. "Especially you, jerk-off."

I bite my lip and slide my sunglasses on to hide my expression.

"I mean, I have to say . . . you boys over here at East sure do love getting naked together." She shrugs. "But whatever. I'm here, and a sports bra is as good as it's gonna get. No string bikini, no bathing suit bottoms. Dream on."

She glances over her shoulder, and we follow her gaze. The first cars are starting to pull into the lot, overeager girls honking loudly, rolling down their windows and sending catcalls in our direction.

"And no one's coming near my skin with body paint," Eve finishes. She extends her hand in Brendan's direction. "Now hand me a damn sponge and let's get this over with."

Most of my teammates follow her instructions, quickly turning their attention to the group of girls excited to get the party started. But me, I'm left staring at her, wishing she'd look my way so I could smile at her.

Wishing for a lot of things, actually.

The way she just got out of the car and stared us all down . . . looking like *that* . . . There's this weird part of me that's whispering, *She's mine* in my head, smiling about that fact. It makes me want to acknowledge it outright, approach her, put my arm around her, but . . . I shake my head . . . we're not doing that.

Frustration grips me. I don't know what we're doing.

I push away the confusing thoughts and feelings and join my teammates, doing what I do best.

And what I do best . . . I do really, really well.

There's this unspoken competition among the guys about who can score the most requests for body paint. So I'm quick to approach every car, those I recognize and those I don't, leaning over their door frames, offering quick smiles and winks, telling them, "Glad you showed up today, sweetheart. I was hoping you would."

When Eve is within earshot, sponging off rear windows or bumpers, her eyes almost roll out the top of her head.

By one thirty, I've had my chest painted with hearts, phone numbers, and various girls' names about ten times and been hosed off just as many times. Eve's still playing it cool, but I know girls just a little bit, and if it's not getting under her skin at all, well, the girl really is made of steel.

I grin as I jog over to her, knowing I'm going to piss her off, anticipating her reaction. "Don't be jealous," I whisper as I pass. "Does it make you feel better knowing you're the girl I'd actually like to leave here with?"

Her face shows absolutely no sign of reaction, but when I run off, a sharp blast of cold water hits me directly between my shoulder blades, making me jump and twist in the air. I'm still smiling, though.

I knew I could count on her.

Then at 2:20, when we're getting ready to close up shop—and to be honest, I'm feeling kind of waterlogged—one last familiar car pulls into the lot. I tense up when I recognize Naomi's ride. She's been an ice queen since I dissed her the night of the spaghetti dinner, and these days, I never know what I'm going to get from her. Whether she's going to ignore me entirely or give me shit in one form or another.

I quickly glance toward Eve from the corner of my eye. Today, I'm hoping Naomi decides to ignore me.

After Naomi parks her car and steps out, I catch her gaze flick in Eve's direction, too. I brace myself, because Eve has caught Naomi's attention before, and today, looking like that, she's sure to catch it again. Naomi used to just dismiss her, but more and more, it seems like it's been harder for her to do that.

But I guess the opportunity to have the undivided attention of the entire team is more appealing than hassling Eve, and instead of focusing on the single girl on the scene, she moves on to all the guys.

"Knew it paid to wait," she says, sauntering toward the team. "Now I can have my pick of any Pirate I want." The smile slides off her face and she nearly snarls at me as she walks by. "That's not going to be you, by the way."

I'm not sure why she's acting so hurt about what happened that night. From what I heard, she just went and found Brendan, went home with him instead. We've never been exclusive; she's never pushed the issue.

I turn my back and ignore her as she makes a big show of deciding who she wants to paint, relishing being the final customer of the day, that no one else is around to steal her thunder. I shake my head. Naomi was always cool because she wasn't overbearing, but when she starts acting like this, I have absolutely no time for her.

It's after she's hosed off Brendan that I catch her looking in my direction, lips pressed together in frustration that I'm not watching her little show, that I'm not giving any reaction to it. She cracks, and tugs on the waistband of my shorts to pull me aside before she leaves. "Hey, can I talk to you for a sec?"

I try to sneak a discreet look in Eve's direction. She's walking toward the school, helping Scott and Pat take some stuff back inside, and her back is toward us.

"Okay."

Her expression softens. "For the record, I'm still pissed about the way you disappeared and didn't answer my texts that night. But." She lifts her face and finally smiles at me. "Prom's next month, and I still want to go with *you*."

It takes a second for me to process it, that we've reached that point where prom is only a few weeks away, where girls are starting to make sure they have dates. *Shit.*

Before, it was just the money thing, but now . . .

Naomi touches my forearm. "I'm going to assume that feeling is still mutual, that you know if you're going to go and actually have a good time, I'm your girl."

I still can't seem to speak. Before, a comeback, a slightly lewd confirmation would've been waiting on the tip of my tongue, but today I have nothing.

"So you might want to think about apologizing for how you've been acting. Other guys are already starting to ask. I'm only going to wait on you for so long."

Naomi wags the tip of her tongue at me before turning to go.

Anger rises up within me like bile.

I shouldn't feel so angry, I remind myself. She's just playing the only game we've ever played, and it's not her who's acting differently. It's just today I don't feel like playing—I don't feel like playing at all—and I have no idea how to forfeit.

All I can do is be thankful that she's back inside her car and on her way before Eve emerges from the building. I feel a strange combination of relief and panic when she appears, and when I have the opportunity to talk to her without everyone staring, I do so, eager to get back to the *good*, to shove all the other shit out of the way, even if I know it's not really going anywhere.

"Pssst," I call when she walks by.

She trains her death stare on me. "I'm not a cat."

I roll my eyes, take my hat off, place it across my chest, and give a half bow. "Excuse me, Miss Marshall. Would you perhaps be able to spend a few moments in my company after this wraps?"

This makes her smile, but still she shakes her head. "I can't. I rode with Scott."

I pause for a moment. Then, "So tell him you're staying."

My challenge, the inherent meaning behind it, hangs in the air between us. We're locked in a staring contest, an unspoken question awaiting an answer: *Are we really going to do this? Here? Now?*

Eve ducks her head and nods, bowing out first. "Yeah. Okay."

I feel immensely victorious, happier about her answer than I should.

But I'm close enough when she offers up an explanation to Scott, when she grabs her sneakers from the floor of his car, tying them on and telling him she wants to go running at the park the next block over.

I don't call her on it, and she doesn't call me on it when Nate asks what I'm doing and I answer, "Nothin'. Just working later."

Neither of us says a thing about how we wait them out at opposite ends of the property until everyone's left, until it's a completely empty parking lot we walk across to meet in the middle.

I just look her in the eye, pretending there's nothing weird about any of this. "Want to walk to Wawa and pick up some lunch?"

"Sure." I swear she glances over her shoulder a final time to make sure everyone's gone. "I could eat some lunch."

Eve leaves a foot of space between us as we walk. We barely look at each other on the way, talking about everything except the fact that we're walking together, apparently.

We both order meatball subs and share a bag of chips at the dilapidated picnic table behind the store. I silently admire the way she puts food away, that she doesn't seem to think twice about eating in front of me, two scoops of ice cream, an entire sub, or more than her share of a bag of chips. And just like that I'm softening toward her again, hoping I'll say something to produce one of those genuine smiles, eager for the next barb she comes up with to launch at me. When no one's watching.

And by the time we're walking back to the school, the temptation to grab her hand and hold it as we go is so strong, I have to bring my hands together, crack my knuckles a few times to keep from going for it. I'm guessing she's not a hand holder. I mean, neither am I, but . . .

I pull a pack of gum from my back pocket, offer her a stick, then glance at the sky as we go. Clouds have appeared from nowhere, so I guess maybe the weather gods only gave us a brief reprieve for our event. The meteorologists may have been right after all.

"So whatcha up to later?" I ask her as we walk.

"Marcella's big state pageant's tonight," she says. "I promised her about five years ago if it ever came about, I'd go. Luckily, it's on this side of the state this year, downtown Philly. I'm going to take the train down with Brian to watch."

"Sounds like a blast."

"Oh, trust me, I am counting the minutes," she says sarcastically. "Can't think of anything I'd rather do."

"Is Marcella actually going to win, you think?"

Eve shrugs. "I can't imagine a girl being more motivated, dedicated, or authentic about wanting it, I know that much. So if that counts as much as how you look in a ball gown, then yeah, I'm pretty confident she has a shot."

She lifts her face to the sky. The sun is still shining behind the clouds, but a few drops have started falling, creating a sudden sun shower. It's still warm, and the drops don't really bother us as we head back to school.

"You have to text me your commentary, all right?" I say. "I picked up an extra shift tonight, and I'm sure your comments will be entertaining."

She glances at me and sneaks a smile. "I have no idea what you're talking about. I will be fully embracing my feminine side."

This actually makes me snort.

Eve sticks her hand out before her, bigger, faster raindrops falling on it. "Is it just me or is this pleasant little shower about to turn into a downpour?"

I feel some heavy drops pelt my shoulders, watch a few more turn my T-shirt dark gray. "Uh, yeah . . . you might be right."

We cross the final block leading back to school, but we still have all the sports fields to cross before my Jeep comes into view. So when the sun disappears from view entirely and the raindrops turn almost violent, without speaking the two of us dash into the nearest dugout before we get drenched.

Inside, Eve swipes at her shoulder, wiping away the raindrops. "What the hell was that?" She laughs. "That came out of nowhere."

"Yeah." I stare out over the infield, the force of the rain now stirring up a dust storm as it pelts the field. "Guess we could've made it to the cars, but I don't feel like getting drenched."

I collapse onto the low bench, and a few seconds later, Eve joins me.

More than a few times over the course of my baseball career, I've huddled in a dugout during a sudden shower, waiting it out with my teammates beside me, either praying a game wouldn't get called, or that it would, depending on the score at the time. It's not a bad place to hole up, with the sound of the rain hitting the roof overhead, the fresh smell of grass and dirt and *baseball* reaching you inside.

I look at Eve, and there's this really unfamiliar *peaceful* expression on her face. I can tell she's thinking the exact same thing as I am, and I stop resisting the temptation to hold her hand. I reach for it, finding it cold and damp. "Kind of nice in here, though, right?" I ask quietly.

She turns and looks at me, the expression on her face that one I sort of love, stripped of defensiveness, seemingly soft. She nods, just once, before glancing down at our hands. Nods again.

And just like that, we're kissing again.

Or, we're trying to. But our hats are in the way, and we're

both laughing as their bills push against each other, keeping our mouths from making contact. She pushes hers off, and I turn mine around so I can get to her, eagerly finding her mouth once there's nothing in the way.

At first her lips, her cheeks, her skin feel chilled against mine, still damp from the rain, but Eve warms quickly at my touch, her breath warming me in return in those few seconds we break apart to grab some air before finding each other again.

My hands ghost over her shoulders, fingers run down her back, finding more exposed skin, more chilled patches in need of warming. Guiding her back with my hands, I ease her down onto the bench, covering her body with mine, kissing my way down her neck and planting kisses on her shoulders.

Her hands make their way under my T-shirt, running up and down my back, and gradually her hands turn warm and transfer their heat to my skin.

God, this is hot.

Making out with a girl on the field, or at least in the dugout, has always been a fantasy. When I reach up to touch her hair, I'm suddenly aware of the knotted wood beneath her head. She isn't complaining or anything, but it doesn't seem comfortable. So I pull away from her, and in a quick second pull my T-shirt overhead, balling it up in one hand and sliding it beneath her head like a pillow.

It doesn't escape my notice the way her face flushes at the sight of my bare torso above her, the flash of something unfamiliar and eager in her eyes, and I lower myself over her again, meeting my lips to hers.

Desire grips me in that second.

I swear, I'd only been thinking of her comfort when I took my shirt off. But the result is the bare skin of my stomach rubbing against hers, affecting me viscerally, making me want more. Making me want to touch her more. Kissing is falling short of fulfilling how I'm feeling today.

It's lying here with her . . . it's remembering the sight of her getting out of the car, hot as shit and untouchable in her work-out clothes.

I can't lie—the whole thing is turning me on, and today, I want to do more than kiss her.

I get that it's Eve. I get that there are limits, but . . . I just want to touch more of her.

And the way she's kissing me in return, the way she's wound her hands around my neck, pulling me ever closer, I get the sense she wouldn't mind if I touched her a little more today, too.

One of my hands is under her back, keeping her close, steadying her on the bench. My free hand, it creeps up over the waistband of her pants, slowly making its way up across her stomach, then on to her rib cage.

She stops breathing when she becomes aware of its ascent up her body. I feel it, and my hand pauses.

Then she starts kissing me again, at first somewhat restrained, guarded, but within minutes, it's as hot as it ever was, her skin growing even warmer beneath me.

My hand starts moving again. It reaches the bottom of her sports bra. My fingers inch beneath it.

Eve sits up in a flash, her forehead nearly slamming against mine.

"Sorry. I'm sorry," she gasps.

She won't meet my eye, not as she stands up, adjusts her

clothes, twists pieces back into place. Her entire torso is flushed with color, but it still pales in comparison to her cheeks.

She gestures vaguely toward the field. "It's a little . . . a lot . . . public, so . . ."

Eve spins around in a circle, trying to find her hat. When she does, she slams it onto her head, pulling it low, hiding her face.

It takes me a second to get my bearings. I stand up, too, disappointed, hell yes, but mostly concerned.

"You okay?" I ask quietly.

"I'm fine." She turns toward me for a second, flashes a small, pained smile before turning around again.

"Sure?"

"Yeah." She nods emphatically, still struggling to meet my eye. "I mean . . . it wasn't . . . you didn't do anything wrong, just . . ." Then she gives this small embarrassed laugh, squeezes her eyes shut. "Nothing. Never mind. I'm sorry."

I'm not sure what she's apologizing for, not sure what's happened at all.

But clearly, Eve is ready to go, ducking her head outside, saying, "Looks like it's letting up," even though I'm not sure it really is.

"We should probably make a run for it now," she says. "I need to get ready for tonight."

I just nod, not sure what to say.

Eve looks like she's ready to take off and sprint across the field. But just before she goes, her stance relaxes, and she doubles back. "Ummm . . ." She leans toward me, kissing me on the lips, finding my hand for a second. "Text you later, okay?"

"Definitely," I reply weakly, watching her take off, feeling rooted in place.

I collapse back onto the bench, not so much in the name of cooling off, but in confusion. I feel like I missed something, misread her cues, even though it sure didn't feel like that at the time.

I let my head fall back against the concrete behind me, confusion turning to frustration, frustration turning to something like anger. I've always known how to read girls, how to read them and how to give them what they want from me.

But Eve is turning out to be just as complicated as I'd imagined she would be, clamming up out of nowhere, and bolting away more often than not. It's unnerving, how she can shift so quickly from feeling right there with me to somewhere else entirely, how just like that she goes back to needing to establish these boundaries, where it feels like I'm on one side and she's on the other.

I close my eyes and inhale deeply, the breath vibrating in my chest.

It's fucking impossible to tell whether we're on the same team if I don't even know what game she's playing.

Chapter 23

April 26

Eve

For the last four days, Marcella has been on top of the world. Pretty much since the second that crown was placed on her head, she hasn't stopped beaming. I bet she's even smiling while she sleeps.

It might not be quite as noticeable, but in truth I've been smiling right along with her. It doesn't matter that I don't really "get" the *nature* of her competition; I get competition. I understand commitment, and work ethic, and the thrill of being rewarded after days, weeks, months of hard work. So I'm proud of Marcella. I'm happy watching her experience this victory.

Her winning the Miss Pennsylvania Teen crown has been a big deal at school, especially with the East kids who hadn't yet learned about Marcella's pageant life. A huge picture of her, taken in the final moments of the pageant when confetti rained down, was on the front page of the *Farmington Reporter*. There was even a quick blurb on the local news. This week has been victory week, the crown seeming the focal point of Marcella's life these days.

So when she bursts into my room at ten forty-five on Wednesday night, eyes red, trails of makeup on her cheeks, still wearing the top she had on at school with a pair of pajama pants, all I can think is that something happened to that crown. I feel panicked at once, wondering if some missed factor made her ineligible, if she failed to meet some requirement that was uncovered after the fact, resulting in her losing the crown.

I scurry out of my bed when she appears in my room, pushing the door shut behind her. "What's wrong?"

Marcella hurls herself at me, collapsing against my chest, sobbing so hard it's actually soundless. So I don't hear her crying; I feel her crying, her body quaking so violently it's hard to stay upright.

"Marcella, you're making me worry," I say. "What's wrong?"

She pulls her head back, only long enough to gasp, "NO!"

I wait as she tries to take a few deep breaths and attempts to talk. But then her face just crumples anew, and she slides down the side of my bed, curling into a ball against it. Silent tears start running down her cheeks. "It hurts too much to say it," she finally admits. "I can't say it out loud."

I sit down next to her, wrapping my arms around my knees, and wait.

"Brian . . . ," she finally whispers, voice cracking as she says his name. "He ruined everything. He ruined it."

Her admission surprises me. Brian wasn't even on my radar. I reach for the box of tissues on my nightstand and hand it to her.

"Thanks," she says, taking one, balling it up in her fist, but neglecting to use it to wipe her tears.

After a few more minutes, Marcella finally turns her face to look at me. She looks ashamed, which makes absolutely no sense to me when she finally spits it out. "He kissed someone else."

"What?" I shake my head. It doesn't compute. Brian would never hurt Marcella. He adores her. *"Who?"*

And what idiot would ever mess with what Brian and Marcella have, anyway?

"He wouldn't tell me." She squeezes her hand into an even tighter fist. "Some girl from East; I don't even know her name."

Oh. *Right.* An idiot girl from East would mess with it. Because she doesn't really know Marcella that well; she doesn't know them. She wouldn't care.

"When?"

I can't seem to stop asking questions, like any of these details matter.

Marcella's lips start shaking. "Saturday," she says, hands going to her face as she crumples all over again.

I inhale sharply, understanding her hurt on a new level. While she was at the height of happiness, having just realized her dream, Brian was out doing *this*.

Which makes me feel really pissed off. I'd been with Brian on Saturday night, and I sort of feel betrayed by association. Sure, on the train he'd been sort of . . . distant. His enthusiasm about the pageant seemed halfhearted in comparison to past events. I'd just assumed maybe he was getting a little tired of all of it, maybe feeling miffed about how it had taken so much of her time and attention recently. And when we got off the train

together, Marcella having stayed at the venue for follow-up inter-
views and pictures, he hadn't said a *damn* thing about heading
somewhere other than home.

"It happened Saturday," she continues, taking a deep breath.
"But he only bothered to tell me tonight." She waves her hand
and rolls her watery eyes. "I guess he wasn't going to, but the guilt
got to him. He said it was stupid, a mistake, just . . . all these
new people around after we'd been together for so long." She
pounds her fist against the carpet. "I hate this stupid school."

It's not fair, that she should have to hurt like this. She's tried
so hard; she'd been so open to changing schools. I was the one
who put up a fight every chance I got. It's not fair that it ended
up biting her in the ass.

"He was crying," Marcella tells me. This makes her start crying again. "I've never seen Brian cry, but at my house, he was
crying. I mean, I actually felt bad for him. I know he feels really
bad about it; I know he probably regrets it. I know he *loves* me,
but . . . I don't think I can, Eve. I don't think I can forgive him."

My best friend's looking at me, waiting on something. Like I
have *any* idea what the right answer is here.

She shakes her head. "I just can't look at him the same way.
He's not my Brian anymore; he just isn't. *My* Brian wouldn't have
done this, especially not weeks after we . . ." Marcella starts
looking a little queasy. "It makes me want to throw up. It's like
after he got what he wanted . . ."

I jump to my feet, rushing to the hallway bathroom to get her
a cold washcloth.

"Thanks," she says, managing a feeble smile as I drop back
down beside her and press it to her cheek.

We're both quiet for a long time as she uses the washcloth

to wipe her face, then lets her head fall back against my bed and covers her eyes with it.

"He still wants us to go to prom together. He knows how important it is to me, and he says even though I'm really mad at him, he thinks I'll regret that we don't have memories of it together. But I'll feel like a complete fool. Even if no one else finds out about this, I'm sure *she'll* be there. She'll know. And I won't even know who she is.

"And I can sit here and say, 'Oh, it's just human nature, he's a guy, he'd had a couple of beers, girls are flirty and throw themselves at guys, even guys who have girlfriends.'" The washcloth slides onto my carpet as she shakes her head again. "But I can't," Marcella whispers. "I hate him, and I love him, and right now I just *hate* him for this."

"I do, too."

Fact.

Marcella's tired red eyes drift to my clock and she sighs heavily. She looks back at me, her expression tentative. "Can I sleep over?"

"Of course," I answer instantly. It's been a while since life has necessitated a midweek sleepover, but it's not like it's never happened before. "Sleep in my bed with me."

I stand up, gathering some extra throw pillows and another blanket. I push my stuff to the side of the bed, making room for her. When I look down at her, she's gazing at the mirror on the back of my door, lips parted.

"I've known something was off. And I just thought . . . if I ignored it, it would go away, things would go back to normal.

"It's funny, except *funny* is the absolute wrong word for it," Marcella tells me, struggling to her feet. She drops the unused tissue into my wastebasket. "He's the one I don't recognize, but it's like . . . I feel like I don't know me anymore, either. For so long, one of the biggest parts of me has been as his girlfriend, and if I'm not . . . I just don't totally recognize myself."

My mouth drops open, but Marcella puts her hand up. "Don't. I can imagine what you're going to say, but please . . . tonight . . . just . . . don't." She steps closer, gives me a hug, her chin coming to rest on my shoulder. "Can we please just go to sleep?"

"Okay." I crawl back into bed, scooching over so that my body is pressed against the cool wall, waiting for my friend to crawl in beside me, and pushing my oldest stuffed bear into her arms.

She wraps her arms around him and smiles before rolling over to turn out the light.

Several minutes pass, but I know she's not sleeping, and it makes it hard for me to fall asleep beside her. So I'm wide awake when her words reach me through the darkness.

"You're right, Eve. And you're *smart*. You'd never let anyone hurt you like this. Because boys just aren't worth it," she finishes wearily.

I suck in my breath, certain she'll make out my reaction in the quiet enveloping us.

There's your cue, I think. *There's your opening.*

Since the weekend, I've been on the lookout for one. After Saturday, telling Marcella about Jamie was feeling more and more necessary. It was feeling like more of a burden to keep it a secret, especially with the way he's approaching me, publicly, when I don't know what to do or even what to call it. Marcella is obviously the best person to confess to, and I've been thinking about it. Even with how caught up she's been with the pageant, I've been looking for an opening.

Plus . . . I needed help. I needed someone to talk to, a girl-friend to offer some guidance given my complete lack of experience. Someone who could tell me what the hell to do when the guy you kinda-sorta like is on his way to feeling you up and you're still uncomfortable with the idea of your boobs because you walk around wearing an Ace bandage half the time.

I feel my cheeks flare in the darkness, remembering. If I'm going to keep doing . . . this . . . with Jamie, I need backup.

I listen to my friend breathing evenly beside me.

Not now, I decide. Marcella's a mess, and tonight isn't about my problems. It would be selfish to expect her to weigh in tonight.

And besides . . .

I squeeze my eyes shut.

I don't frighten easily, but Marcella just scared the crap out of me. She's right—the Eve she knows would never let a guy break her down like that; the Eve she knows would never give him the chance to. I'm not sure I like the idea of her looking at me differently.

I sure as hell *don't* want to set myself up to be hurt the way she's hurting tonight. I don't want to give a guy a part of myself only to be made a fool of weeks later. I don't ever want to look in a mirror and not recognize myself because of the way a guy has transformed me.

If this is what happens when you put what you want with someone before what you want for yourself . . . I'm not really sure I want any of it.

Chapter 24

April 29

Eve

I'd heard of Farmington East's legendary pirate parties way before I'd ever stepped foot in one of East's classrooms, way before I'd ever put on a Pirate uniform.

Julia Dawson's pirate parties are notorious, tales of them reaching South every spring. Apparently they were started by Craig Dawson, about a decade ago, then taken over by Drea Dawson, who still shows up with her college friends and the alcohol. The Dawsons are exceptionally rich, and their parents travel internationally a few times a year. Their parents refuse to tell them when until the day before in an effort to derail party plans, but this tactic has never actually been successful in thwarting a pirate party, based on the wild tales that circulate every year.

Apparently, the Dawsons *always* serve "grog," a horrendous-sounding mixture of dark rum and orange soda. If you attend, you are obligated to talk like a pirate the whole time and have to take a shot if someone catches you slipping up. Girls scare up the skimpiest pirate outfits they can pull together with a day's notice. And then there's the story I call bullshit on, the one about the Dawsons setting up a piece of plywood for those brave/stupid/drunk enough to "walk the plank" across their small indoor pool.

Pretty much every weekend since I've been at East, there's been speculation that it could be *the* weekend, which is so utterly lame. So when it's confirmed by none other than pirate maiden Julia Dawson herself on Friday, I'm sort of glad the notorious event is finally upon us so that we can get it over with and everyone will shut up about it already.

I have no interest in attending and no plans to attend. When Scott mentioned it on Friday afternoon, I made it perfectly clear. "Yeah, there's not a snowball's chance in hell I'm dressing up like a pirate whore in the name of a good time."

He just grinned and said, "Why do you have to be so *arrrgu*mentative all the time?"

I gave him a Look, and that was that.

I was counting on the fact that Marcella, still devastated and crying more often than not, would want to hole up with me Saturday night, maybe agreeing to order Chinese and watch a movie. I was pretty sure she hadn't washed her hair since the breakup, and when it comes to Marcella, that's saying something. So the last thing I expected was her showing up at my door at eight o'clock, clearly having done her hair and her makeup, wearing heeled black boots, a red skirt with jagged edges, and a ruffly white top that showed her belly button and hung off her shoulders.

I stand in the doorway and stare down at her boobs, very much on display. "What the hell is that?"

She plants her booted feet firmly before me. "We're going to the pirate party."

This makes me laugh out loud. "Uhh, no, we're not. Please take that off as quickly as possible."

But she holds her ground, lifting her chin and staring me down, eyes still looking watery behind thick black liner and a couple of coats of mascara. "I'm not going to run and hide like I'm the one who did something to be ashamed of." Marcella swallows hard as her voice starts quivering. "What if they're there together or something? I'm not going to make this easy for him."

I collapse against the door frame, closing my eyes and inhaling through my nose. "This is a bad idea. Things like this, they never end well."

"I don't care."

"Yeah, well, as your best friend, I can't endorse that attitude. Plus, Marcella, you know I don't party when I'm in season."

"You're always in one season or another. And I don't need you to drink. I just need you to have my back."

I have no intention of folding. We lost on Friday, and I made a couple of errors on the mound. My period is due literally any minute and my mood is actually dangerous. And . . . there's another reason I was aiming to stay as far away from that party as possible, something having to do with Jamie's inevitable attendance, the likelihood that pirate skanks would be swarming him for all to see.

But then Marcella stops demanding and starts begging, her voice quiet and shaky. "I know I've asked a lot of you lately. But I also know you know that if the situation was reversed, I'd do the same for you. I still feel like I'm falling apart inside, but when you're with me, I feel a million times stronger. Because you're so strong."

Well, damn it.

She's right and I know it. If the situation was reversed, Marcella would do anything I asked. I can't understand exactly what she is feeling, but I can still tell how torn apart she is right now. So I hear myself opening my mouth against my will, agreeing to go with her.

"Only so you have a DD," I tell her, snatching my keys and sliding into my sneakers. "And only to keep you from doing anything desperate."

"Got it. Thank you."

Marching past her to my car, I yank on the top of her shirt, pulling it up a few inches. "Seriously, Marcella, Girls Across America would take back the crown if they saw you right now."

....

My first impression is that a Party City warehouse exploded inside the Dawsons'. The girls went overboard, setting up plastic chests overflowing with foil-wrapped chocolate coins, inflatable parrots, and torches around the patio. I'm sure it looked festive at some point, but it's not even ten o'clock yet, and the place is wrecked. The sink is filled with empty rum bottles and crushed Solo cups. There's an orange stain on the white couch. And someone has put one of the plastic parrots in a compromising position with the life-size Jack Sparrow cardboard cutout in the living room.

Ten minutes into scoping out the party, we've yet to see the girls who live here, or anyone we know, really. Kids are spread out over the expanse of the huge house and its yard, and it's a mixed bag of attendees—the pirate party faithful who have gone all out in their pirate garb, us first-timers from East, some dressed up, some not, and people I don't recognize at all who I assume are crashing from other nearby schools.

Marcella accepts a hefty serving of grog, served in a skull-and-crossbones mug, from one of those guys we don't recognize. He appeared at once, like her boobs had beckoned him, but after getting her drink, Marcella's on the move again. We wander from the living room to the kitchen to the game room, stopping to say hi when we see people we know, moving on when we don't. Most of them respond with a resounding "Arrrgh!" leaving me to wonder how long, exactly, I'm expected to endure this.

The party thing's just not my scene, and I don't really know how to have normal conversations with people when they're drunk.

Even one of my best friends becomes difficult when he's had too much grog, apparently. I do a double take when Scott goes tearing past us, wearing nothing but bulldog-print boxers, bath towel tucked under his arm.

I grab his elbow and pull him aside. "Oh my God, what are you doing? Where are you going?"

He raises his mug of grog in the air. "Preparing to go overboard to win the he*arrr*t of a fair lady, me matey."

"What?"

Scott leans closer. "Jessie Hembrow is in the pool. That means I'm going in, too."

I shake my head. "Just don't drown."

He takes off with a spirited "Arrrgh."

"Ahoy, matey!" Marcella appears beside me, calling after him. "Go get 'errrr, ya scalawag!"

I rub my forehead, notice she's gotten her hands on a second mug of grog. "Take it easy, okay?"

She just laughs, pulling on my arm. "Come on, let's go."

We wander out back, finding a group of kids huddled in the yard, and back through the living room. Marcella claims she wants to check everything out before committing to a spot to hang out for a while, but I know she's looking for Brian, the way her eyes sweep each room we enter, how a small disappointed frown appears when we don't find him.

I'm keeping an eye out for someone, too, but in truth, I'm hoping I *don't* find him. Because I don't know what I'll find, or who I might find him *with*.

We run into Jasmine in the kitchen. She's just arrived and is sober, and I'm extremely happy to add her to our group. Then we decide to try to track down this infamous indoor pool with the plank, curious to see how much of a fool Scott is making of himself, and after a few wrong turns end up in a two-story room in the back corner of the house with floor-to-ceiling windows.

It feels about twenty degrees hotter than the rest of the house, the air damp and foggy, and the heavy smell of chlorine assaults my nose the second we enter.

"Marrrshall!"

I hear a male voice calling my name from across the room, but it takes me a few seconds to get my bearings, to figure out where it's coming from. Eventually I see the crowded table in the corner of the room, where a bunch of guys are playing some sort of card game. Chris Jamison is waving to me, but my eyes immediately go to the person seated at the end of the table.

I exhale in relief, letting go of a breath, and a worry, I didn't even realize I was holding on to. It's all guys at the table. I quickly check out his outfit—he's wearing a red bandanna and a torn white T-shirt, and it looks like someone drew a scar on his cheek with eyeliner or something. On a scale of one to Jack Sparrow, he's only about a three; there's nothing too obnoxious about his appearance. He's not visibly wasted, and again . . . no pirate skanks on the scene.

After witnessing Marcella's breakup almost firsthand, I walked in tonight with my defenses up. But now . . . I'm *almost* happy to see him.

So when Chris sort of beckons me over after I wave back, I walk toward the table, seeing a bunch of my other teammates— Nathan, Brendan, and Pat—sitting there as well.

"I did *not* expect to see you here tonight," Nathan says at once.

Before I can answer him, my eyes dart to Jamie's face again, the one place I'm trying not to look.

I get the sense he didn't expect to see me, either, but his expression is inscrutable, leaving me with no idea if my presence is a good or bad surprise.

Brendan lifts his bottle of Bud Light. "Don't rat us out to Coach, okay?"

I shake my head. "I'm not going to tattle, Brendan."

Honestly, why does everyone think I'm so uptight? Just because I'm focused doesn't mean I'm going to give people shit for partying. I'm here, aren't I?

But as hard as I try, it's impossible to relax while I'm standing there, trying to have a casual conversation with my teammates when Jamie's in the group, present but silent. My body is tense and my neck hurts from making sure I don't look in his direction, and after three minutes of trying, I'm done.

"Sit down." Chris scoots over, leaving room between him and Jamie. "You girls should join the game. We're just about to deal out the next hand."

I turn to my friends at once. "Actually, can we go back to the den?" I make a big deal of taking a breath. "This chlorine makes it hard to even breathe."

They nod, and I'm this close to getting away from the guys when a rogue pirate blocks our path. It's Brian. He's staring mournfully at Marcella, face pained. "You're not even going to say hi?" he asks her quietly.

At first, her expression matches his. Then she squares her shoulder and presses her lips together. "No."

He takes a step closer. "Can we just talk? Please? Just for a minute."

When she doesn't answer him, I take her elbow. "Let's go."

Brian puts his hand up in my direction. "Eve, I just want to talk to her for a minute."

I look at Marcella. She looks back at me, eyes pleading, and I know what she wants to do. As much as I want to make the decision for her, it's not my place, and I release her arm. "Three minutes," I tell her, looking at my watch. "Then I'm coming to get you."

She nods, then slowly walks toward Brian. They disappear together behind a row of potted palms. Jasmine and I are left standing there, ready for a recovery mission, serious and silent.

And as a result, we're subjected to the conversation coming from the table, whether we want to be or not. Just as I've started letting my guard down, just as I've started to think maybe he's ignoring the girls tonight for a reason.

"Shit, do you remember what happened last year?" Brendan

asks, pointing toward the pool. "When Matty slipped on that kick-board, landed on his ass, and slid right into the pool in his clothes?"

"Jules was so pissed. He had his cup of grog with him. Five minutes into the party, and it's already in the pool," another East kid continues.

Nathan cracks up. "All I remember is Jamie following Drea around, poking her with his sword and asking if he could 'plun-der her booty.'" He falls forward, laughing so hard I think he might choke.

I tense up infinitesimally, hoping that's the end to the story.

But of course, it's Jamie, and it isn't.

"No, that was two years ago," Brendan corrects him. "Last year he hooked up with Jules. I remember, because I walked in on them."

Nate shrugs. "Drea was more impressive. She was a senior when we were sophomores. And Abrams was only a freshman. That was a helluva lot of game for a freshman."

My back is stiff, and my heart has started pounding in warning.

I'm not looking at him. It may have been hard a few minutes ago, but now there's less than zero desire to look his way. I'm facing away from the table, wishing my ears would stop working. I don't hear him deny it. I don't hear him protest. What I think I hear is some hand slapping, the resulting laughter.

"Damn, Drea's hot," Nate says. "Is this the year you hook up with both of them at the same time?"

Finally, Jamie puts an end to it. "Shut up."

He sounds irritated. But it's not enough. It's not enough to make any of it untrue.

"Yeah right," Matty agrees. "Abrams has already worked his way through the Dawsons. Maybe he'll leave them for the rest of us this year."

"Damn, you're all interested in my sloppy seconds," Jamie says. "Why don't you worry less about my life and more about your own?"

As she leans closer, the horrified sneer on Jasmine's face suddenly clues me in that she's been listening to them, too. "He is so gross," she mutters under her breath. "Seriously, who would hook up with him at this point? It just sounds dirty."

I can practically feel my cheeks turning pink, a very clear image of me lying on my back in the dugout popping into my head. I feel like it's being projected onto a screen, like Jasmine can see right through me, like it's obvious I'm one more idiot girl who's been seduced by Jamie.

It's torture standing there, the only relief being that no one knows about us, that I'm not the punch line, one more joke of a girl who's involved herself with him, that no one's publicly dissecting me or what I may have done with him.

And without meaning to, I'm turning, glancing over my shoulder, glaring at him.

He's already looking at me. He stares for a beat, then starts to stand. I whirl back around toward Jasmine, already tugging on her hand and marching toward the door. "Let's get out of here."

"But what about Marcella?"

Shit. What about Marcella?

I pause, and just like that, Jamie's heading toward us.

"Eve," he calls. "Wait up a sec."

I'm tempted to turn around. But I'm even more tempted to get the hell out of there. I just need to grab Marcella.

Unfortunately, before I can actually do so, something heavy and wet knocks into me from behind. It's Scott, wrapping me up in a damp bear hug, eyes hazy, grinning like he won the lottery.

"She said she'd go to prom with me!" he announces.

Not bothering to smile, I glance toward Jamie again. "That's great, but can we discuss it inside?"

The door is only a few feet away. I'm going to make it.

At least that's what I think. But before I can push the door, it opens from the other side, and she comes strolling through, blindsiding me. In that moment I'm about to escape, I have no idea I'm about to be pushed further down into the depths of hell.

It's Naomi, with two of her friends in tow. She's got a bikini top on and a mermaid-print towel is wrapped around her hips. She scans the room, eyes landing on Jamie, who's almost caught up with me.

"I've been looking for you all night," she says. "Have you been dodging me or something?"

Just for a nanosecond, I allow my eyes to flick to his face. It's evident he wants to disappear.

Naomi taps a finger against her Apple watch. "Tick-tock, tick-tock," she says in a singsong. "Jules and Erika are going dress shopping tomorrow. I would *like* to go with them. Prom is, like, two weeks away. Are we going or what?"

I turn my back entirely.

Just say yes, I mentally urge him. *Do what you do. Make this go away.*

"This" being the really shitty feeling of being a girl who's foolishly involved herself with you. Who's started to see you as something different than you really are.

(274)

When he finally responds to her, Jamie's voice is cool and steady. "Come on, Naomi. Did you come tonight to party or just to call me out in front of everybody?"

In my peripheral vision, I see her fold her arms. "You're stalling. Yes or no? If you don't want to say yes, then say no. But if it's no, then you at least owe me a reason why you've taken so long to say so, because I thought this was pretty much a given, us going together."

There's a moment of silence, and no one moves, even though this particular drama has nothing to do with any of us. Well, any of *them* at least. The scene is disrupted when Marcella comes tearing out of the trees, head held high, face proud, but she slows down at once, confused at what she's stumbled into, the tension on the pool deck suddenly feeling thicker than the humid air.

"What's going on?" she whispers.

"Shit's about to go down . . . ," Scott mumbles back.

I look around. They've definitely gathered a crowd. Naomi has her friends with her, and a couple of others have gathered behind her. All the guys from the team have abandoned their game to watch. There's me, Jasmine, Scott, and Marcella. Brian's wandered out from the trees. And a few other people inside the pool room have stopped talking so they can eavesdrop.

At last, I hear Jamie speak up, his voice cracking the silence if not the tension in the room.

"It's no. And *no*, I don't owe you a reason."

"Really? Are you kidding me? Just like that, after letting me think all spring that we were going together? Just no, like I asked you if you wanted a stick of gum." Naomi's glaring at him. "This is *prom*."

Jamie's gone silent again. He's glaring right back at her, giving her nothing.

But Nathan, ever so helpful, chooses that moment to speak up. For someone I've written off as moronic in the time that I've known him, he chooses this particular instance to turn astute.

"You really need to ask?" Nathan grins, jerking his thumb in my direction. "Umm, the reason is pretty frickin' obvious. Jamie's got a thing for Marshall. I mean, has no one else been paying attention?"

My heart turns to a motionless rock inside my chest, and I become aware of an icy sensation inside me, like even my internal organs are breaking out in a cold sweat.

There is a deep hole. Right beneath me. There must be. And any second now, it will open, swallow me up, and take me away from this moment.

But no matter how hard I wish for it to be true, it's not, and instead I stand there, paralyzed and silent as the eyes of the group turn on me.

Scott cracks up. He slaps Nathan's shoulder. "Good one."

Naomi turns and stares at me over her shoulder. She looks back at Jamie. "I don't know if he's joking, actually."

"You kidding me? Eve can't stand him," Pat chimes in. "That's the only thing that's been obvious around here. Where did this come from?"

"Yeah, I mean . . . what the hell?" Scott turns and looks at me, shock and disbelief all over his face. "Eve?"

I stand there, feeling naked, exposed, and miserable under their scrutiny.

Marcella's eyes are about to pop out of her head, her mouth in a surprised little O.

"Sure. Maybe if there's some other idiot named Eve Marshall out there," Jasmine murmurs, nudging me.

It's an awful feeling, because I'm used to looking people in the eye, staring people down at the plate, fearing nothing and no one, despite the various ways people have tried to intimidate me over the years. And I could do what I've always done. I could lift my chin and look them all in the eye. I could tell the truth and let them make whatever the hell they want to out of it.

I could admit that I like him, that I sort of *really* like him, the Jamie I've gotten to know. I could admit that I hate hearing about him with other girls, that it's rude and offensive talking about anyone like that. I could admit that I secretly cheered when he told Naomi he didn't want to go to prom with her, when I secretly believed I might be the reason why.

God.

I could finally admit all of this, not only to myself, but to everyone, publicly.

I could put it out there before he does, because they're asking me the question. They're asking me to acknowledge something that Jamie himself has never really said out loud.

Sure.

I could do all of this, and I could set myself up to lose. *Big-time.*

I shake my head. I let it fall and stare at the ground. "I don't know what the hell you're talking about," I murmur.

But seconds later, the group hasn't broken up, the focus hasn't shifted back to Naomi.

No one looks convinced. They're all still staring at me, so unused to me *cowering*, and my eyes go to Marcella. She's looking me straight in the eye, and I blush, because lying to Marcella is a whole other thing entirely, and it's hard to pull off when she's looking at me.

I turn my back on her. I stare at Nate instead. "You're out of your mind." My voice is firm now. "Clearly, there's nothing going on between me and Jamie and there never will be."

I lift my chin and square my shoulders. Finally I sound like myself again, and this is the person they'll listen to. Believe. I push past the girls, determined to get out of this room, this party, once and for all.

The only problem is . . . Nathan is standing right next to Jamie, so Jamie's face is the last I see before I go. And as I turn away from all of them, attempting to remove myself from the group with some kind of dignity, it's impossible to miss his expression.

And my motivation changes in an instant. When I leave the pool room, it's not to escape them anymore, it's to get away from him—his face, the flash of disappointment . . . hurt, even . . . that I saw that first instant.

Before it immediately converted itself, turning back into a face I still remember—the cold, angry mask he used to wear when I first met him.

....

Jamie

Her words are swift and brutal. The shock of her betrayal reminds me of the time I cut the palm of my hand with a serrated knife at the Burger Barn and didn't realize what had happened for several seconds after the blood poured from the wound.

Fuck, it hurt. It hurt in a sneaky way, because I hadn't even felt the knife slicing my skin.

Her words have the same damn effect as that knife. And the resulting hurt is so overpowering in the same way, too—confusing because I didn't see it coming.

Confusing because I'd never have expected her words to have that kind of damaging power in the first place. Confusing and paralyzing.

She gets to walk away. And I'm left standing there, at the receiving end of Naomi's fury, Eve's friends' contempt, and my teammates' amusement. I feel all these things pouring over me, rushing into the open wound she created.

And it only takes seconds for the sensations to transform into one cohesive emotion—fury. It expands within my chest, produces spots of red behind my eyelids. Suddenly I feel hot all over, and my brain feels like it's pounding against my skull.

No way in hell she gets to walk out of here. No way in *hell* she gets to walk away unscathed.

I push away from the table, shoving Scott out of my way as I go. Don't even bother looking at Naomi as I storm past her and her crew, intent on getting out of there and away from all of them.

Not that escape, or isolation, is my mission. Hell no.

I push my way past a couple of drunken pirates, their stupid eye patches irritating me, amping up my agitation. Screw this party, and screw Naomi. Screw her for thinking this was all some kind of game, for needing to be the center of attention for everything, at all costs.

A thought interjects itself into my consciousness, causing the hurt to flare up. It's an unwelcome intrusion, but even after she denied *everything*, I can't deny it to myself.

I was actually going to ask Eve *to prom.*

Before everything even started going to shit, I was going to. I'd been thinking about it. And I'd made up my mind.

I was going to . . . put it out there. Make it clear to her—beyond stupid text messages, and a few kisses, and some random sports competitions—that I was into her.

That I was into the idea of being *with* someone in maybe a way I hadn't ever been into such a thing before.

If she wouldn't start the conversation, then I would.

I was gonna ask her after the game, hopeful for a win, thinking she'd be in a good mood, joking and approachable. But then we lost, and I thought I'd better wait, assuming a prom invite wouldn't cheer Eve up like it might some girls.

I waited till today, trying to find the nerve a few times during the day, trying to figure out why I was struggling in the first damn place. I waited, and I waited too long, until this stupid party, until she overheard all that bullshit from the guys, until Naomi showed up.

Until . . .

Until she killed the idea before it ever had a chance to make its way out of my mouth.

I feel my face heat up all over again, and my teeth grind together. I punch the wall as I continue down the hallway.

She shut me down so quickly and succinctly, it knocked down anything we'd built together in two seconds flat. I stared at her, and she had that face on again, that tough, hard mask she seemed to depend on so much. I stood there watching her, reminded of someone who wasn't on my side, someone who was rooting against me, against us.

So fuck that, and fuck any good intentions I had about the whole thing.

And the unbelievable nerve of her, thinking she gets to turn and walk away, thinking she gets to leave unscathed, getting to say her piece, getting to end things *her* way, without giving me any chance to do so.

Maybe she's forgotten who she's been kissing. Maybe she's forgotten the person I was before she screwed with my head.

I tear through a few rooms before it hits me—Eve's not going to hide; Eve's going to leave. So I immediately double back through the kitchen and rush through the foyer, throwing the door open and jogging down the steps and the long, winding driveway.

I can make out a lone figure in the distance, rushing down the dim path, and I take off in her direction, grabbing her elbow the second before she reaches her car.

She startles, throat convulsing as she swallows suddenly, glancing left and right for someone, anyone, like she's actually scared that I've found her. If I wasn't so pissed, her reaction might actually make me *sad*.

I get myself together, letting go of her arm. But still I position myself between her and her door, because she may be trying to drive away, but I'm not going to lie down and let her run me over on her way.

I look her in the eye. I stare for a long time, trying to see the girl who sat beside me on the bench at Mitch's, the girl who'd been in tears the first night I kissed her, the girl who liked the smell of the rain from inside a dugout.

But I can't. She won't let me. Her eyes are cold and hard.

I shake my head and curse toward the ground. "Shit." I look

up at her again. "Did you really think I was going to let you walk out of here like that?"

"Oh, give me a break. Don't stand there acting so *wronged*, Jamie." She waves her hand in the direction of the house. "Like you've always treated girls with the utmost respect. We've all heard the stories. Apparently they're endless. You're a hypocrite, acting so appalled about all this."

My hands go to either side of my head for a second, trying to focus, because all this nonsense she's spewing . . . it's just confusing everything. That's not what this is about.

I'm trying to focus, to find the words, but Eve won't stop talking. She inserts herself between me and her car, shifting her weight to wedge in there and open the door. "Look," she says coldly. "What did either one of us think was honestly going to happen here? The truth of the matter is we don't get along. That's been blatantly obvious since day one." She shrugs one shoulder. "I probably just saved both of us from it being any worse in the long run."

Eve turns her back on me, fiddling with her keys.

"*That's* what's been blatantly obvious?"

She nods.

"Yeah, well, I think there's something else that's blatantly obvious, and it's not that, Marshall."

I wait for her to turn around, because it's my turn, and I deserve this much respect at least.

"The truth of the matter is, party or no party, Naomi or no Naomi, stories or no stories . . . you never gave me a chance." The anger starts rising in my chest again. *"Never!"*

She opens her mouth, like she wants to argue, but I'm on a

tear now. I move my face closer to hers, because she will hear this—I'll make her, even if she refuses to show it.

"When it came time to actually put yourself out there, put the tough girl act down and actually show you could have some trust in someone else"—I shake my head bitterly—"you couldn't even do it.

"You act so hard." I glance away, laugh once, although there's nothing funny about any of this. "I used to like that you were tough; that you had more of a backbone than any girl I've ever known. But in reality, you're scared. You're not tough at all. And it's actually easier for you to think badly about other people than put yourself out there and take a chance on them."

Something flashes to life in her eyes, like my words have finally hit something human beneath the cold, heartless exterior she's giving me.

So I drop some more truth bombs, hoping they hit their mark, too.

"Tell me a single time, since the night of the spaghetti dinner, shit, since before that, that I've hurt you. That I've treated you badly. That I've made it seem like I didn't care."

She's quiet, her eyes going to the ground.

"You can't, can you? All you can do is dredge up stories from before we even met, because facing the reality of what's happening here is too hard for you. Because . . . as I've always said, you're just too stubborn for your own good, too stubborn to admit that maybe you're wrong."

I study her face, thinking some more. "Captain. Standout. All-star." I can't help but huff. "When the truth is, you know nothing about being a team player. Putting yourself on the line for someone else. Not when it actually matters. Not when it means there's even the smallest possibility you might lose."

I take a step back. I wait on her. Because a minute ago it looked like she had something to say, but suddenly, she's clammed up again. She's silent, and rigid, looking past me into the distance, eyes focused on nothing.

I wait on her, but she waits me out. Waits for me to shut up and leave her alone.

My shoulders collapse. My head falls forward, and I rub at the back of my neck, all of a sudden feeling sore and tired.

"Now you have nothing to say," I mumble. "All right."

All the anger, all the everything drains from my body, and when I manage to speak again, my voice sounds as flat and emotionless as her face looks right now. "If it's easier to make me the bad guy, because of stupid stories people are telling or how things used to be between us, well . . . have at it, Eve. If it's easier to pretend nothing has changed in the name of protecting both of us . . . I guess go ahead.

"I mean, whatever it takes to win, right? Go ahead. Walk away. Tell yourself whatever you have to so you can feel good about that, so you can tell yourself that you were right, that you *won*."

I only look into her eyes one final time. "You're making the wrong call here, Eve. And the sad thing is . . . there are no winners." I shake my head, swallowing hard. "This time everyone loses."

Another glimmer of emotion flickers in her eyes. But now it's my turn to walk away.

She's almost made it easy.

Chapter 25

May 7

Eve

My brothers come home for Mother's Day weekend, as is the expectation, as they do every year, regardless of where they're living, stationed, or being educated come May. We have to celebrate a week early because Evan has an obligation at his base on the actual holiday, but we're all present and accounted for. My family spends the whole weekend together, taking the train down to the Phillies game on Saturday night. Then we celebrate Mother's Day like we always do. We go to church. We give her a bouquet of flowers. We go to brunch.

And then we play ball.

It's pouring when we leave the restaurant, but rain doesn't put a damper on the yearly tradition. My mom opens the fitness center, which is closed on Sundays, and we have access to a huge gym with a full basketball court. We play three-on-two while my dad, the least athletic of the bunch, refs the game. Mom and

I play together and call Evan over to join our team. Basketball wasn't his sport as much as the rest of us, and it evens things out a bit. We'll cream my brothers, even with Mom playing in her less-than-layup-friendly floral skirt. She has a pair of sneakers in her office, and she's good to go.

During quick water breaks, I glance at my mom's slightly shiny face. I watch her watching us, blissfully in her element— on the basketball court, with all four children in the same place at the same time, getting along. Which, for the record, is a million times easier now that we don't all live under one roof. Eric's rubbing the top of Evan's head, still giving him a hard time about his military-required haircut after all these years. Ethan's vying for equal attention from them, the way he always did as the youngest of the pack. And occasionally one of them will try to sneak up on me and grab the ball from the crook of my elbow, but I catch them every time and escape without harm.

We're into our second game, and our team is on its way to a second victory, when the toe of Eric's sneaker catches my calf and leaves a nasty scrape that starts to bleed. Eric notices and forms a T with his hands to call time-out. "Eve's bleeding."

"Badly?" my mom asks as she jogs over.

"No," I answer, wiping the blood away with my hand. I shove Eric away in retribution. "But I probably need a Band-Aid."

"I'll unlock my office," she says. "I have a first-aid kit in there."

The boys linger around the basket, taking free throws, and I follow my mom out of the gym, down the hallway, and into her office. She disappears under her desk to retrieve the kit, and when she comes back up, she finds me staring at a framed eight-by-ten picture on her desk.

It's a picture of my mom, wearing the jersey I recognize from her time playing ball overseas. In it, her face is bright red, most of her hair has escaped its messy ponytail, and she's bent over at the waist, one hand resting on her thigh. With the other hand, she's holding a "number one" up in the air.

I tap the picture as she hands me the Band-Aid. "I never saw this one," I tell her. I smile wryly over her shoulder. "You look like you're about to keel over."

She chuckles, leaning down to wipe my scrape with a cleansing pad. "I was," she admits. "I had a hundred-degree fever and a strained hamstring, but that was my last game and there was no way I was going to miss it."

"Your last game in Germany?"

"My last game ever," she says. "Well, my last game that wasn't in a rec league."

I slap the Band-Aid on, and when I look back up, she's smiling fondly at the picture. "I didn't know at the time I'd be married and pregnant within the year."

"Because you met Dad?"

My mother shrugs. "Not because I met your father; not really. He probably would have supported me, tried to work something out, if I'd decided to stay in Europe. But he was being sent back to the States, and our relationship was too new for me to be traveling around Europe and him going from base to base back here and have any chance of surviving. So . . . that was my last game."

I tilt my head and stare at the picture some more. Her love for the game practically oozes from the photograph, which is now over twenty-five years old. It's still tangible. "You just gave it up?" I hear myself asking. "Just like that? For . . . Dad?"

She throws her head back and laughs. "I *kind* of think your father would be offended to hear you put it that way."

Then her face grows serious. She reaches out and touches her image behind the frame. "I loved playing ball with my whole heart. I loved being this girl. I loved how tough she was; I loved winning; I loved feeling bulletproof. And it wasn't an *easy* decision, when I had to choose between staying in Germany and coming home to be with your father." She turns and gives me a quick smile. "I mean, I'd loved basketball my whole life; I'd only just met him. But then I realized something," she continues. "Yes, I loved basketball with my whole heart, but . . . it was sort of a one-sided relationship." My mom looks at me. "I realized the game can't love you back."

Her words feel like an unexpected punch to the gut, and I struggle to keep my face from revealing how they knock the wind out of me.

"I thought I liked that," she tells me. "The other choice was scary, moving and marriage and everything. Relationships . . . they take everything—your tears and your energy and your patience. But . . ." My mom reaches for the other picture on her desk. In it, all four of us kids are eating Fudgsicles on a particularly hot summer day. We're sweaty and messy from playing outside. My brothers are shirtless and chocolate's everywhere—running down chins, arms, legs, and bellies. "Relationships give you back even more if you take the leap." I notice her throat tightening as she puts the picture back into place. "And I wouldn't change anything I did for the world. Over time, I started seeing it differently. Putting your heart on the line and being weak aren't the same thing."

The watery pressure in my eyes surprises me with its quickness, how my tears betray my attempt to stay emotionless, and

I bat my eyelids furiously in an attempt to keep the tears from showing themselves. But my mom notices anyway, or maybe she notices my hands curling into fists at my side, or the way my chest is quaking, the way I'm physically protesting everything she's speaking of. Putting my heart out there or being weak . . . I'm not sure I know the difference yet.

I hated the way it hurt, how hurting felt like losing, after I let him in and then had to be reminded at every turn about the girls who had come before me. I hated how it felt, having my private business put on public display at the party. I hated the way it hurt, even after I tried to shut him out, remembering those accusations he made, realizing they were true.

Your brain is telling you to wise up, but your heart is asking you to listen to something other than reason.

And the struggle . . . it *hurts*.

My mom's mouth falls open as she watches me. "Eve? Baby?"

"I don't like the way it feels," I whisper, afraid my voice will crumble if I speak any louder, "putting myself out there. It doesn't feel like me."

"I understand." She nods. "It feels like you're trying to wear someone else's skin, and it doesn't fit right, and it makes you uncomfortable inside and out."

"Pretty much," I mumble. She's quiet, waiting me out, and eventually I continue. "I just want to run away from the feeling. Go back to the old me. But"—I pause, feeling the tears on the verge of forming again—"it's like, I can't quite find my way back there, either."

"You've had to be tough for so long. Stand up to people's comments and underestimating you, even mocking you. Stepping into situations where it's felt like you didn't have too many allies. It's scary to let down your defenses after building them up." My mom considers this for a minute. "But sometimes when you stop resisting change, it doesn't feel so awful or overwhelming anymore. It's not as painful when you decide to let it happen."

She glances downward, from the corner of her eye, purses her lips like she's thinking about something. "Speaking of painful . . ." She hems and haws a bit more before finally spitting it out. "You might want to give up the Ace bandage. That doesn't feel good. And it makes it hard to breathe."

My head jerks up in surprise and my cheeks heat. "Oh my God, you *know* about that?"

"Been there, done that," my mom answers sagely. She points to her own chest. "These revealed themselves at a really inconvenient time, too."

"*Mom!*" I'm mortified, and appalled . . . and laughing away my tears.

She sighs and gives me a hug. "My tough girl. I never would've wanted you to be any other way. But . . . for the record . . ." She steps back, hands on my shoulders, studying me at arm's length. "I'd be okay getting to know the other parts of you, too. It doesn't make you weak to acknowledge them."

I don't say anything, thinking our conversation has just about reached maximum cheese capacity.

"Does all this have something to do with Jamie?"

The question takes me by surprise, and I inhale suddenly, answering her question without meaning to. A sharp pang of regret hits my gut, and I quickly shake my head. "Not so much," I tell her. "I'm pretty sure that situation is botched beyond recognition."

"Too bad," she says a minute later. She strides toward the

gym, preparing herself for a quick getaway before offering a final opinion on my life. "He was kind of charming."

I linger in her office, collapsing on the corner of her desk, needing a minute or two to collect myself before going out to face my brothers and my dad. I feel about ten times girlier than I did walking into my mom's office, and I can't seem to bring myself to head back to the court.

I stare at my mom's blank wall, thinking back on the week.

It sucked.

Me, the girl who generally avoided parties altogether, ended up being the focal point of one of the most talked-about stories to come out of the Party of the Year. I endured Marcella's endless questions, stares on Monday from people I didn't even know, and, worst of all, the tension on the field as Jamie and I did everything to keep our distance at the same time our team was trying to secure a trip to districts.

I could barely even look at him. I'd gotten over feeling disgusted by the stories his friends were telling; now I was disgusted with myself. The night of the party, sometime around midnight, it occurred to me that the things Jamie had said to me were incredibly similar to the things Marcella had said to me after the fashion show. *Too* similar. And if Jamie and my best friend actually saw it the same way, then . . . maybe there were some habits I needed to own up to.

But I couldn't do anything about it, not really. Lingering anger surrounded him like a force field, making him entirely unapproachable, not like I had the words to fix things even if I ever found the courage to approach him. So I suffered in silence, doing the best I could to keep my head in the game when we were on the field. All the while knowing that with every day that passed, there was another day between us, another day taking us back to the place where we had started. If neither one of us did anything, we'd be back there all too soon. And regardless of how the series turned out, regardless of who got the trophy . . . Jamie might be right after all.

We might both end up losing.

Chapter 26

May 10

Jamie

I'm about a mile away from the school when I notice a person walking on the side of the road, heading in the same direction. I tense up when I get close enough to recognize the curls bouncing over her shoulders, the purple bomber jacket, and the fit of those tight jeans.

Just keep driving, man.

It's been over a week since the party, but I'm still not really feeling too friendly toward Naomi. No, she wasn't the cause of the problem, but she sure as hell was a catalyst. And she's definitely pissed off at me, from the way she's been stopping abruptly and turning on her heel when we end up in the same hallway and staring right through me if we happen to end up in the same group together.

I don't owe her anything. And I'm already running late.

But just as I'm about to pass her, I see the way the wind

lifts her hair, how she clutches the sides of her thin jacket together, trying to keep warm on an unseasonably cold morning, and decency gets the better of me. I slam on the brakes, the Jeep coming to a grinding halt in the gravel, causing her to startle and lurch into the grass.

I lower the passenger window, immediately finding her glaring at me through it.

"Thanks for the early morning heart attack." Naomi turns away, tosses her curls, and keeps walking.

I hit the gas again, driving a couple of feet and idling beside her. "Just get in."

I'm trying to be nice here, but I'm not really in the mood to kiss her ass.

She still won't look at me. "No thanks."

"Naomi. We're, like, a mile away from school and it's already seven fifty. Just get in so neither of us is later than we need to be."

"I said no."

But she makes the mistake of looking over at me, and damn it, I can see hurt there, hiding out behind her indignant pride. And I'm kind of tired of hurting girls when I never even meant to, when I was just trying to . . . I don't know . . . do something *differently* for once.

So I slam on the brakes a second time, put the car in park, and jump out and jog around to intercept her path. She stares into the distance over my shoulder, chewing on the inside of her cheek, like if she just keeps ignoring me long enough I'll vanish.

I inhale a deep breath, trying to work up the motivation for this. "Look. I'm sorry about the prom thing, okay? I know you thought we were going, and I know it's a big deal to you. I didn't mean to screw you over. My head was . . . somewhere else."

"*With* someone else," she says.

I look down, kicking at the dirt with my sneaker. "Yeah, maybe."

"You should've been honest. And a hell of a lot sooner."

Then, even though in all these years I've never seen Naomi cry, I swear her eyes start looking a little shiny as we stand there on the side of the road.

"I don't want you as my boyfriend or anything, just so that's clear." Her shoulders fall and she leans against the side of my car. "But I did . . . I don't know . . . depend on you to be there." She glances over at me with a small, wry smile. "I always thought we were actually, you know, friends apart from everything else. I always felt like you had my back. It sucked when all of a sudden you didn't."

I look at Naomi. "I'm sorry," I repeat. I've said it before, but this time, the regret makes my throat tighten, because she's right—both of us know what it feels like to have people let us down, time and time again, and I don't want to be one more of those people to her.

She studies me for a long minute, eyes narrowed, like she's evaluating the sincerity of my apology or considering how she wants to play this.

"Guess I'll think about letting you make it up to me," she finally says. "Since it wasn't like I ended up without any options. Brendan's *happy* to be going with me."

"Did you really think you'd end up without any options?"

"Not really," she admits after a beat. She grins. "It's me we're talking about."

Naomi pushes off my car. "Enough of the deep conversation this early in the morning. Are you gonna drive me to school or what? Piece-of-shit car wouldn't start today."

"Yeah. Get in." Before walking back around to my side, I give her shoulders a quick squeeze, just to reassure her. "Anytime."

....

The next day, after showering and changing into my school clothes after gym class, I linger in the back hallway, outside Coach's office. His door is closed. It's weird to find his door closed, so I pull the crumpled pass out of my back pocket to check on the time. I glance at it, see that I'm here at the right time, shrug, and lean against the wall to wait for him to show up.

But after all the other kids filter out of the boys' and girls' locker rooms and the next class files in, after the bell rings and the corridor becomes quiet again, when I see a figure making her way down the hallway, my back stiffens and I stand straight again. Suddenly I feel trapped in the dead-end hallway, because it's not Coach approaching. It's Eve.

I recognize her walk now—long, purposeful strides without any sway in her hips. I recognize the fiery orange Nikes, the ones she's put yellow-and-black laces in. As she gets closer still, I recognize something else, and it's the punch-to-the-gut sensation of a familiar scent, the kind only a scent from the past can deliver, because your brain identifies it as a scent from the *past*. Eve doesn't smell like "yummy cupcake" or "just-peachy-and-cream" or any other ridiculous girly scent. Eve smells like Tide-washed cotton straight out of the dryer, with a touch of worn leather mixed in, from spending so much time with her glove, I guess. She comes all the way into view, and I recognize one final thing, something I've almost forgotten. That look on her face, the one that reveals nothing. I used to see it all the time—her ready-for-battle face, her chin slightly jutted out, her nostrils slightly flared.

Eve's face relaxed for a while there, but . . . here it is again, forcing me to forget the girl I'd started to get to know, reminding me that in no time at all we've ended up on different teams again.

She doesn't acknowledge me whatsoever. She waits on the other side of the door frame, adopting a posture identical to mine. Eve crosses her arms over her chest and stares dead ahead. I notice a similarly crumpled pass in her fist.

Coach called us here at the same time. I consider for a minute whether Coach would actually sink so low as to involve himself in our . . . personal lives. Sure, he's involved himself in mine, he's crossed the line between professional and personal, but . . . he wouldn't, would he? As much as I hate how things are between me and Eve right now, I think I hate the idea of Coach playing guidance counselor even more.

Seconds tick by on the old clock overhead in slow motion. Standing there, the tense energy radiating off Eve's body, it seems like a magnet is trying to pull the second hand in the opposite direction as it struggles to move forward. There's still not a sound behind the door, and I can't even tell if there's any light escaping from beneath it.

I glance at her again in my peripheral vision. This is torture.

Two minutes later, I turn all the way toward her, surprised to find she's actually turned to look at me, too, that her expression has softened almost imperceptibly.

Over the weekend and into the week, my anger toward her had flared periodically, engulfing any other feelings, the more painful ones, she'd stirred up at the party. Anger I'm used to. Anger I can handle. It reminds me I could write her off and be done with it, tells me I *should* write her off.

But looking at her today, the anger's extinguished just like that, leaving me with pangs of regret and loss nudging at my heart, telling me something else. Maybe someone different is worth being different for. Maybe worth working for, challenging as it can be sometimes.

Not that I know how to fix things. All I know is how relationships *don't* work, how eventually it's every man or woman for herself when they turn ugly. My hands curl in frustration at my sides.

I want better than that. I got a taste of what better can be like, and I want it back.

"Eve," I finally whisper, all the while knowing I have no idea how I'm going to follow up the single word. Because I don't really know how to communicate with the girl who walked down the hallway; never did.

My hands twitch nervously at my sides, but before I can begin to figure out what to say next, Coach's door finally opens.

Thank God, I think, my body rolling off the door frame and into his office.

I'm disappointed at the same time.

"Hey, Abrams," Coach murmurs, gaze toward his carpet. "Sorry I kept you."

He leaves the door open and stands just inside it, expectantly. There's no movement outside it, and finally he ducks his head outside. "Marshall," I hear him say. "I believe your pass was written for fifth block, too. Get in here."

She's actively rolling her eyes, dragging her body inside against her will, and I could almost smile, because I'm pretty sure she's gotten the sense that we're in for a joint guidance lesson, same way I did. And she's every bit as disappointed in Coach.

Guess we always had more in common than we thought, before we messed everything up.

Coach tugs on the brim of his hat before collapsing into the chair behind his desk and staring at us. He exhales a long sigh through his nose. He stares at us some more. He makes a tent with his fingers and looks from Eve, to me, then back again. He nods a few times. Sighs again.

A nervous laugh escapes me. "Uh, did you want something, Coach? You're the one always reminding me to get to class on time."

"Zip it, Abrams," he says, removing his ball cap, running a hand through his matted hair, and putting the cap into place again.

He looks at both of us, hard, one more time. Then, finally, he gets around to talking. "I've got myself a problem here." He slaps a file folder onto his desk, lips pressed together in a thin, frustrated line.

Eve and I wait, silently, for him to elaborate.

Coach gazes out his window as he continues. "The spring sports banquet is just about three weeks away," he says. "And by the end of today, I need to get back with the athletic director about whose name to get engraved on the Cy Young trophy."

Every muscle in my body tenses. I sense the exact same reaction coming from the chair beside me.

"And I think we can agree," he continues, "that I'm in a god-damn no-win situation."

I listen, motionless, feeling frozen inside.

This is it.

"In the past, it's been easy to identify the standout. That's the thing about standouts; they're easy to spot." He shakes his head back and forth slowly. "And I've never been given a man-ual, any kind of guidelines about pitch counts, about games won or lost, about weighing strikeouts versus RBIs. This has always been a discretionary award, and I know I'm not going to get any help from analyzing stats for comparative purposes anyway. That wouldn't bring me peace of mind."

My heart pounds as I listen to him give a brief recap of the season and review highlights from games at home, games on the road. He talks about our record, how our performances on the mound supported it.

"The fact is, and it's a fact I know you two are keenly aware of, why things between you remain so . . . complicated . . ."

There's something in the way he says it that makes my head jerk up, something that hints he knows a lot more about the extent of our relationship outside the bullpen. And it all hangs in the balance in that moment . . . but ultimately, Coach stays a coach. He doesn't play guidance counselor. He keeps talking baseball.

". . . is because you're both standouts, and that's hard for both of you to take." A hint of a smile appears at the corner of his lips. "You both had outstanding seasons, you both demonstrated sportsmanship in the toughest of times, you both were leaders in your own way. We've got a few other pitchers on the team, but everyone knows that this award belongs to one of the two of you."

Coach takes off his hat again, anxiously runs his hand through his hair, and resituates the cap. "And if there's one thing I know for certain, it's that I'm damned if I do and damned if I don't."

He lifts his hand in my direction. "Could give it to you, Abrams. And the stats would back me up that you deserve it. The team would back me up that you deserve it. But you know . . .

you got the honor last year." He shrugs. "And there's a good chance you'll get it next year. And there will be people out there, talking in whispers behind my back, saying that I never would've given it to Eve, that I never would've given it to a girl, no matter how fully she proved herself. That's the bitch about this being a discretionary award; I have no strict guidelines to follow."

Then he looks over at Eve. "Or I can just give it to you, Marshall."

Suddenly I'm biting back a protest, by instinct.

"Again, the stats would back me up, and so would the team. And there would be people out there, talking in whispers behind my back, saying that you got the award because in some way I had to give it to you; how would it have looked if I didn't? I'm pretty sure there are few things you'd hate more than people thinking you got the award for any other reason than fully deserving it . . . and again, all I could say is that it's a discretionary award." He hangs his head. "I have no guidelines," he says quietly.

"Or I could just ask the AD to order two trophies. He'd probably say yes." Then Coach taps the file folder on his desk one more time. "But why do I get the sense that this would be the ultimate cop-out, and neither one of you would want to take a trophy home if I did that?"

Coach looks at us expectantly, like he's waiting for us to speak, and it sinks in for the first time during this exchange that he's actually come to us for help, that he actually expects us to weigh in.

We sit there in joint silence instead.

"I mean, I can make whatever bullshit decision," he tells us. "And I can let the odd man out know after the fact, before the banquet, so he or she is adequately prepared." Coach leans forward. "But I wanted to talk to you ahead of time, because I have no idea what I'm going to do, but I do know that the decision is not going to get any easier. So, once I do figure this out, if it's what you want, I'll tell you privately ahead of time." Coach stares at us, sitting there silent. A long minute passes. "Either of you have any thoughts on that?" he finally asks.

My mouth does in fact fall open, but no words come out.

I'm dumbfounded.

And in that instant, I realize it's not because I'm not sure what *I* want to happen, because that's obvious. I feel it on a visceral, competitive level. I want the trophy. I deserve the trophy. And in some way I'm still well aware that I really need the trophy.

I'm dumbfounded because I'm wondering . . . *What does she want?*

And I'm wondering if there's a way I can still make her happy.

As furious as I've been at her, as disappointed as I've been that she copped out when everything was on the line . . . damn it . . . I'm still finding myself caring about her.

I'm jolted out of my stupor by the sound of Eve's chair scraping the floor loudly as she pushes it back and stands up. "Give the trophy to Jamie," she says, eyes trained on Coach.

My head whirls around in shock.

What?

"What?" asks Coach.

She only glances at me for a second, long enough for me to see her swallow hard, before turning her attention back to the coach. "Give the trophy to Abrams," she says. "I'm okay with that."

My mouth is still hanging open; I can't pull it together to acknowledge that I'm not sure if *I'm* okay with it.

Eve is gripping the strap of her backpack, like it's giving her strength or something. "Jamie was more consistent. He got us out of trouble a few more times than I did. I've seen the way he rallied the team when we needed it. Got everyone fired up to maintain the lead he set from the mound."

She shrugs, her voice quieter now. "That's the reality of the situation, and I'm not going to stand here and try to deny it." Eve lifts her chin. "I had an incredible season, for sure. I overcame some things probably hundreds of people thought I couldn't, or at least couldn't anymore. And if the award encompassed all those things, yeah, it would be mine. But I know what's what, and if we strip all that other stuff away, the award belongs to Jamie. And I'm okay with that."

Listening to her speak up on my behalf, painful feelings stir in my chest, crippling me from talking or moving. I don't think I've ever felt so brokenhearted to learn a baseball award was about to be mine.

Even though we were fighting, even though she had an opportunity to try to screw me, she didn't. She was being honest, and she was conceding this to me. The girl who never conceded anything was giving me this, putting me before something I know she really, really wanted for herself.

"You sure, Marshall?" Coach asks. "I'm not asking anyone to play the martyr, just to be clear."

"I'm sure, Coach." She pulls her backpack all the way up on both shoulders, squaring them like she's getting ready to go. "And I appreciate you talking to us like you did. I appreciate the respect you showed me. Today . . . well, to be honest . . . the whole season." Eve turns her back on us and makes her way to the door. Then she smiles over her shoulder at Coach. "Almost makes me proud to say I'm a Pirate."

Seconds later, she's gone. And even though she just gave me something—something huge, something I desperately wanted—it feels like she took something even more important with her when she walked out the door without looking back.

Chapter 27

May 12

Eve

Coach ends practice twenty minutes early. Yesterday we secured our spot in the district playoffs, and it's prom weekend. The guys are talking about last-minute haircuts, corsages they forgot to order, and what time they need to pick up their tuxes.

I guess I'm sticking with my plan to go with some of my friends from the basketball team, now that Marcella's got a date. When Ethan was home last weekend, we all ended up hanging out together like old times. I've always suspected he had a little bit of a crush on Marcella, and so when it came up that she needed a last-minute date, he was more than happy to offer to take the train back down and hang out at his alma mater's prom.

Everything got squared away just in time. The weekend will be . . . fun.

I close my eyes, already picturing it—him walking in, cool and confident in a tux, with whatever girl took Naomi's spot. Jamie, arriving at prom, without me. I mean, never in a million years, even when we were . . . whatever . . . did I fantasize about going to prom with him, but the idea of him showing up with someone else . . .

I push the image aside, busying myself in an attempt to ignore the pain in my gut, the feeling of my throat tightening for about the hundredth time this week. I know I did the right thing in Coach's office the other afternoon, as an athlete and as a person. It wasn't an attempt to fix things; it was just an attempt to do something right in that gut-check moment.

Turns out doing the right thing doesn't necessarily go so far in making you feel any better. Any less sad.

I linger down at the field until the coaches and the rest of my team have left, not into being part of the bustle back up at the school, wanting to be alone. I hide in the dugout, picking up empty sunflower seed bags and Gatorade bottles that have been left behind during the season and pulling together a small pile of batting gloves and sweatshirts to take up to lost and found. It's officially prom weekend, and I can't seem to make myself face it.

When I emerge, I stop in my tracks, staring at the infield. I didn't realize I wasn't alone down here, that someone else had also hung back. He seems to be pretending to be busy the same way I am, standing on the mound and fiddling with a leather strap on his glove with an unnecessary amount of concentration.

He's looking down at his glove, not at me, but my heart starts pounding anyway, because it seems like he's hanging out for some reason. If he were still totally angry, he'd have made sure not to get stuck down here alone with me.

And if I'm going to speak up, if I'm going to say what I want to say, then now's the time.

I wait, and wait, and eventually he looks up. He doesn't seem surprised to see me standing there.

Rubbing my neck and clearing my throat, suddenly feeling like I've swallowed the entirety of the infield, I call out to him weakly. "Can I talk to you for a minute?"

Jamie nods, expression blank, but he doesn't move. He waits on me, and slowly and very unsurely I walk out to join him on the mound.

I try to assess his face under his hat. He still looks kind of scary, the way he used to, but I close my eyes briefly and try to recall the not-so-scary person who'd shared ice cream with me, wound plastic wrap around cars, and held my hand for just a minute there.

Taking a deep breath, I dive in. "I owe you a huge apology." I pause. "Well, actually, I owe you a few apologies, and they're all so embarrassing to acknowledge it's almost painful to admit them out loud. But I will." I take another breath. "I'm sorry for how I acted at the party. I'm sorry for how I acted after when you tried to talk to me. And I'm sorry it's taken me over a week to say it to your face."

Shaking my head, I finally admit it out loud. "You were right, Jamie. All of it . . . it had less to do with you and more to do with me. And I was mean and unfair. Because I was scared."

I force myself to meet his eyes. "You didn't deserve it. And I'm sorry. I'm really, really sorry."

He just regards me, silently, for another moment, and it's so unsettling that I finally turn to start back.

I walk away, swallowing back the hurt, telling myself I said what I wanted to say, that he had listened, and I should be satisfied.

"Marshall."

My head whips around at the sound of my name. I think I detect the smallest of smiles on his face as he beckons me back to the mound with his index finger.

When I'm standing before him, he finally crosses his arms and nods his head at me, the small smile turning into that patented smirk. "I know saying that was probably the most difficult thing you had to do this spring," he acknowledges. "So thank you." Jamie sighs loudly. "It sucked, that scene at the party, but . . . I'm getting over it. Seems like no matter how many times you piss me off, I still kinda like you. And you know . . . I was confused about how you felt, what you wanted. But on my end, I didn't speak up soon enough, either, so . . ." He shrugs.

"So . . ."

"So I'm not mad at you. And I think . . . maybe . . . we should give this a shot."

My heart hangs in the balance, hesitant but hopeful.

Jamie reaches around to his back pocket and pulls something from it. "On one condition . . . we do this for real, we do this in public."

I stare down at the two tickets he's grasping within his fist.

My eyes widen. "You want to go to prom?"

"Nah." Jamie shakes his head, smiles, and extends his palm to reveal the face of the tickets. "Something better."

I stare down at them. Two tickets for tomorrow night. To the Reading Phillies home game.

"I was going to ask you to prom, for the record," he tells me, surprising the crap out of me. "Before you very ruthlessly and cruelly dissed me in public. But then I thought . . . we'd have a better time at the game, anyway."

I feel a strange pressure in my chest and a tightness in my throat.

"See, Marshall . . . I've always meant what I told you that one day, that I like you a lot the way you are. I like *us* a lot the way we are, sarcastic and competitive and . . . not your average girl and guy counting down the seconds to prom." He raises his eyebrows at me. "So we could do formal wear and crappy chicken parmesan. Or we could do ball caps and those amazing hot dogs." His voice drops to a whisper. "You tell me what you want. And I'll want to be with you either way."

I swallow hard, blinking back the tears I swore I'd never let a boy bring about. Because this boy, who I believed was the last person who would ever get me, might actually, truly get me. I snatch the tickets from his hand. "Choice B," I tell him. "Definitely choice B."

"I'm going to show you the receipt," Jamie continues, looking at me meaningfully. "Bought these on Tuesday. Before you did what you did yesterday in Coach's office."

I smile bashfully at the ground, inexplicably pleased to learn he was ready to forgive me before I'd given up the trophy.

When I look up, he's staring at me, suddenly wide-eyed. "So we doing this, Marshall? Like . . . for real? Like . . . maybe I'm your boyfriend and maybe you're my girlfriend?"

I stare back at him, well aware that I'm probably looking suddenly as panicked as he is. Because, holy shit, I'm going to be someone's girlfriend. And hearing him say the words aloud just made me really freakin' happy.

"I think we are."

Then I turn and stare toward home plate. "I mean, I have no idea what I'm doing here. And maybe you don't have any idea what you're doing, either." Glancing over my shoulder, I narrow my eyes at him, the challenge revealing itself in my voice. "But tell me either one of us would ever be willing to forfeit a game just because we might *possibly* lose."

Jamie throws his head back and laughs loudly. "Hell no."

"Hell no is right," I tell him.

I keep staring at him.

Jamie's kissed me a bunch of times.

This time, I kiss him.

Grinning up at him, I turn my cap around so there's nothing in the way, push off the back of my cleats to bring my mouth to his, and find his lips. His hands go right to the small of my back, drawing me all the way close. The last thing I see before I close my eyes is his—now the color of the ocean lit by the sun when it emerges from behind the clouds.

We kiss and kiss on the mound. It's still the place where I belong, only I've finally learned to share it.

We're both probably still a little bit scared. We're definitely sweaty and dirty. But it doesn't stop us.

Because we're pitchers.

We're Pirates.

We're perfect.

Acknowledgments

Kat Brzozowski—so many thanks for tackling this project with me! Your support and enthusiasm took this story from a manuscript I'd put aside several times to a final product I'm proud of. Thank you for embracing Eve and her fierceness.

Lauren Scobell, Holly West, Jean Feiwel, Emily Settle, and Kelsey Marrujo—the encouragement and kindness that is Swoon HQ is incomparable. I am forever grateful to be part of this squad and for the faith you have in me. Thank you.

My Swoon sisters (and bros!)—this journey wouldn't be half as fun without you, and I'd be lost without you all to navigate it with. Kim, Danika, Jenn, Katy, and Sandy, thank you for making this a team effort—it truly feels like we win and lose together—big hugs to all of you. Mel. A match made in heaven, an instant friend, the little I never had. One more thing I have Swoon to be grateful for—thanks for all the love and endless baseball puns. #karomel for life

M.D.—thanks for the inspiration; you're everything amazing.

James—thanks for answering my questions and keeping the eye rolling to a minimum, and most importantly, for watching *Pitch* with me "in the name of research." Love you.

Lu and Christian—thank you for inspiring me every day, for

sharing in the writing world with me, and for making me smile always.

Laine, Aug, and Irene—thanks for your endless excitement, belief in me, and support. Thanks for embracing your feisty little girl, and her feisty little girl, too.

Thanks to the Swoon Reads community and the Sweethearts of YA. I'm honored to be part of both.

Kristen, Jacob, Danielle, Michael, and Tanya, thank you for making me fall in love with my characters anew. You perfectly captured their personalities in a single image, and I am grateful you all shared your artistic talent with me.

Lastly, thanks to my readers. You're why I do this, and your reactions and thoughts mean more to me than any other aspect of this endeavor. Thank you, thank you, thank you!

DID YOU KNOW...

this book was picked by readers like you?

Join our book-obsessed community and help us discover awesome new writing talent.

1 **Write it.**
Share your original YA manuscript.

2 **Read it.**
Discover bright new bookish talent.

3 **Share it.**
Discuss, rate, and share your faves.

4 **Love it.**
Help us publish the books you love.

Share your own manuscript or dive between the pages at **swoonreads.com**

**Check out more books
chosen for publication
by readers like you.**